Dear Reader,

What a joy to spend time with you in Marble Cove! To me, it's like coming home. When my husband and I were first married, we lived in New England. Miracles of Marble Cove brings back wonderful memories. I recall numerous trips up the Maine coast, with its quaint villages and breathtaking coastline. I loved the winding narrow roads, rock walls, stately old trees and historic homes. We spent many weekends immersed in the history around us, exploring the countryside and the old cemeteries with glowing epitaphs and wise sayings on the gravestones. I loved the lobster-clam bakes on the beach—a whole lobster, corn-on-the-cob, steamer clams and a potato, baked in a basket, buried with hot coals in the sand. Served, of course, with melted butter, rolls and cole slaw. Yum!

I love the cross-generational friendships Margaret, Diane, Beverly and Shelley share. Their interactions bring glimpses of our own struggles and joys in their experiences. I hope you find encouragement and pleasure in *With Grateful Hearts,* just as I found in writing the stories of these women. I pray you will see miracles around you. They're so easy to miss when we get busy and problems crowd in. May God send you a special miracle today and give you the eyes to see it amid the distractions of the day.

Blessings,
Sunni Jeffers

MIRACLES *of*
MARBLE COVE

WITH GRATEFUL HEARTS

SUNNI JEFFERS

New York

Acknowledgments

Every attempt has been made to credit the sources of copyrighted material
used in this book. If any such acknowledgment has been inadvertently
omitted or miscredited, receipt of such information would be appreciated.

"From the Guideposts Archive" originally appeared in *Guideposts* magazine.
Copyright © 1998 by Guideposts. All rights reserved.

Cover and interior design by Müllerhaus
Cover photo by IStock
Typeset by Aptara, Inc.

Printed and bound in the United States of America
10 9 8 7 6 5 4

WITH GRATEFUL HEARTS

Chapter One

W hat do you think? Are we wasting our time here?" Shelley and Margaret stood in front of a rock-and-brick entry sign reading Bayview Estates by Calder Construction. Next to it, a large red-and-white sign promised A Vote for Dennis Calder Is a Vote for Prosperity and Progress.

"Maybe, but these residents need to know there's an alternative to voting for Dennis Calder. As long as we're here, we might as well try to convince them to vote for Beverly," Margaret said.

"You're right." Shelley straightened the aquamarine button on her jacket to be sure the words *Embracing Our Heritage: Vote for Beverly!* were clearly visible. She followed Margaret and pushed the stroller up the concrete driveway to the front door of a two-story, blue-and-white Cape Cod house. A forlorn young maple tree stood in the middle of the manicured lawn, a few tenacious red and orange leaves clinging to it.

Only three homes were occupied in the new neighborhood, which was close to downtown. They seemed somewhat out of place for Marble Cove, where most of the houses were older Victorians or Craftsman-style cottages.

It was warm for the first day of November, and billowy clouds played hide-and-seek with the sun. Leaves in an array of reds, purples, yellows, and oranges skittered past them along the road, driven by gusts that carried the threat of winter.

Shelley maneuvered the stroller with her sleeping toddler up the single step of the long covered porch as Margaret rang the doorbell. A middle-aged woman answered the door. She looked at Margaret, then at Shelley, and down at Emma.

"Yes? How may I help you?"

"Good morning. I'm Shelley Bauer and this is Margaret Hoskins. We live near the beach. Margaret owns the Shearwater Gallery downtown. We're campaigning for our friend Beverly Wheeland, who's running for mayor. The election is next Tuesday." Shelley felt a little awkward, as if she was rattling off a memorized spiel. She smiled. "Have you registered to vote here?"

"Yes, I have, and I know a little about Beverly, but I'll take one of your brochures." The woman smiled and held out her hand.

Margaret handed her a flyer. "We'd appreciate your vote. Beverly is highly qualified, but she's also passionate about helping Marble Cove preserve its small-town charm and history."

"Aren't you the baker?" the woman asked, peering at Shelley. "I bought one of your blueberry crumb cakes at the Old First dinner auction. It was amazing."

"Beverly planned that fund-raiser," Margaret told her.

"I was very impressed with it. If she can manage the town like she ran that event, she has my vote."

"That's wonderful. I'll tell her. She'll be encouraged to hear your praise."

"I'm Rose Jennings, by the way. My husband is on staff at Sailors Memorial Hospital. We fell in love with Marble Cove, so we decided to settle here."

"Welcome to the town," Shelley said. "You have a beautiful home, and it looks like you're going to have more neighbors soon." As much as she hated to give Dennis Calder credit, since he was Beverly's rival and seemed bent on ruining the town, he did build nice houses.

"Yes, welcome," Margaret said. "We're having a surprise celebration for Beverly at the gallery after the results are announced on Tuesday night. We'd love to have you and your husband join us. We hope it'll be a victory party, but whether she wins or not, we want to recognize her hard work and thank her supporters."

"What a wonderful idea. We'll come if we can, thanks. I have to admit, I already feel a bit proprietary, now that we're residents." She gave them a sheepish grin. "I'd like to close the gate so we don't grow too big. The town is the perfect size."

Shelley couldn't help smiling. It was nice to have new residents who felt the way she did. "If you need any baked goods for the holidays, or anything at all, please call me." She fished a business card out of the diaper bag and handed it to Rose.

"That's kind of you. I may just order some of your pies for Thanksgiving."

"Please do," Shelley replied.

"It was nice to meet you both," Rose said.

"You too," Margaret said. "Have a wonderful day."

No one was home at the next house, so they left a flyer on the front door. As Shelley wheeled the stroller down the sidewalk, she heard little noises from Emma. Her daughter was waking up. "One more house."

"Yes. Then I need to get down to the gallery. Allan would rather watch the gallery than go door-to-door, but he has work to do this afternoon."

They went up to the door and Shelley rang the doorbell. When no one answered, Margaret started to leave a flyer. Suddenly a woman appeared, looking irritated.

"Yes?" she barked.

Shelley didn't recognize her, but she put on her best smile. "Hi. I'm Shelley Bauer." She introduced Margaret and reached out her hand. "Welcome to Marble Cove."

"We're not new here. We just moved into this neighborhood." The woman crossed her arms.

"Oh. Well, we'd like to give you this information about Beverly Wheeland. She's running for mayor—"

"Oh no, I don't want that. We're voting for Dennis. He built our house, you know. My husband works with him." The woman backed into the house.

"Well, have a nice day," Margaret said, as the door shut firmly in their faces. The sound brought a cry from Emma.

At the curb, Shelley pulled back the hood over the stroller to see her daughter. Emma blinked and reached up with both arms.

"Mama. Get down?"

"Hello, sweetie. You can get down when we get back to town. Let me get you some juice."

"No. Down now." Emma's face puckered up.

Shelley sighed. If she let her out now, she'd end up carrying her. She rummaged in the diaper bag and pulled out a sippy cup of apple juice, which Emma took eagerly. Relieved, Shelley glanced at her watch and then at Margaret. "It's time for me to get Aiden from pre-K already. Is Diane coming to the gallery?"

"She said she would. I hope she's feeling up to it. She told me she's having trouble sleeping."

"I noticed she looks tired lately. I'm afraid when she starts chemotherapy, she'll feel even worse."

"I know she doesn't want to bother anyone, but we've got to figure out ways to help her."

"Agreed."

They had reached town. Shelley turned toward the preschool. "I'll get Aiden and meet you at the gallery."

"See you in a few."

* * *

Diane opened the front door of Shearwater Gallery and held on tight as a gust of wind tried to wrest it from her hand. The effort of walking to town had worn her out, which disturbed her. She was used to walking every day, and the jaunt to town only spanned a couple of blocks. Stepping inside, she firmly shut the door behind her. Margaret was standing on a step stool near the back, removing orange and black streamers from the ceiling. "Hi. Sorry I'm late." Diane reached up and finger-combed her windblown hair into place.

"You're not late. I just got here a few minutes ago."

"Oh, good. Can I help you?"

"Sure. I'll hand these down to you. There's a plastic tub for the decorations on the work table."

"Okay. Let me put my bag down." She removed her windbreaker and set it and her bag in the back. She turned around just as the door opened and Shelley came in. Aiden pushed past her and burst into the room.

"Miss Diane!" He rushed forward and hugged her, then turned toward the ladder. "Miss Margaret!"

Margaret descended the ladder and managed to get her feet planted on the floor as Aiden reached her and threw his arms around her.

"Aiden, be careful. You're going to knock Miss Margaret down," Shelley said.

"It's all right," Margaret said, handing the streamers to Diane, then giving the boy a smile and a hug.

"Up." Emma reached to her mother from the stroller, so Shelley lifted her out and set her on the floor. She toddled after her brother, who started running in a circle.

"Sure wish I had their energy," Diane said. She rolled up the streamers and carried them to the plastic bin.

"Me too." Margaret got a big sheet of butcher paper and a tub of crayons and spread the paper on the floor. "Aiden. Emma. Do you want to draw a picture for me?"

"Okay," Aiden said, plopping down on the floor.

"'Kay," Emma said, flopping next to him.

"Do you have more to do? We can help," Diane said.

"I think I got it all. Sit down at the table. I'll fix some tea." Margaret put the kettle on in her office, and then carried cups and tea bags to the small table. She set out cream and sugar.

"Margaret and I have been campaigning door-to-door," Shelley said.

"That's great. How's the response?" Diane asked.

"Mixed. Some people haven't decided, so we talked up all of Beverly's great qualifications and passed out her pamphlets."

"I think we gained some votes," Margaret said. "Shelley even got a few orders for Thanksgiving goodies too."

"Yeah. I wasn't expecting that. And we invited a few people to our election night surprise party," Shelley added.

"I've mailed a number of invitations and handed out a few from the gallery too. I think we'll have a good crowd." The teakettle whistled. Margaret filled their cups with hot water.

"I feel like a slacker. I haven't done anything to help lately," Diane said. She hadn't felt up to campaigning this week, in part, perhaps, because she'd overdone it the week before.

"Nonsense," Margaret said. "You helped Beverly with her brochure and you're supplying the victory plates and cups and napkins. That's plenty."

"There isn't that much left to do at this point," Shelley said.

Margaret turned to Diane. "You're having your first chemotherapy treatment Friday, right?" Margaret asked. "You just rest and take care of yourself. We want you feeling well enough to attend Tuesday night."

"That's right," Shelley said. "We've all got to be there with Beverly when they announce the election results. Afterward, we'll sweep her away to the gallery. I don't think she suspects a thing."

"I'm sure she's going to win, but I know she's worried," Margaret said. "Dennis and his friends have been telling everyone that Beverly doesn't understand the town or the people here. They're calling her a newcomer, and that's anathema to a Mainer."

"Well, she might be new to Marble Cove," Shelley conceded, "but she was raised in Maine, and her dad has been here for years."

"People are smart," Diane said. "They recognize Dennis for what he is. And Lee Waters—I don't think he wants to be mayor. He's running because of his mother. She wants the position to remain in the family. It's tradition."

"Well, the tradition is about to end," Margaret said.

"Agreed," Diane said. "I don't know how I'll be feeling on Tuesday, but I'll be there if I can."

Diane saw the look Margaret and Shelley exchanged. It was comforting to know her friends cared, but they hadn't been through chemotherapy and couldn't know how much it would drain her energy. She already felt lousy. Whether it was the power of suggestion or her body was tired from its internal battle, she didn't know.

"Didn't you say you're having lower doses of treatment?" Shelley asked. "Maybe you won't feel as bad this time."

"Yes, but I'll be having one every week, instead of every three weeks."

"Well, we're all going to pitch in to help you any way we can," Shelley said. Margaret nodded in agreement.

"Thank you." Diane knew her friends were there for her. She was learning, slowly, to let other people help her. But it was still hard. She hated to burden her friends.

Shelley glanced at her watch. "I'd better get these kids home. Diane, did you drive down or walk?"

"I walked." Diane was glad Shelley changed the subject. "Are you ready to go? I'll walk back with you."

"Aiden, Emma, let's get ready to go," Shelley called out.

"Can we take our picture, Miss Margaret?" Aiden asked.

"Certainly," Margaret said. "Let me roll it up for you."

"Okay." Shelley looked surprised and pleased as Aiden put his crayons back in the bucket without prompting and Emma followed suit.

Diane put on her jacket and took her bag as Margaret helped Shelley get the kids out the door.

Margaret blinked against the bright sunshine. She turned to Diane and put a hand on her arm. "Hope to see you at the party Tuesday night."

"I hope so too."

"I'll be praying it's a victory party," Shelley told her friends.

"Me too." Diane shuddered in the November wind. "I don't want to live in a town run by Dennis Calder."

CHAPTER TWO

Beverly zipped up her light jacket. The black fabric absorbed the sun's warmth, but the breeze was nippy as she walked to town. A wisp of her dark, shoulder-length hair blew across her face. She pushed it back behind her ear. The Webinar sponsored by the Maine Municipal Association had given her a lot to consider. In their small town, just how much influence did the mayor have with the town council in making decisions? Or was she more of a figurehead? Marble Cove didn't have a town manager, and Evelyn Waters seemed to be involved in everything. But then, she was at least a second-generation mayor. Would the council want more control after she retired at the end of the year?

Beverly didn't want to jump the gun. There was a good chance she would lose the election. With Dennis Calder and his cronies taking potshots at her, and Lee Waters running as the incumbent's son and a lifelong resident, her competition was stiff.

She recognized the group coming toward her. With the stroller and a little boy running ahead, it had to be her friend Shelley, and the other woman looked like Diane. She waved. Aiden ran to meet her. He bounced up and down and squinted at her.

"Hi, Miss Beverly. I drawed a picture at Miss Margaret's."

"You did? What did you draw?"

"A bi-i-i-g boat," he said, stretching his arms out wide.

"I bet it's beautiful," Beverly said.

Aiden nodded. "Emma drawed one too, but it's just lines."

The toddler was walking behind the stroller, hanging on as if she were pushing it.

"Hi. How was your Webinar?" Shelley asked.

"You must have talked to Margaret. It was good. I was typing notes as fast as I could. So much to remember. That's *if* I get elected. How are you feeling?" she asked, turning to Diane.

"I'm doing all right. A bit tired. I thought the fresh air would be good for me, but I'm ready to sit down and put my feet up."

"Margaret and I did some door-to-door campaigning this morning," Shelley said. "We covered Dennis' new housing development."

"Really? How did that go?"

"We got one very positive response. One of the homeowners works for Dennis, so you can imagine how that went. We left a brochure on the door of another house where no one was home. We went to several other neighborhoods. A lot of people were undecided. Let's hope we gained their votes today."

"I can't tell you how much I appreciate your help. Dennis is doing his best to paint me in a bad light. I've heard that I'm an outsider, an interloper, an opportunist, a bureaucrat, and a paper-shuffler because I worked at the State House, and that I'm stuck in the nineteenth century, which is ridiculous. I hope people don't believe him."

"The ones who matter won't," Diane said. "His comments seem personal. I think people will question his character, not yours."

"I hope you're right." Beverly wondered if Dennis' vindictiveness had anything to do with her refusal to date him, or if he was just a fierce competitor. "I'm going to put one more last-minute ad in the *Marble Cove Courier*. Just a reminder to vote and a thank-you for considering me. It might not help, but it can't hurt."

"Good idea. I like your positive campaigning. It makes his claims seem even cruder, if you ask me," Shelley said.

Diane nodded. "And to think, I once tried to play matchmaker. Thank goodness you had the good sense and good taste to choose Jeff."

"Jeff is very persuasive. And Dennis is too pushy. That's okay in a friendship, but not a dating relationship. Dennis' 'self-confidence' can really rub a person the wrong way."

"Let's hope it rubs the voters that way too," Shelley said.

Emma started pushing on the stroller. "Go, Mama," she said.

Beverly laughed. "Looks like someone else is feeling pushy. I'd better let you get home. I'll see you later."

As they parted, Beverly wished they'd had more time to visit. She missed sessions when they met at the Cove for coffee or at the gallery to chat. She especially missed their walks on the boardwalk along the beach. She still jogged daily to keep in shape, but she'd gotten so busy with her campaign and building her business that she didn't have as much time to enjoy her friends. If she won, that could get worse.

Her thoughts on her friends, she almost didn't hear the long, steady whistle. It grew louder, pushing into her consciousness. It sounded like a train. She turned her head toward the sound, toward the old train station. Definitely a train whistle. All four of the friends had heard it before, which should be impossible, since no trains came close to Marble Cove and hadn't for over half a century. She looked around. It seemed to be coming from a distance, not a nearby store or residence. People walked along the sidewalk, but no one else acted as if they heard the out-of-place sound. She glanced back toward her friends, but they were out of sight. Should she go after them and ask if they'd heard it? No. She had an errand to do. She continued on to the newspaper office.

Abby Lane was at the reception desk at the *Courier*. She looked up when Beverly entered. "Good afternoon, Beverly. How can I help you? Another campaign ad?"

"Hi, Abby. Yes, I want to place an ad. I suppose my opponents have been in?"

"Only Dennis Calder. Lee hasn't done much advertising. Guess he figures everyone knows him. Don't know that I'd count on his name to carry the day, though. Do you have ad copy, or do you need help with that?"

"I have it here." Beverly took a sheet of paper out of her bag. "It's not very long."

Abby accepted it and read it. Then she looked up. "Short and sweet. Are you sure you don't want to say more? Dennis had a big ad."

Beverly wanted to ask what Dennis had to say, but thought better of it. She didn't want to seem too curious, and she didn't want to spoil her day.

"Beverly, I thought I heard you out here." Gerald Kimball, the paper's lone reporter, came out of a back office. "If you've got a minute, I'd like to talk to you."

"Sure."

"Good. Come on back to the office."

Beverly followed him to an office in the rear of the building. He offered her a chair across from a big oak desk.

Gerald sat down and looked at her, his fingers steepled together. "I just had a visit from Dennis Calder. He asked me to investigate your business."

"What? Why? There's nothing to investigate. It's a very simple business."

Gerald frowned. "He insinuated that you are running for office merely to further your personal business and finances. That the position of mayor would give you unfair advantage in advising your clients and possibly even line your pockets with investments."

Hot pressure started up from Beverly's neck, flaming and pounding toward her temples. Her integrity and reputation were above reproach. How dare he malign her! She gripped the arms of the chair to keep from jumping to her feet. It was so dishonest and unfair. Her heart racing, she took a deep breath, closed her eyes, and took another deep breath. Overreacting would not help her win the election. She opened her eyes.

"That's preposterous." Her hands were shaking. She hoped her voice sounded calm. "I had all kinds of inside information when I worked at the State House, and my reputation is spotless. Call and ask my colleagues there. I'll even give you their names and phone numbers."

"Good idea. I don't believe his accusations, but you would be wise to refute him."

"I don't believe such slander warrants a response. I won't stoop to his level."

"What about your local clients? Would you not be tempted to advise them about something that might affect their business?"

"Fair question." Beverly thought for a minute. She had several local clients. Shelley, and Victoria Manchester, who owned the Landmark Inn, and a couple of owners of bed-and-breakfast inns. She'd helped them with marketing and computer systems. She'd have to be careful to keep her business and her elected position—if she should win—separated. "Well I'm getting a larger clientele of out-of-towners who have no interests in Marble Cove. The only local ones I have aren't likely to benefit from any information I might gain, and I can assure you I will be scrupulous in keeping my business and my town duties separated. Besides, I might argue that Dennis Calder's business is local and involves property development. Any insider information is far more likely to benefit him than me. So it's odd that he is trying to cast stones."

Gerald was busy entering notes on his computer. After a moment, he stopped and looked up. "Calder is planning to develop a mini-mall at the site of the old train depot. He says it is part of his strategic plan as future mayor to bring in more jobs and revenue for the good of the town, but that you would stop any kind of progress. Do you have a response?"

Beverly was stunned but hid her feelings. So Dennis not only planned to go forward with destroying the train station, but he was using it as a campaign promise. "I am in favor of quality progress that will maintain the friendly and historical flavor of Marble Cove. That's why people love living here and visiting here. I will have to see plans and study impacts on any proposed projects before I will approve or disapprove them."

"Sounds reasonable. I'll make a few calls, and I've noted your comments. I'll publish an article in this week's paper. I'll be fair, I promise you."

"From everything I've read, you are always fair." Beverly rose. "Thank you for bringing your questions to me."

"Of course, as a reporter, I'm impartial, but I wish you the best. Good luck in the election." He held out his hand, and Beverly shook hands with him before she left.

She was still fuming as she walked down Main Street. Then she thought about the train whistle she'd heard. It had seemed like a warning or an alarm to her, just like the impossible light shining at the decommissioned Orlean Point Light and the ringing of the old, walled-off bell at Old First Church. Few people had seen or heard them, and they only happened at some crucial moment, to alert the friends to vital clues, or when there was danger.

She'd been skeptical about the miraculous nature of the light. She'd become less skeptical when the ringing bell in the

Old First tower had saved Maddie Bancroft's life and warned them to get out of the old bell tower when lightning struck it and burned that part of the building.

So what did the train whistle mean? Was it a warning about Dennis' attempts to discredit her? Or was it even intended for her? She needed to talk to Margaret, Diane, and Shelley and see if they'd heard the train whistle.

As Beverly turned the corner on Main Street and headed toward the gallery, Dennis came walking out of the post office right in front of her. He was looking straight ahead, and she hoped he wouldn't see her. He stepped into the street. *Phew. Saved!* she thought, but then he turned to get into his car and looked right at her. His face seemed to turn to stone. Did he despise her that much?

"Hello, Dennis." What else could she say?

He gave her a curt nod. Then his mouth turned up on one side. A smirk. He got into his car and drove off.

Well! So much for being cordial. Obviously, he had no intention of being friendly. And from his cocky grin, he didn't consider her an opponent. In his mind, he'd already won the election. More than ever, Beverly hoped he was wrong.

★ ★ ★

Margaret set aside the bin of Halloween decorations to be stored for next year. She'd cut large maple leaves out of magenta, purple, and forest-green foam craft sheets for her Thanksgiving harvest theme. She was arranging a rattan cornucopia of small gourds and colorful Indian corn on top of several leaves when the front doorbell tinkled. She looked up.

"Hi, Beverly. How was your Webinar?"

"Good. I just stopped by the *Courier* to place a final campaign ad. I'll be so glad when this is all over."

"I don't blame you. It's been a hard campaign."

"That's an understatement. Dennis is still at it. He wants the newspaper to investigate me."

"Whatever for?"

"Conflict of interest. Supposedly I'm only running for mayor so I can line my pockets."

"Ha! He's the one with the pecuniary motives, if you ask me."

Beverly laughed. "Wow, now there's a descriptive word. You'd think you were an accountant or something."

Margaret laughed. "Well, he stands to gain a lot financially if he can manipulate the town to accept all of his real estate development plans."

"I hinted at that to Gerald Kimball. He told me Dennis is pledging to build a mini-mall on the train station site as a campaign promise to bring jobs and revenue to the town. I sure hope he doesn't get a chance to keep that promise. At least Gerald talked to me and warned me about Dennis. He's going to do an article. I gave him character references of people I worked with at the State House. I hope he puts me in a favorable light."

"I'm sure he will. And you can bet that mini-mall would bring Dennis a tidy profit. He makes my blood boil."

"Thanks. At least I'm not alone. My blood pressure was about to pop when I came out of the *Courier*. Then I ran into Dennis. He wouldn't even speak to me. I think he considers me the enemy." Beverly shook her head.

"That's crazy."

"It's laughable. By the way, did you hear that train whistle?"

"Today?"

"Yes, about a half hour ago. I was on my way to the newspaper office when I heard it."

"No. I didn't hear a thing. I did have music on though."

"Oh. I wonder if Diane and Shelley heard it. I passed them right before the whistle blew." Beverly looked toward the kitchenette area, where the extra teacups were still sitting on the table.

"They were here for a few minutes," Margaret told her. "Shelley and I were out campaigning for you earlier."

"That's what she said. I can't tell you how much that means to me. I know you're both busy with your businesses and families."

"We all want you to win. The town needs you."

"Thanks for the vote of confidence. Diane was quiet. How did she seem?"

"She said her energy levels were way down. Shelley is going to make some high-protein dishes for her. Something easy to digest, she said. I'm going to look for recipes online that Allan can make. I doubt if she'll feel like fixing food, but she'll need good nutrition to keep her strength up."

"I can look for a few ideas too. I'm not much of a cook, but maybe I can get Mrs. Peabody to help. She's done a great job finding diabetic recipes for my father. I offered to take Diane to her treatments, but she intends to drive herself. I know she doesn't want to cause anyone inconvenience, but I wish she would accept my help."

"Me too. I think she's getting better at it, but it's hard for her."

When Beverly left, Margaret breathed a sigh of relief that she hadn't had to explain why Diane and Shelley were there without her. Not that they always had to be together, but she felt guilty hiding their meeting from Beverly, even if it was to plan her surprise party. The four of them had been drawn into a tight circle of friendship that shared life-changing experiences. Their differences in age and background were insignificant. On Tuesday night, Beverly would understand.

★ ★ ★

As Beverly entered her father's Victorian home, where she'd moved to care for him in his elder years, she heard gentle snoring coming from his study. Moving quietly, she peeked in at him. He was slouched down in his favorite chair, a book open facedown across his lap. *Collective Memories of Maine: A History.* Beverly smiled as she went down the hall to the kitchen. Her father loved to read, and loved history above all subjects. But his books often put him to sleep these days. She hadn't seen that book before. He had passed his love of history to her, and she thought she'd seen all of his extensive library.

Hungry because she'd skipped lunch, she went back to the kitchen. Mrs. Peabody was standing at the sink, scrubbing potatoes.

"Good afternoon."

The elderly lady looked over her shoulder and smiled. Her white hair had curled tighter with the warm humidity in the kitchen. She turned off the faucet. "Hello, Beverly. I'm making beef stew for you and the mister for dinner, so I wanted to start early. It needs time to simmer and let the flavors meld, you know."

"Sounds wonderful. I'll just get a yogurt and get out of your way."

"All right. How is the campaign going?"

"As well as can be expected." She was not going to talk about Dennis or his backstabbing. Mrs. Peabody loved to gossip, and Beverly didn't need any more talk about her opponent and his opinions. She knew Mrs. Peabody was on her side, but her idea of support could backfire.

"I told everyone at the Mercantile that they'd better vote for you and not that shyster, Dennis Calder."

"Oh. Well, thank you. Now I'd better get to work."

Mrs. Peabody nodded, then went back to her task. She didn't like to share the kitchen when she was working. Beverly took a peach yogurt out of the refrigerator and carried it upstairs to the office she'd set up in a spare bedroom. She settled at her computer and opened a spreadsheet with her business plan and projections. She'd been thinking about her consulting business since she talked to Gerald at the newspaper. Becoming mayor of Marble Cove could present a challenge. She felt confident she would keep her business and town duties separated, but she couldn't let any hint of impropriety mar her reputation or that of the office of mayor.

Beverly had to have facts. She needed a black-and-white response that she could present to anyone who might question her motives, and she wanted that information for her own reassurance. Financially, she was in a good position. Her business was growing. As she had worked with clients on their budget needs and helped build business plans and long-range goals, she had discovered a talent for marketing and graphic design. Those abilities helped with corporate clients, and much of her work could be done online, from her home office in Marble Cove.

She loved her adopted hometown. Marble Cove maintained its cozy seaside atmosphere and managed to avoid the tacky T-shirt and souvenir shops and shabby tourist attractions that had taken over many similar towns. But the town needed some progress to stay alive, and the residents needed secure local jobs. She could help. She and her friends had already been instrumental in saving the Orlean Point lighthouse and finding a priceless portrait whose sale at auction was helping restore Old First Church. Now she wanted to help save and restore the old railroad station. It was part of the history and fabric of Marble Cove—a history Dennis Calder wanted to destroy. His brand of progress might bring money to the area, but at what cost? Marble Cove could lose its identity and the charm that made it unique.

She was at a loss concerning Dennis' claims against her. The services she offered to her local clients helped them develop their own potential. None of them would conflict with town duties. Perhaps she should limit her future professional budget analysis and growth projections to corporate, out-of-town clients. That should satisfy anyone concerned about her business conflicting with the town's.

Beverly made a note to speak with Charlotte Vincent, the chamber of commerce chairwoman, about putting together a pamphlet on creating business plans for the local businesses. She could make the information available to everyone and perhaps she could give a couple of seminars on business planning through the community center. There might be others in town, like Shelley, who could start small cottage industries from their homes. That way she could use her skills to help the town without being concerned about conflict of interest. In fact, she wouldn't wait for the election. She could offer her services even if she didn't win the election. She picked up her cell phone and dialed the chamber of commerce office. That should silence Dennis and his friends. How could they accuse her of profiting from the town if she volunteered her expertise to help the local business owners?

CHAPTER THREE

Diane woke to Rocky's wet nose nudging her hand. When she stirred, he whined.

"*Hmm*. What's the matter? You need to go outside? What time is it?" She lifted her hand and glanced at her watch. Four o'clock. She'd fallen asleep on the couch soon after she'd gotten home from town. "Well, I didn't intend to sleep the day away," she said out loud. Rocky watched her with compassionate eyes. At least it seemed that way. When she sat up, his tail moved side to side. When she pushed to her feet, his mouth opened into a grin. She couldn't help smiling.

"You're not really a dog, are you, Rocky? That's just a shaggy disguise." His tail pumped harder and faster. Especially when she went to the kitchen and got his leash. She put on a jacket and draped a scarf around her neck, as it was likely to be windy on the beach.

He pulled her along, which was good, since she had no energy. When they reached the boardwalk, she unhooked Rocky's leash and let him run. He dashed down to the water and danced along the edge of the surf. Oh, to feel so lively and carefree.

What was wrong with her? Was the cancer really affecting her that much or was it psychological? If she hadn't been diagnosed, would she be feeling so drained? Was it knowing she was going it alone this time?

A wave of loneliness hit her, washing cold over her as startling as the salt water hitting Rocky's feet. But she couldn't dance away. A tear trickled down her cheek. She missed Eric so much. In the years since his passing, she'd adjusted to being independent, or so she'd thought. But now his absence hit her anew. So many times he had held her and rocked her and comforted her. He had fed her and taken care of the menial tasks when she'd been ill from the cancer and the treatments. Justin had called often and sent cards, and Jessica had prayed and held her hand when she'd felt weak. Now both kids were away, and Eric was gone.

As much as she wanted to be independent, without her family, she needed her friends. She didn't want to be a burden, but Beverly had offered to take her to her first treatment. Diane had refused, but now she realized she didn't want to go alone.

She called Rocky. He looked up from his investigations and came running. He stopped short of running into her, then loped ahead of her toward home when she turned around.

After putting Rocky in the house, Diane walked down the street to see Beverly. She reached up to ring the doorbell, but the door flew open. Mrs. Peabody stood there in her familiar plaid Pendleton wool jacket, her curly white hair framing her face. She put her hand over her heart.

"Gracious me, Diane. You startled me. I was just on my way out."

"Hello, Mrs. Peabody. How are you?"

"Fit as a fiddle. Come on in. Beverly is up in her office and the mister is in his library. I'd love to chat, but I don't have time just now." She stood back to let Diane in, then shuffled out the door and down the steps.

Diane marveled at the energy of the little white-haired lady, who was in her early eighties. Beverly preferred not to spend too much time in the kitchen, and though her father wouldn't admit it to her, he'd hinted to Diane that he preferred Mrs. Peabody's cooking.

Diane stopped at the library doorway and peered in. Mr. Wheeland was sitting in his leather chair, his glasses perched on his nose, reading. She stepped into the room.

"Hello, Harold. Mrs. Peabody let me in on her way out."

He looked up, then set his book down. "Diane, come in. Beverly is around here somewhere."

"Mrs. Peabody said she was in her office. How are you?"

"I'm just fine. Sit and warm yourself by the fire until Beverly comes down. It's turning chilly outside."

"Yes, it is. I suppose winter will be here before we know it." She moved over by the fireplace, where a cheery fire danced and crackled. She removed her jacket and sat down, facing him. "What are you reading these days?"

He raised the book so she could see. "It's a collection of stories about Maine from old journals and letters and memoirs. All firsthand accounts. Very interesting. I read this years ago, but I'd forgotten. I was just reading about Marble Cove and the old rail line."

"Really? Does Beverly know about it?"

"Not yet. I haven't had a chance to talk to her."

★ ★ ★

No sooner had Beverly concluded her call with Charlotte Vincent than the cell phone rang again. The caller ID lit up the name: Jeff Mackenzie.

"Hi, Jeff. How are you? Where are you?"

Hearing his deep chuckle made her smile. "Hello, sweetheart, I'm so glad to hear from you. I'm in North Dakota."

"You called me, and I *am* glad to hear from you. So what are you doing there? I thought you were in Texas."

"Have camera, will travel. It gets me around. I'm doing shots for an article on the natural gas hydraulic fracturing industry. There's a modern gold rush going on up here. And no four-star hotels. No place to stay, actually. I'm in an eighteen-foot travel trailer."

"Isn't it cold in North Dakota?"

"Thirty-seven degrees right now."

"Colder than here. Are you keeping warm?"

"It's not too bad. I borrowed an insulated coverall. I've got a subzero sleeping bag. Want to come up here?"

She laughed. "Not this trip. Besides, I've got my hands full with this election." She told him about her interview with Gerald Kimball.

There was a pause on Jeff's end. "I'd like to have a few words with that Calder." Beverly could hear the irritation in his low tone.

"So would I, but it wouldn't do any good."

Jeff's reaction sounded like a growl. Just knowing Jeff was angry on her behalf and wanted to defend her boosted her spirits. "Maybe it's a good thing we don't confront him. I did point out that he has more to gain financially than I do."

"I hope your newspaper reporter gets his facts straight."

"Gerald's been fair so far. Will you be back in time for the election?"

"I'll try to. I wish I could vote for you."

"You . . . oh. You aren't a resident here. I forgot that." Beverly wondered when he planned to move to Marble Cove, but now wasn't the time to ask. "Stay warm."

"I will. I'll see you next week. I miss you."

"I miss you too."

Beverly hung up and started back downstairs. It hadn't hit her before that Jeff couldn't vote for her. He didn't live in Marble Cove. She had mentioned before that they could live with her father or find a place nearby, but they hadn't settled where they would live after they got married.

Jeff knew she'd moved there to care for her father. When she talked to him about running for mayor, he had encouraged her. She'd assumed he intended to move to Marble Cove too, but he hadn't said so. She liked to have her life organized. They needed to come to a mutual decision on their future home. Planning their living arrangements moved to the top of her to-do list. If she won the election, she needed to stay within the town limits.

She hoped Jeff made it back for the election. His presence gave her an extra measure of confidence. And then they could talk about their future.

She heard voices coming from her father's library and went to investigate. As she walked in, Diane said her name.

"Hi, Diane. What haven't you had time to tell me yet, Father?"

"Ah, there you are. I was just telling Diane that I found references to Marble Cove's railroad in the book I'm reading."

"Really?" Beverly sat across from her father and Diane. "What did it say?"

"It gives accounts of the railroad hauling casks of lime from the limestone quarry at Marble Cove. I remember reading about a quarry around here somewhere, but I've never investigated it. I think it's out near the point of the cove. They mined the limestone, then heated it in kilns to reduce it to powder, which was used in making plaster and mortar. Lime from our quarry was shipped to Boston and to Washington, DC, for use in the capitol buildings. Shipping by rail was safer than by sea, as the lime powder it produced was highly flammable when it got damp. I hadn't realized that. Quite a few ships were lost to fire from transporting the lime casks."

"That's amazing. No wonder they switched to shipping by rail. I assumed the railroad was brought here because of the Cannery. Between the two industries, Marble Cove must have been pretty prosperous," Diane said.

"The railroad was part of a rich heritage. All the more reason to save the station as a historical building. What else does it say, Father?"

"Not much. The Marble Cove route shut down in the early fifties, when demand for lime fell." He paused. "Oh, and the depot was designed by a young architect who went on to become quite famous. The name escapes me now."

"Another reason it needs to be preserved," Diane said decisively. "The Cannery closed later, but the old photos show trucks shipping the sardines, so I suppose the railroad became obsolete."

"That reminds me, did you hear the train whistle this afternoon, right after I talked to you and Shelley?"

Diane's eyes lit up. "No. And Shelley would have said something if she heard it. Was it like what we heard before?"

"Very similar. If you didn't hear it, and Margaret said she didn't hear it, then I was the only one. It sounded like a warning, right before I went into the newspaper office." She told Diane about her conversation with Gerald.

"I think you're right. It was meant for you." Diane cocked her head to one side. "Interesting. I wonder why?"

"Maybe the four of you are so attuned to local history that you're hearing and seeing glimpses of the past in your minds' eyes," Mr. Wheeland said. "You have a writer's mind, Diane. You have to be able to inhabit your story world. It seems you've rubbed off on my daughter and your other friends. A true gift."

Diane smiled, but didn't comment. Beverly wondered whether the whistle only sounded to someone who needed it or could respond to a warning, like the lighthouse light and the old bell at Old First.

Beverly knew how much Diane enjoyed researching the area's history. She'd been key in finding out the history of the Orlean Point lighthouse and Old First. And maybe she needed a distraction from her cancer. "Do you want to go out to the train station with me again? I'm beginning to wonder if the train whistle is somehow tied to my political race. Dennis is determined to demolish the station and to keep me from interrupting his plans. We need to find out more about the railroad's history and importance. I don't want to oppose all progress, and I won't try to block Dennis if he has a beneficial project. He initially wanted to save Old First, just as we did, but the train station is a different situation. I don't want the town to lose an important part of its heritage."

"Yes, I'd like to go out there again. It better be soon, though. I don't know how I'm going to feel once I start treatments."

"Can you go tomorrow morning?"

"Sure. Maybe Margaret and Shelley would like to come along. Then we could stop at the Cove for coffee and some of Shelley's blueberry coffee cake. Last time I had treatment, I couldn't drink coffee. Even the smell of it made me sick."

"Oh dear. I know how much you love your coffee. Did tea bother you too?"

"No. I could drink herbal teas. Beverly"—Diane paused— "I was wondering if your offer is still open to drive me to my treatment Friday."

"Of course. I'll be happy to drive you to all of your treatments."

"Oh, good. I realized I don't want to go alone. I might be fine, but driving home could become a challenge."

"Then we have a standing date. Every Friday."

"Thank you, Beverly. It means a lot to me." Diane stood. "I'd better get back to Rocky. He'll be wanting his dinner."

"Would you like to join us for dinner? Mrs. Peabody made beef stew."

"Thanks, but I have leftovers that I need to eat up. I'll see you in the morning. I hope the weather is nice so we can look for the quarry."

"I'll contact Shelley and Margaret to see if they can come along." Beverly walked her friend to the door and watched her move down the sidewalk. Diane was putting a brave front on her cancer battle. She was independent, which Beverly understood. Diane wouldn't ask for help unless she really needed it, but she was alone, facing a tough fight. Beverly was happy to help. Margaret and Shelley wanted to help too. They would make sure she had all the support she needed. How blessed they were to have such a special group of friends.

★ ★ ★

Shelley tied an apron around her niece Hailey's slender waist. The nine-year-old was tall for her age, making her a bit awkward and gangly. "Let's pull your hair back so it won't get in the food." Shelley smoothed back Hailey's strawberry blonde hair and secured it in a ponytail.

"Would you like to stir the sauce or grate the cheese."

"I want to stir."

"Okay. Stand on the stool and use the wooden spoon. Stir to the bottom of the pan so it doesn't stick as it thickens."

Hailey climbed up, then turned her head to look at Shelley. On the stool, she stood eye to eye with Shelley. "I know how to do this. I fixed dinner all the time at home." Her niece's blithe comment saddened Shelley. Her sister's irresponsible lifestyle had forced her young daughter to be the caretaker, just to survive. All Shelley wanted was to love her and care for her and let her be a child.

Shelley said a quick prayer for guidance. Raising her own children was hard enough. She wanted Hailey to feel at home, which meant being a part of the daily routine, yet she didn't want the girl to feel required to help. She wanted her to enjoy helping. "I know, and you're a big help in the kitchen. I think it's more fun when there's two people working together, but you don't have to help me cook if you don't want to. I remember being your age and cooking with my mom. I think that's why I love baking so much."

Hailey shrugged. "It's okay." She turned and began stirring.

Shelley prepared three kinds of cheese. It was a splurge. She'd always bought blocks of American cheese when it was on sale because it melted easily and went with everything. But she wanted to step it up a bit. A quarter pound of sharp cheddar, a quarter pound of jack cheese and a tablespoon of mustard made a big difference to mac and cheese. With bites of hot dog, they'd have a gourmet comfort food dinner. As she passed the shredded monterey jack cheese to Hailey, Aiden came bursting into the kitchen and slid to a stop in his stocking feet.

"I'm starved! Is dinner ready?"

Shelley stifled a laugh. Aiden sounded just like a miniature Dan. "Not yet. We'll eat when Daddy gets home."

"Oh. Can I set the table then?"

Shelley stared at her son. He'd never offered to help before. "Sure. That would be wonderful. Thank you for offering, Aiden."

"It's okay, Mom. Then we'll be ready to eat." He marched to the cabinet and opened the silverware drawer. He took out a handful of forks and carried them to the table.

Shelley shook her head, stunned. "Did aliens abduct my son and replace him with a robot?" She glanced at Hailey, who was grinning.

"Naw. It's Aiden."

"What brought that on, I wonder?" Shelley asked.

"He's making points so he can get on Santa's good list," Hailey said.

"Santa? What made him think of that?"

"One of his friends at school said his father was putting up Christmas lights."

"Already? It's not even Thanksgiving yet."

"I set the table, Mom," Aiden said, coming back into the kitchen.

"You did? Did you put plates and napkins and silverware at each place?"

"What? All that?" His shoulders sagged as if he'd been saddled with a heavy backpack. Shelley kept a straight face.

"Well, we can't eat off the place mats."

"Oh." He looked glum. Shelley doubted he could keep up his helpful streak until Christmas.

"Here are the plates. Take them one at a time, please."

He gave her a long-suffering look. Hailey giggled.

When he came back for another plate, Shelley asked, "To what do I owe your helpfulness?"

"Huh?"

"I appreciate your help. Thank you very much. I just wondered what spurred your sudden desire to help?"

Aiden gave her one of his beguiling smiles. "Will you tell Santa I helped?"

"I don't know when I'd see Santa. You can write him a letter."

"I can't spell." Aiden had learned to print his name and most of the alphabet. "Will you help me?"

"Of course. What do you want Santa to bring you?"

"A train," he said without hesitation.

"You have a train."

"That's just Thomas. He's not a real train. He's a baby train. I want a train like Benjamin's. It's black and makes smoke and he can make it whistle."

"*Hmm.* I see." Benjamin was Maddie Bancroft's son, and the Bancroft children had all the coolest toys. Aiden loved to go to Benjamin's house to play. Shelley wondered what a train set cost. She had a feeling they were expensive, and her Christmas budget was not large. And this year Hailey would be with them. Shelley had no intention of trying to keep up with the Bancrofts, but she could see Aiden and Dan playing with a shiny black metal train set. Dan would love it. She'd have to take another look at their budget. If she could come up with something unique for her Thanksgiving holiday offerings, maybe she could earn enough to buy her boys a special Christmas gift.

CHAPTER FOUR

Shelley slipped two large pans of pumpkin pecan coffee cake into the oven and set the timer. The children were in bed. Dan was watching television. She made a cup of tea, then sat at the table with a pad of paper. With Thanksgiving less than three weeks away, she needed to start baking and freezing baked goods for the Lighthouse Sweet Shoppe. Two orders had come in this evening as a result of her door-to-door campaigning for Beverly. She hadn't expected to gain from helping her friend, but it was a nice bonus.

She really needed to concentrate on getting through Thanksgiving. Local deliveries she could arrange, but anything to be shipped had to go out three to four days before the holiday to ensure arrival. She had to consider freshness too. Timing was a priority.

She took out her recipes and started a list of holiday specials. This year she wanted to try pumpkin and gingerbread whoopie pies. She wasn't sure if they would ship well, so she needed to make a batch and try them. Then she came to her biscotti recipes, and that gave her an idea. Biscotti shipped well and kept well. She'd never tried Thanksgiving-specific biscotti. Her basic recipe could be adjusted to make pumpkin spice biscotti and apple pie biscotti. She set the recipe aside to work on.

The oven buzzed and she removed the cakes from the oven and put in two pans of maple oatmeal muffins.

"Smells mighty good in here. Got anything for a hungry electrician?" Dan wrapped his arms around her shoulders and kissed her cheek.

"*Hmm.* When you ask so sweetly, I'm sure I can come up with something. How about a chocolate chunk cookie and a glass of milk?"

He sat across from her at the table, ran his hand through his short, sandy hair, making it stick up like spikes, and grinned at her. "Whatcha working on?"

"Thanksgiving list for my Web site. I need to offer a few specials."

"A few? Looks like a lot!" He took a bite of cookie, swallowed it, and licked his lips with a little smack. Aiden ate cookies the same way. "Are you sure you have time to make all of those?"

"No. I'll pare it down. I don't want to have to buy too many specialty ingredients. If I don't get the orders, then it runs my costs up. I'd love to include some maple recipes that use real syrup, but it's pricey."

"If you think they'll sell well, maybe you should give it a try."

"But I don't want to go over my budget."

"You can put more of your money back into supplies since I'm working full-time. And my income is going to get better as I get more experience. Wayne said it looks like we'll have plenty of business with Dennis Calder's company once they start their commercial developments."

Shelley pursed her lips. "What if his developments don't fly? If he doesn't get elected, he might have a hard time getting approval. He wants to tear down the old railroad station, but it's a historic building. The town might want to preserve it."

"It's got to be a mess, Shell. It'd cost a fortune to restore it."

"But it would add to the historical heritage of the town. Beverly wants to research the possibilities before it's too late. If she's elected mayor, she'll probably take it on."

"As long as she's realistic. A convenience store would bring revenue into the town. A historic building in need of repair will only drain it."

Shelley nodded. Dan's argument made sense. "You know Beverly. She has to run all the numbers and look at every angle. She won't do something unless she can prove it will work in the long run. I went out campaigning for her today. I think she has a great chance."

"I hope you're right. I admit I'd rather have Beverly for mayor than Calder. She's more likely to listen to all sides of an issue. He acts like the world revolves around him. And there'll be electrical work either way. That building will need complete rewiring."

"True. We're going to take another look at it tomorrow morning."

"Watch out for broken glass and rusty metal. Don't want anyone getting hurt."

"We'll be careful. Did you know Aiden volunteered to set the table tonight without my prompting? He carried his dishes to the sink afterward too."

"Really? What gives?"

Shelley grinned. "He wants me to write to Santa Claus for him."

"Already? Christmas is two months away."

"I know. That's what I said. One of his friends at pre-K said his father is putting up Christmas lights. That got the class talking about Christmas."

Dan shook his head. "I hope he doesn't want me to put up lights yet. Let's get through Thanksgiving first."

"He didn't mention lights. He's more interested in telling Santa what he wants."

"What does he want?"

Shelley thought for a moment. On one hand, she'd love to surprise Dan, along with Aiden, if she could pull it off, but she didn't know anything about trains. And Dan would have the fun of shopping for one if they could afford it. "A train. A black metal one that runs by itself and blows smoke and whistles."

"A train, eh?" Dan's eyes lit up. "Good choice. I loved playing with trains when I was his age. We had a really cool one in my family." Dan laughed.

"Do you think Aiden is old enough to take care of a real train set?"

"Sure. Boys take care of mechanical things. It's in our genes."

Shelley laughed. Then she sobered. "Aren't they expensive? We don't have a big Christmas budget."

"Well, maybe we can make it stretch. I'll do a little research. And I think we can afford to splurge a little on Christmas this year."

"I just don't want us to go in debt for toys. We have to pay cash."

"Agreed."

The oven timer buzzed. Shelley got up and took the muffins out of the oven. Dan stood and stretched. "You about done for the night?"

"I've got one more batch, then I'll clean up. How about you?"

"I need to spend a little time online with my classes, then I'll turn in. Thanks for the cookie." He gave her a kiss, then took his laptop computer to the dining room table and logged on.

For the next hour, they worked silently. Shelley was proud of Dan's hard work and determination to better their lives. They'd struggled for so long. She'd pinched pennies and made food and clothes and supplies stretch as far as possible. Could she really relax? Perhaps a little. But she wanted security. She needed to know they had a cushion, in case tough times came back around. That was prudence.

As she wiped down the granite counters, Shelley marveled at the journey they'd been on and the blessings they had. Relying on the Lord was a huge adventure. Dan's new profession was the beginning of a new phase in their lives. This was his time to shine. Where did she fit into the journey?

Dan didn't have the time to help her as he had when he'd been out of work. And now they had Hailey. At first that had seemed like a temporary situation, but Shelley had come to terms with the fact that Hailey was part of their immediate family. She hoped Hailey would be reunited with her mother someday, but right now, Hailey needed the stability of a secure environment and unconditional love. More and more, her family needed her attention. Less and less, they needed her income. All the changes left Shelley feeling a bit unsettled.

★ ★ ★

Low clouds obscured the sky as Margaret backed her minivan out of her driveway and up to the curb in front of Diane's cottage. Before she could honk, Diane came out the front door.

"Good morning," her friend said, sliding into the passenger seat. "I'm prepared for bad weather." She had on a waterproof windbreaker and held up her travel umbrella.

"I hope the rain will hold off. I'm excited to see what we might find," Margaret said as she pulled across the street and stopped in front of Shelley's house.

Shelley stepped off her porch toting a child's car seat in one hand and a folded umbrella stroller in the other. Emma toddled along right behind her. Margaret got out to help.

"Go ride. Go ride," Emma said, her little voice raised insistently.

"Yes, we're going for a ride," Margaret said.

Shelley buckled the seat in place, then swept her daughter up and into the seat in one motion and scrambled in next to her. Margaret marveled at her young neighbor's efficiency and energy. She climbed back into the driver's seat, then saw Beverly walking up the street. They waited for her.

"Good morning. Looks like we're ready for an adventure," Beverly said as she settled into the backseat next to Emma.

"Go benture," Emma said, showing a toothy smile and bouncing in her seat.

"That's right, sweetie." Margaret always felt like an adventurer when she set out with her friends. She never knew what their escapades would reveal, but their time together was never dull.

Debris had blown up and collected against the old train station. Weeds poked through the broken sidewalk in front of the building. The paint had peeled from the trim, leaving bare gray wood, and boards were tacked up over some of the windows, giving it a forlorn, long-deserted appearance. It looked sad, but Margaret could picture it with a good cleaning and fresh paint and barrels of flowers. It could be charming.

The four friends stood on the wooded path, surveying the old station. Emma tried to squirm out of her seat belt to get down.

"Sorry, sweetie, but you'll have to stay in your stroller. There's too much glass and old metal and trash, just like your daddy predicted."

Beverly stood with her hands on her hips. "I really think we've got our work cut out for us."

She walked over to the door and tried to open it. It didn't budge. "Someone must have fixed it and locked it after we were here. I'll try the back door." She disappeared around the back.

Shelley pushed Emma in the stroller around the overgrown yard area. The toddler was leaning half out of the stroller, reaching for things on the ground. Shelley handed her a sippy cup, and that occupied her for a while. She came back to where Margaret and Diane were inspecting the building.

"It looks sound to me, but then I'm not a building inspector," Margaret said.

"I was thinking the same thing. A coat of paint would do wonders."

"Maybe we could get Randy McDonald to come look at it. Maddie Bancroft got him to inspect the bell tower at Old First. I'll ask her how to get ahold of him. Maybe she'd even help."

"It's worth a try," Shelley said. "Maddie is very concerned about preserving our history. When I wheeled Emma out by the old tracks, I could see where they once extended out toward the point. Now it just looks like a gravel road, but it seems to be in pretty good shape."

"That must be the track to the limestone quarry. Beverly's dad was telling us about it last night. He found it in a history book. Evidently it was a pretty prosperous quarry in its day. The clouds are lifting," Diane said, looking up and squinting. "Let's go see if we can find it."

"Are you sure you feel up to it?" Beverly asked.

"I feel fine. A walk in the woods is just what I need."

"I'm game," Margaret said. "I've got my camera ready."

"Dan talked about a quarry around here somewhere. They used to go swimming in it when he was a kid, but they blocked it off. Said it was too dangerous. I've never been out there, but I don't think it's very far."

As they started down a wide, leaf-strewn path, Margaret stopped and turned back toward the station. The sun filtered through the clouds, shining on the old red roof, showing a few missing shingles. It needed repair, or perhaps a new roof. From her experience with the gallery, that could get costly.

The trees forming a border in back of the station toward town were mostly bare and gray now, their leaves fallen off. She snapped a couple of pictures. Sixty years ago, any train coming from this direction would have seen the spire on Old First and some of the downtown roofs in the background.

"Mama, Mama, Mama. Down." Emma's little voice carried in the tree-canopied lane. The maple and birch trees had grown tall and reached their branches to touch overhead, creating a wide tunnel. Fallen leaves padded the path in a thick layer of yellow, red, and brown leaves. The bare limbs let a little light filter through. The rain had pressed the leaves, making a cushioned carpet.

Shelley lifted her daughter out of the stroller and let her walk along with them. She stopped every few feet to examine the colored leaves. Then she would run forward, squealing with joy, to catch up. When Emma surged ahead, her arms raised to the sky, Margaret snapped several quick pictures. If only she could capture that explosion of life and joy on canvas, she would have a masterpiece.

"If those turn out, I want copies," Shelley said.

"You bet."

"If it comes out clear, it'd be great on a brochure to advertise the Marble Cove Railroad Walking Path," Beverly said, her eyes twinkling.

"That has a nice ring to it," Diane said. "I love walking on the beach, but this is a nice alternative."

Margaret pictured their brochure. The glossy, full-color cover had all of them walking side by side through a canopy of trees in full autumn regalia. Among the five of them, including Emma, they represented every phase of life. Anyone watching them would never guess the women were all best friends. They were an eclectic group. Perhaps their differences made their shared experiences and their miraculous faith journeys all the more in tune.

After about a quarter of a mile, they stepped out of the tunnel of trees. In unison, the friends stopped to stare at the breathtaking scene.

The path curved along a ridge above the cove. Thin strands of clouds threaded through the branches of the pine trees on the ridge and meandered out along the rocky point that framed the cove. Ribbons of mist floated above the white-tipped waters where the cove opened to the bay. The sun shot rays of light out from behind a golden-tipped cloud. Margaret aimed her camera, but the scene was too grand to capture. She took several shots of the trees and the point and hoped they would be interesting enough to paint.

The path curved gently downhill toward the ocean. The land became more barren, with rugged rock formations and clumps of tall, dry grasses and low bushes. The ground beyond the gravel track turned powdery white. As they rounded a rocky outcropping, the path ran smack into a ten-foot-tall chain-link fence. A large padlock with the initials BOLQ secured the gate.

Diane examined the padlock. "This looks old. The initials must stand for the limestone quarry. I wonder what the BO stands for?" She tugged on it. It didn't budge.

"Those must be the old kilns," Beverly said, pointing to a crumbling wall of hewn rocks. The crumbled ruins of three towers stood close together. Blackened rock like charcoal covered the ground around the base of the towers. Beyond the kilns were mounds of white that looked almost like snow. "That must be limestone."

"I'd like to get in there and look around," Diane said. "Maybe there's a break in the fence." She moved along the fence a ways. "I can see the quarry. It's filled with water. Come look!"

The others walked out to where Diane was standing on tiptoe, peering through the links in the fence.

"I see the lake. Why, it's beautiful," Beverly said.

"I'm too short. Where's something I can stand on?" Margaret asked, looking around. A pile of boulders rose like steps just in back of them.

"It looks big enough for both of us up there. I'll give you a hand," Shelley offered, picking up Emma and climbing the rocks. She reached out for Margaret's hand. With a little help for balance, Margaret climbed up next to her, then turned around to see the view.

A serene lake filled the old quarry. Beyond the white sandstone ledges that formed its shore, a stand of white birch trees, bare of leaves, with the characteristic peeling bark and stripes of black knots and wrinkles, stood straight and tall like legs on a herd of zebras. Clumps of tall golden marsh grasses swayed gracefully in the breeze. Several tall, chimneylike structures made of large blocks of rock stood watch along the northern edge of the quarry. They looked newer than the crumbling kilns they'd first seen.

"It's gorgeous. And I don't see anything dangerous-looking. The kilns, perhaps. They could be fenced off."

Ha-ha, who-who-who, ha-ha! Raucous laughter, loud and mocking, erupted from the direction of the lake.

Emma screamed, making Margaret jump. She managed to keep her balance and looked at Shelley, who was clutching her daughter. "What was that?"

Suddenly, a flock of birds rose from behind the rocks across the lake, calling out their cries in a cacophony of wild laughter and swooping down over the water and darting back and forth above their heads.

Margaret clapped her hand over her heart, then started laughing.

At her laughter, Emma stopped crying and looked up at the birds. She reached out her hand toward them, her little fingers waving at them. "Birdies," she said, giggling at their sounds.

"What are they?" Diane asked.

"They're laughing gulls. I haven't seen any around here before, but I believe they are rare. Oh my. I have to paint this."

She raised her camera and started shooting pictures. "I wish that fence wasn't there, blocking the view. I wonder who owns the quarry. I've got to get in there and paint."

Diane had walked farther along the fence, but came back. "The fence is secure. I don't see any way in, unless we can get a key from someone."

"I'll ask around and see who owns it," Beverly said. "This is too beautiful to hide. It should be a park or a nature preserve. We've got to save it and make it available for others to experience."

Margaret sensed that Beverly's excitement matched her own. How could she have lived so close and not known this special spot existed? "If we had a visitor's center or something at the old train station and a nature preserve down here, it would make a wonderful place for people to come visit. I'm going to paint this scene and the railroad station and display them. That might get some notice."

"I'll see what I can dig up at the library and historical society," Diane said.

"Great idea. I'll help you," Beverly said. "I can't wait to see your paintings, Margaret. We'll need all the attention we can get, so people will want to help save it."

CHAPTER FIVE

Diane scrolled down through the list on her computer screen. *Chemotherapy and Nutrition.* The article talked about the difficulties of eating well during cancer treatment. Diane remembered losing her appetite and how many of her favorite foods had become unappealing and even repulsive. Taste buds disappeared. Textures and smells changed. Eric had tried so hard to serve enticing foods that she'd eaten just to keep him from getting discouraged. But this time Eric wasn't with her.

How was she going to manage? She looked at the grocery list she'd started. Yogurt. Eggs. Bananas. Soup. She'd have to eat more than that. She tried to think of things she liked that would give her good nutrition. With the added problem of low blood sugar, she needed to make sure she ate well. But nothing sounded appetizing right now, and that would only get worse.

She knew she wouldn't want to cook, so things she could fix from a can or frozen food would make it easiest. She stared at the paper. Whoever heard of having writer's block with a grocery list? She wasn't sure whether to laugh or cry.

Her cell phone rang. She looked at the number. Jessica. She hit the button to answer.

"Hi, sweetheart. How are you?"

"Hi, Mom. I'm fine. The question is, how are you? Are you sitting there dreading tomorrow?"

Diane laughed. "I'm trying to make a grocery list. But I can't think of what I want to eat."

"Ah. Do you have peanut butter on your list? And how about some fancy nut butters, like almond or cashew butter on crackers or celery sticks? You could even add chocolate. I read that it's supposed to be high in antioxidants, but it has to be the good, dark stuff."

"Now that sounds like a diet I could live on." Diane added nut butter and chocolate to her list. Just hearing her daughter's voice cheered her.

"You should get some of those canned protein drinks too, just to supplement your meals. I wish I could be there with you, Mom. I've got my Sunday school class praying for you every day. And I'll call. I plan to come for Thanksgiving, and I'll do the cooking, so don't worry about fixing anything. I'm going to try to get a week off over the holiday to spend some time with you."

"That'll be wonderful, darling. And thanks for the prayers. And the food suggestions. I'm going shopping this afternoon so I'll be stocked up."

"I know your friends will help you too. Let them. They can pick up groceries for you and make some meals."

"They've already offered. I don't want to be a pest, though."

"You? A pest? Never! You know the saying 'It's more blessed to give than to receive'? Let them get a blessing by helping you."

"Yes, ma'am. You'll be happy to know Beverly is going to take me to my treatments."

"Good. I wish I could be there with you."

Diane's throat suddenly got a catch in it. "I wish that too, but it's going to be all right. I can't wait to see you for Thanksgiving."

"Me too. I love you, Mom."

"I love you too, darling. So very much."

Diane hung up and just sat there for a few moments, waiting for the tightness in her throat and the moisture in her eyes to clear. She was so blessed. She added a few more things to her list, then got her jacket and bag and headed to the store.

★ ★ ★

After dinner, Margaret dug out a box of photographs from days gone by. The sight of the old limestone quarry that day had reminded her of a trip she and Allan made years ago, before Adelaide was born. They'd visited a park in Minnesota that had once been some kind of quarry. She remembered that the chain of lakes in the old quarries had created breathtaking scenery. She had taken pictures and made sketches, hoping to paint pictures of it someday. Surely they were in this box somewhere.

The albums on top were more recent. Pictures of Adelaide throughout her school years. Vacations. Family reunions. She pulled out a sketchpad from college and a small journal that had trip diaries with dates and places they'd visited. Glancing through it jogged her memories. It startled her to realize she'd forgotten more than she remembered.

Near the bottom she found a leather-bound journal. Opening it, she read the date and realized she'd written it while she was still in college, more than two-thirds of a lifetime ago.

The first few pages were attempts at poetry—musings on life. Reading it, she couldn't help but laugh at her attempts to put her thoughts to verse. She flipped through the pages until she came across a list. Reading down through the items, she realized it was her bucket list. One hundred things she wanted to do and see in her lifetime. *Learn to fence. Climb Mount Whitney.* That hadn't happened. *Learn to scuba dive.* Nope. *Play an instrument.* She'd tried the violin. When the cat screeched and ran out of the room, she'd given that up. *Visit every state in the United States.* Hadn't done that. She scanned down the list, realizing she hadn't done most of the items. *Go to Paris and live like an artist. Visit all the art museums and paint street scenes and parks.*

That had been a major dream. She'd wanted to rent a room in a garret and drink thick, sweet coffee and eat croissants in a sidewalk café on the Champs-Élysées, and wander the streets with an art satchel so she could stop and paint a scene at whim. Thinking about it left an ache in her heart. She could imagine herself as a starry-eyed young artist in Paris. Instead, she'd become an accountant and given up that dream. She sighed and set the journal aside.

At the bottom of the box, she found the photo album with the trip to Minnesota. After locating the pictures of the park and the quarry lakes, she set the album aside with the leather journal and repacked the rest of the pictures and sketchpads.

The photos would show her friends what the limestone quarry could become if developed into a park. She wasn't sure why she kept out the journal. It was a reminder of what could have been, but would never be. And yet she couldn't resist looking back and remembering the longings of her youth.

★ ★ ★

It was still pitch-black outside as Shelley carried a box of baked goods into the back door of the Cove. The light was on in the kitchen. Shelley set the box on a counter and turned to get another load.

"Hey, Shelley, let me help you."

Shelley was surprised to see the owner of the Cove so early in the morning. "I have one more box."

Rusty followed her out to her car and carried the box in. "Your baked goods are sure popular. Business has grown since we started selling them."

"That's encouraging. Thanks."

"I was hoping to catch you this morning." Rusty ran his hand through his hair, the source of his nickname. In the light, Shelley noticed a liberal mix of silver among the red strands of hair.

"I wondered why you were here this early. I'm putting together my list for Thanksgiving items. I'll start bringing some in next week. That'll help people get in the holiday mood."

"Good. Speaking of the holidays, the wife and I are thinking of going to spend Thanksgiving with Freddie. He can't get leave to come home."

"That's wonderful. I imagine he gets homesick sometimes."

"Yeah. We miss him too. He loves the army, though. He intends to make it a career. I don't see him ever coming back to take over the Cove."

"That must be disappointing for you."

Rusty shrugged. "It's all right. I want him to do something he loves. But that leaves me with a predicament."

"Oh?"

"I've been thinking about retirement. Not right away, but we want to do some traveling while we're still healthy enough to enjoy it."

"Sure. That'd be great." Shelley wondered what he was getting at. Was he going to shut down the Cove? That'd be terrible for Marble Cove. It was a hub of social life for the town. Everyone stopped in at the Cove on a regular basis. The Cove was her biggest customer. If it closed, she doubted she'd have enough business to keep going.

"I want you to take over running the Cove."

"What? You want me to manage the coffee shop? I can't..."

"Not right away. Probably not for a year or so. I want to be sure we're ready for retirement, but the time is coming."

Shelley was stunned. With all her dreams about having her own bakery business, she'd never imagined running a business like the Cove. She just wanted to bake. "Why me?"

Rusty leaned back against the counter and crossed his arms. "I've watched you since you first started baking for me and using the kitchen. I didn't know if your proposal would work, but you have determination and perseverance, two of the biggest requirements for success. You're an excellent baker and you're organized. You're punctual. You're clean. You have a talent for pleasing people, and people like you and want to please you too, which is huge if you're going to manage employees. I believe you have all the attributes needed to keep the Cove running successfully."

"Wow. I don't know what to say." Shelley shook her head. "I have young children at home, and Dan and I decided a long time ago that I should be at home with the kids while they're growing up. That's why he built the commercial kitchen for me."

Rusty nodded. "I have a great staff here, so I rarely do any of the daily tasks. Some days I don't even come in. Brenna is very reliable. She can open and set up. She keeps an inventory going so I know what I need to reorder. You'd be able to work around your children's schedules. I know this is a lot to consider, but for now, just think about it. Okay?"

"Okay." Shelley laughed. "I doubt I'll be able to think about anything else now."

"No stress. Take all the time you need to think it through. Like I said, I'm in no hurry. It won't happen tomorrow. Maybe not even next year."

"Well, thanks for thinking I could do it. That's a real compliment. But now I've got to make some more deliveries." Shelley backed toward the door. "See you later!" she called as she let herself out.

She made three more deliveries. When she got home, Dan was pacing, waiting for her so he could leave for work.

"Sorry," she said. "Rusty wanted to talk to me."

"Oh. Well, I've got to run. Wayne gets upset if I'm late." He gave Shelley a quick kiss, grabbed his lunch, and dashed out of the house.

Shelley sighed. No chance to talk to him about Rusty's proposal. Perhaps it was just as well. She needed time to think it through.

"Mom, I can't find my Spider-Man shirt. I want to wear it today," Aiden said, barreling through the living room and skidding across the dining room floor.

"You're going to wear out your socks that way," she said. "Your shirt is in the laundry."

"But I want to wear it!" His mouth turned down in a pout.

"We'll find something else. Have you had breakfast?"

"No. I want pancakes. Dad said I'd have to wait for you to get home."

"Sorry, no pancakes today. Oatmeal or cold cereal."

"But I want…"

"Aiden, I don't have time today. You can have an applesauce muffin with your cereal."

He let out an exaggerated sigh. His shoulders slumped. "All right."

Shelley was afraid he'd learned the sigh from her. She'd have to watch her reactions around the children.

"Let's go get your clothes on. Scoot."

Aiden turned and ran upstairs, with Shelley right behind him. He bumped the wall as he passed Emma and Hailey's room.

"Mama, Mama, Mama!" Emma's voice got more and more insistent.

"Just a minute, Emma. Hailey? Are you dressed?"

"Almost. Can you help me with my hair?"

"Sure. Just a minute. I've got to get Aiden started."

Aiden had pulled all the shirts out of his dresser drawer looking for his Spider-Man shirt. Shelley stifled a sigh. As she dug through the shirts, she almost laughed. How could she possibly handle running the Cove? She couldn't even handle her own household. She must be crazy to consider it for even a second.

CHAPTER SIX

The headlights of Beverly's dark-gray Ford punched holes in the predawn darkness outside Diane's house as she walked down the sidewalk. The only other light came from Shelley's house across the street.

"Good morning," Beverly said as Diane got into the car. "How are you? Did you get any sleep?"

"Not much. But I might get to sleep while they put my port in. They'll do a local anesthetic, but they'll give me something to relax. You know, you don't have to stay with me. It's going to be a long day."

"That's all right. I brought my laptop, and I have a book to read if I get tired of working."

"This will be the longest day." Diane turned to look at her friend. "I can't tell you how much I appreciate this. I know you have a lot to do with your business and the election."

"You're my friend. I want to be there with you. My goodness, you've helped me, you've encouraged me, you've listened to me whine and complain, and you've given me tons of your time when I know you should have been writing. This is nothing."

"No. It's everything. I've been feeling very alone. Last time I had Eric and Jessica with me. This time, they're not around."

"Well, I'm glad I can be here. What about Rocky? Will he be all right?"

"Shelley will take him for a walk if we're not back by two."

It was ten o'clock by the time Diane got through all the admission procedures and was finally wheeled in to get her port. They'd given her an intravenous medication to relax her, and it worked. She woke up in the recovery room. A nurse was leaning over her bed.

"Diane, I need to take your blood pressure again."

There was a blood pressure cuff on her upper arm. The nurse pumped it up, then listened with a stethoscope as it slowly released. "Good." She checked her pulse. "How do you feel?"

"Groggy. How long have I been in here?"

"Not long. About a half hour. Everything went well. You can go back to sleep. You'll be here for another hour at least. Then we'll wheel you down to get an X-ray."

"Okay. Thanks." Diane closed her eyes and drifted off. When she woke, Beverly was sitting in a chair next to the bed. She was typing on her laptop.

Diane moved, and she felt an ache in her chest beneath her shoulder bone. She groaned, and Beverly looked up.

"Are you all right? Do you need the nurse?"

"No. Just sore where they put the port in. How long have I been asleep?"

"About an hour." Beverly smiled. "You were right. You've had a good nap."

"Whatever they gave me really knocked me out."

"That's good."

The nurse came back. "Good, you're awake. It's time to send you down for an X-ray."

An orderly came in and wheeled her away. She felt a little sore, but she was so relaxed that she had a hard time getting her legs and arms to move. The X-ray confirmed that her port was in the right place, and the orderly wheeled her back to the recovery room. As soon as she got there, the surgical doctor came in to see her. He checked her port, told her everything looked fine, then released her to get her first chemotherapy treatment.

A clerk from the infusion center came and escorted Diane and Beverly to a large, open room with eight comfortable-looking recliners set up as treatment stations. They stopped at a reception desk, where Diane had to get checked in.

"Welcome. You must be Diane," a smiling young woman said. "Please sit down and we'll get you registered. Your friend can stay with you." She pulled a second chair over.

"You just got your port this morning?" she asked.

"Yes. The doctor said I could go ahead and start the treatments." Diane was still feeling relaxed. She wanted to get this over with before the medicine wore off.

"I have your chart. It'll take a few minutes to get your medicine prepared." She asked Diane a bunch of questions and double-checked everything to make sure she had the right patient. Then she took Diane and Beverly to a treatment chair and got Diane settled in.

"Hello. Welcome to our special little group," a cheerful voice said. Diane looked around. In the next chair, at least two yards away, an older lady wearing a bright purple turban was smiling at her with a toothy grin. She was very thin and pale, but there was a sparkle in her eyes.

"Hello. How are you?" Diane asked without thinking. Perhaps that wasn't the best thing to ask someone who was getting a chemotherapy treatment.

"Oh, I couldn't be better," she answered, which Diane thought was an interesting response. Either she was in denial or she had a great attitude and outlook on life.

"I'm Mable. Is this your first time?"

"First time here," Diane said. "First time in a very long time."

"Ah." Mable nodded. "You'll do fine. You're not alone, you know."

Diane smiled. "Yes, I do know. We're never alone."

Mable grinned. She might have continued if the nurse hadn't come with Diane's treatment and diverted her attention.

The dreaded moment when the strong medication started flowing through the IV tube came and went with little ceremony. Diane had held her breath, steeling herself against the cold that coursed into her veins, then let it out and tried to relax.

Beverly sat next to her, watching with a slight frown. When Diane looked up at her, she smiled.

"How are you doing?"

"Not as bad as I expected. I guess that's a good sign. I hope I do as well as Mable over there. What a great spirit."

"This doesn't look like it will take too long. The nurse said you can have something to eat. Are you hungry?"

"Not really."

"I could get you a milkshake or some yogurt. Don't want your blood sugar to crash."

"I suppose you're right. Did you get some lunch while I was napping?"

"No. How about I get us both a milkshake?"

"That sounds good." Diane wasn't hungry, but she knew she should eat, and Beverly must be hungry. Besides, this gave Beverly something to do other than sit and wait.

While Beverly was gone, Diane looked around. A younger man, perhaps in his thirties, was sleeping through his treatment. A woman close to her own age was crocheting while she got her treatment. Looked like a hat. She had on earbuds attached to a small device, listening to music or something. Diane had an iPod at home that she rarely used. She could use it as a distraction.

"She makes hats for cancer patients," Mable said. Diane looked over at her. She pointed toward the lady. "Ask at the reception desk when you leave. They have a pile of her hats for anyone who wants one. All colors and styles."

"What a wonderful ministry," Diane said. She wondered what she could do to help others. At the moment, nothing came to mind.

Beverly returned with two tall drinks. "I found a yogurt shop about a block from here. This is a tropical shake, with all kinds of yummy fruit in it. I hope you like it."

Diane took a sip. It was smooth and cold and went down easily. After the initial chill, the chemo hadn't affected her system yet. "This is yummy. Thank you."

"Good. I'm glad you like it." She opened a small sack and held it out to Diane. "I got us each a soft pretzel too. They're still warm."

Diane took one and bit into it. The soft, yeasty dough and coarse salt tasted surprisingly good. She ate the whole thing and drank all of her shake.

Her treatment took less than an hour. The nurse gave her a sack of supplies to clean and dress her stitches where the port was inserted. There were brochures about nutrition and what to expect while she was getting chemotherapy. Her grogginess from the surgical procedure had lifted. She was able to walk out with Beverly without help.

They stopped at the drugstore on the way home so Diane could pick up a prescription for pain pills. She didn't want to take anything, but the doctor warned her that she would have discomfort from the port insertion for a while. Beverly convinced her it wouldn't hurt to have something on hand in case she needed it. The ordeal of the day had caught up with her. Diane was too tired to argue.

Beverly insisted on carrying Diane's bags into the house. Rocky wasn't there to greet her. As Diane hung up her jacket, there was a knock on the door. Beverly opened it and let Shelley in.

"How is she?" she asked, keeping her voice low, but Diane could hear her.

"I'm fine. Come on in."

"I won't stay. I just brought you some chicken and dumplings and bread fresh out of the oven. Margaret took Rocky."

Tears sprang to Diane's eyes. She blinked them away. "Thank you. That's so sweet." Her voice choked up on her words. Had the chemo affected her throat?

"You're welcome. I hope you like them. I put blueberry muffins in the bag for your breakfast too."

Just then, Margaret arrived with Rocky. He was still on his leash, and she held on so he wouldn't rush Diane in his excitement.

"Rocky." She was so glad to see him. It was like having a member of her family there. He wagged his tail and tugged at his leash. Margaret let him go. He came to Diane and gently nudged her hand with his nose. She scratched his head.

"He had a good run. He won't need any more exercise today. Do you want me to come over tonight and take him out?"

"No, we'll be fine. Thank you for taking him for a walk."

"No problem. We had a great time, didn't we, Rocky? I'll take him tomorrow afternoon too. Is there anything else I can do?"

"You've all done so much already, I'm overwhelmed."

"I think you're overly tired after all you've been through today," Beverly said.

"Yes, we're going to leave you alone to rest," Shelley said. "I want to give you a hug, but I know you're sore." She blew Diane a kiss, which made her smile.

"I'm off too," Margaret said. "We'll see you tomorrow. If you need anything, no matter what time it is, call. Okay?" She held her hand up to her head, thumb and pinky extended like a phone.

"Okay. Thanks."

Beverly stayed behind. When they'd left, she said, "Why don't you go change into something comfortable so you can rest? I'll wait, in case you need some help."

"I'll be fine."

"I know you will, but I'll wait anyway. Are you hungry? Do you want a little of the chicken heated up now?"

"No. I'll have some later."

"Then I'll put it in the refrigerator while you change." Beverly went into the kitchen.

Diane put on a loose pair of pajamas. Moving her arms pulled against her chest. Pain from the incisions and stitches for the port radiated out to her arm. Her head was pounding. She took a blanket and pillow and went back out to the living room and sat on the couch.

"I can see the pain in your eyes. How about a pain pill?" Beverly asked.

"Yes. I think I'll take one."

"I'll get it." Beverly went back in the kitchen and came back with a glass of water and the bottle of pills. She waited while Diane took it. Then Diane leaned back against the pillow.

"You know, I could stay here with you tonight."

"Oh no. I'll be fine. I'm just going to rest. I'll go to bed early."

"Do you have your cell phone charged, so you can call if you need anything?"

"My bag is right here by the couch. It's in there."

Beverly looked around. "Okay. I'll go, then. Call one of us if you need anything. We mean it."

"I know. I can't believe I've been blessed with such special friends. Having you with me today made it all bearable."

Beverly reached down and squeezed Diane's hand gently. "I'm glad. And I blocked out all my Fridays so I can take you to your treatments. And it's my pleasure. I want to be with you through this."

Diane nodded and yawned. "I want you with me. And I think my pill is starting to work."

"In that case, go to sleep. I'll see you tomorrow." Beverly put on her coat and left.

"Well, Rocky, it's just you and me."

Rocky whined and put his head in Diane's lap. She petted him for a moment, then lay back. Usually Rocky went to his bed, but today he curled up on the floor next to her. He let out a big sigh, then put his head down and closed his eyes. Day one was over. She'd made it through, thanks to her friends.

Just then her stomach roiled. Bile rose in her throat, choking her. She pushed to her feet and hurried to the bathroom. Nothing came up. She felt clammy and hot, all at once. She steadied herself as dry heaves overtook her.

So soon? She hadn't expected to react so quickly. When her stomach finally subsided, she rinsed her mouth and washed her face, then made it back to the couch. Rocky was sitting, watching her intently. His eyes held pity. Diane sat on the couch and hugged her big, shaggy friend. "How are we going to do this, boy?"

Rocky shifted closer, as if giving her a hug. She clung to him and let the tears flow. "Lord, I feel so helpless. That woman, Mable, said we're never alone. I need to know that. I need to feel Your presence. Help me, please."

She didn't expect an answer. Certainly not an audible one. When the phone rang, she nearly jumped out of her skin. She picked up her cell phone. Justin.

"Hello, sweetheart," she said.

"Hey, Mom. I prayed for you today. How did it go? How are you feeling?"

She laughed and wiped away a tear. Goodness, she was turning into a faucet. "It went fine. Beverly took me and stayed with me. And I feel about like you'd expect. Not great, but not too bad."

"In other words, lousy, huh?"

"I did, until you called. Now I feel much better. Your voice was just what I needed. Funny thing is, I was just praying and telling God I need to feel His presence when the phone rang. For a minute, I thought God was calling."

"That's awesome, Mom. I wish I could be there to help you."

"As much as I'd love to see you, I wouldn't wish that on you. You'd go stir-crazy. So catch me up. Tell me what's happening in your life."

By the time she hung up, Diane had forgotten her unsettled stomach and thoughts of the future. She managed to eat a few bites of Shelley's chicken and dumplings, let Rocky out for a few minutes, and then go to bed. As she lay there, waiting for sleep, she thought about her prayer and Justin's call. *God works in mysterious ways, His wonders to perform.* Was that a Bible verse or something she'd heard somewhere? She wasn't sure, but she knew it was true. Though she dreaded the next six weeks, she knew God would be with her through it all.

Chapter Seven

Shelley was glad Rusty wasn't at the Cove when she dropped off her daily order on Saturday. She had thought about his offer. His suggestion that she could run the coffee shop had hovered on the edges of her consciousness like a carrot, or a dark-chocolate truffle—tantalizing, but just out of her reach. Her thoughts mingled with the demands on her time, causing confusion. She almost wished he hadn't shared his idea with her.

She hurried home, knowing Dan had to leave for work early. He didn't usually work on Saturday, but they had a rush job to finish. It meant overtime, which was great for the pocketbook, but Shelley had hoped he'd be home to play with the kids and give her some uninterrupted time in the kitchen. He met her at the door, going out as she came in. He gave her a quick kiss, then sprinted to his truck.

A pile of dishes filled the sink and counter. Someone had toasted frozen waffles for breakfast. The rest of the package sat on the counter, thawed. A jug of milk and bottle of apple juice sat on the dining room table, which was sticky with syrup and grape jelly. Cheerios and chocolate chips were strewn across the table.

Prize started barking upstairs. Then she heard a screech. "Me, me, me..."

"No. I need it!" Aiden's voice, distressed.

"Emma, let go." Hailey's voice, trying to referee between the two siblings.

Shelley started up the stairs. The three children were in the hall having a tug-of-war over Aiden's blue hoodie. Shelley stepped in and gently pried Emma's fingers off the sweatshirt. She picked up her daughter, who was sobbing now.

"This one is Aiden's, sweetie. Yours is in the laundry." Emma had a hoodie too, but it had a cartoon rabbit astronaut on it.

Emma put her thumb in her mouth, which was covered with chocolate. Aiden had chocolate on his face too.

"Aiden, go wash your face and hands, then get dressed." She turned to Hailey. "I'll take care of these two so you can get dressed."

"Okay. Can we go to the store today and get some stuff for my science project?"

"Yes, but it will have to be this afternoon."

"Hello! Where is everyone?"

Oh no! Frances. Of all mornings.

Emma's eyes lit up with a look of delight.

"Meemaw!" Aiden started to run downstairs, but Shelley caught him. "Not until you finish washing up and get dressed."

Aiden let out a big sigh. Probably like she'd just done. He marched into his room.

"We're up here, Frances. Just getting the children dressed. Have a cup of coffee, we'll be right down."

Too late. Frances was halfway up the stairs.

"Whatever happened here? Is everything all right?" She looked genuinely concerned.

"I just got back from making deliveries. Dan had to leave early, so we're a bit behind this morning."

"Well, give me that baby. I'll take care of her." She reached out her hands, and Emma leaned toward her, stretching away from Shelley's arms.

"She has chocolate all over her hands and face. She'll get it on you."

"Oh, fiddle-faddle. A little chocolate won't bother me. Come to Meemaw, sweetie pie." She took Emma and went into the bathroom, where Hailey was brushing her teeth.

Resigned to her mother-in-law's visit, Shelley helped Aiden get dressed. Frances had taken Emma downstairs. The two of them were picking up toys and clothes in the living room. Frances would put an item in a basket, and Emma would giggle and take it back out. Shelley shook her head. At least Frances had wonderful patience with her grandchildren.

"Kids, you can watch a cartoon while Grandma and I have a cup of coffee."

"Yes, we need to talk," Frances said.

Oh dear. That usually meant she wanted to give Shelley advice. Shelley believed Frances meant well. She'd learned that Frances cared about her and wanted to be helpful, but sometimes her advice felt like criticism. "Give me a minute to clear off the table and make fresh coffee," Shelley said.

"I'll help you." Frances followed her into the disaster that was the kitchen.

Shelley grabbed a damp cloth and trash can and went after the table. She heard the water running and turned to find Frances starting to wash the dishes.

"Why don't you sit down and let me do that? I'll put them in the dishwasher."

Frances gave her a resigned look. "I suppose you have your own way of loading, but really, I can do it. After all, I've been taking care of my house for longer than you've been alive."

"I know, and I appreciate the offer, but you didn't come here to clean."

Frances wiped her hands on a dish towel, then sat down. Shelley started a fresh pot of coffee, then quickly loaded the dishwasher and started it. That cleared the worst of the mess. She put away the milk and syrup and chocolate sauce.

"Your family can certainly make a mess," Frances said when Shelley carried two cups of coffee and a plate of goodies to the table.

"Have a pumpkin biscotti."

"That sounds wonderful. Is that one of your Thanksgiving bakery items?"

"Yes. I added them to my Internet list. They ship well."

She had wanted to bake this morning while the children played. She hoped Frances wouldn't stay too long.

Frances took a cookie and nibbled on it. "Mmm. These are good." She dipped it in her coffee and bit off a bite. "Very good. Would you make some of these for Thanksgiving?"

"Sure." Last year Frances had dropped Thanksgiving dinner in Shelley's lap. She and Dan had hosted the entire Bauer clan in their small home, before she'd had a new kitchen and dining room. This year would be a lot easier. She even had a working dishwasher this year. She wondered if that was what Frances wanted to talk about.

"Dan told his father he's doing well in his electrical apprenticeship. Of course I knew he would. He's very handy and smart."

Shelley smiled. "Dan seems to love it. And I think his boss appreciates his hard work and desire to learn. And his willingness to work overtime, like today."

"I'm sure he does. He's lucky to have such a good employee. Dan losing his job at the wharf was a blessing. Now he has a real career."

"Yes, I suppose it was."

"And with Dan supporting you again, you can quit all this baking and get back to taking care of your family." Frances sat back with a pleased smile as if she had solved all Shelley's problems. She could go back to being Suzie Homemaker and give up her business.

"I have a lot of customers depending on me," Shelley said. "And I enjoy baking for them. That's why Ralph and Dan built this kitchen."

"Yes. But you had to help your family then. Don't you think it's been hard on them, having you constantly baking for someone else? Really, Shelley, the children need you. And now you have your niece to care for. I know you're talented, but you're not Superwoman."

If Frances' comments hadn't stung, Shelley might have laughed at her backhanded compliment. At least she thought Shelley was talented.

"I am here for my family every day." Frances had walked into another disaster that morning. It seemed she had a talent for finding the worst possible moments to drop in.

"Yes, but your time is divided. Think about it. I'm sure you'll see I'm right. Oh, and the reason I came by today—I'm going to have Thanksgiving at my house this year. You did a good job last year, but I missed using my Thanksgiving dishes. It's tradition, you know. You can bring the pies. Pumpkin, apple, and pecan. And homemade rolls. That would be lovely."

Frances stood. "Well, I must get home." She went into the living room and said good-bye to the kids. They let her distract them from the cartoons long enough to give her a kiss and hug.

"Good-bye, my sweethearts. See you later."

"Buh-bye, Meemaw. See you wait-ah." Emma opened and closed her hand in a chubby wave.

After Frances left, Shelley carried the cups to the sink, then stood looking out the window. Should she close the Lighthouse Sweet Shoppe? She loved baking for people. What about Rusty's offer for her to take over managing the Cove when he retired? He thought she could do it. But at what cost? If Frances didn't think Shelley could handle her work and her family now, what would it be like if she took over the Cove? She and Dan had decided she would be a stay-at-home mom and he would support the family, and it seemed they were back at that point. Did Dan want her to quit? Had he said something to his father or mother to prompt Frances' lecture?

Shelley didn't know, but she did have commitments for Thanksgiving, so she wouldn't make any decisions until after the holiday.

★ ★ ★

Beverly peeked into her father's study. He was in his pajamas and bathrobe, his glasses perched on his nose as he read the newspaper. "Good morning, Father. Is that the local newspaper?"

He looked up. "Morning, Beverly. I was just reading the article about you." He nodded gravely. "Kimball did all right by you. He includes quotes from your boss at the State House and even from the secretary of state. They gave glowing statements on your honesty, integrity, and qualifications. When Kimball said it had been suggested that you want to be mayor to further your own business, your boss said that was preposterous. He got quotes from other coworkers and some of your clients. All positive. That should clear up any accusations of your trustworthiness."

Beverly breathed a sigh of relief. She was glad she'd been able to defend herself and give references at the newspaper office. She wondered again at the timing of the train whistle. She hadn't been in danger, but hearing the sound had put her on guard.

★ ★ ★

Diane had woken feeling halfway decent Saturday morning. Pleased, she got dressed, ate one of Shelley's muffins and a couple of tablespoons of yogurt, then got ready to take Rocky for a walk.

A thin layer of fog shrouded the neighborhood. A bright spot showed the sun trying to break through. Across the street, Diane could make out Frances Bauer's car pulling away from the curb in front of Shelley's house. She hoped Frances hadn't ruined Shelley's morning. Her mother-in-law had a talent for upsetting her.

Rocky tugged on his leash, then looked up at Diane as if to say, "Remember why we're out here?"

"I'm coming," she said, turning toward the boardwalk.

They walked for ten minutes, going slower than usual. No one else was out that morning. The fog began to lift like a curtain, showing the shore beneath the layer of gray. Sandpipers scurried along in groups that looked like waves of motion, darting, then stopping, then darting forward again. Diane let Rocky off his leash and he chased after them for the sheer fun of running. The birds scattered, then regrouped ahead of him. He lunged forward again and they repeated their evasive maneuvers.

It felt good to be out in the fresh air, breathing in the salty scents and feeling the misty air. Then a wave of nausea hit her. A taste of bile rose in her throat. She stopped and looked around. Just off the path she spotted a boulder and went to lean against it. Rocky was a mere speck ahead of her, racing along the water toward the rocky tide pools. She didn't have the energy to call him. She reached in her pocket for a tissue.

Then she saw a dark figure coming down the boardwalk. As it got closer, she recognized Beverly, out for her morning jog. Diane stood and started toward her, but the nausea hit again, making her double over.

Beverly veered off the path and came to her. "Diane, are you all right? Where's Rocky?"

"Down the beach." Diane pointed. "I was feeling pretty good, but breakfast isn't sitting too well."

"Give me his leash, then go rest against that rock. I'll get him and help you back home."

Diane nodded. Her stomach roiled. She made it back to the rock and lost her breakfast in the bushes.

Five minutes seemed like hours when Beverly and Rocky returned. Rocky sensed her distress and nudged against her, looking up with soulful eyes.

"Think you can walk back?"

"Yeah. I'm sorry to interrupt your jog, but I was sure glad to see you coming. I didn't know how I was going to get Rocky to come back."

"No problem. I'm glad I was here."

Diane nodded and walked as quickly as she could. She wanted to get back to the comfort of her home and the proximity of her couch and bathroom.

Beverly made sure she was settled before she left to resume her run. She offered to take Rocky, but he lay down next to the couch and didn't want to leave Diane's side.

Diane rested and her stomach settled down. She dozed off, then woke at noon feeling hungry.

She wasn't sure if the muffin or the yogurt had upset her stomach or if the exercise had been too much. She opted for a piece of toast and a soft-boiled egg. After she ate, she went back to the couch and picked up a mystery that she'd checked out of the library. She'd gotten immersed in the story when the phone rang. Leo Spangler. She debated whether to answer or let him leave a message. She didn't want to talk to anyone, but she didn't want to have to call him back, either.

"Hello, Leo."

"Hi, Diane. How are you feeling? I was wondering if I could drop by this afternoon and see you."

"Oh. I'm sorry, but I'm not up to having company. I need to rest today. I tried taking a walk earlier and it didn't work out too well."

"I'm sorry to hear that. How can I help? Do you want me to take Rocky for a few days so you don't have to worry about feeding or walking him?"

She looked down at her companion, who was watching her intently. Rocky might be better off with Leo, but she would miss him. Just knowing he was there, ready to lavish her with devotion, made her feel better. She reached down and scratched him between his ears. His tail thumped against the rug. "Thanks for the offer, but he's no trouble, and Margaret Hoskins is walking him for me."

"All right. Please call me if you need anything."

"Thanks, Leo. I will."

After she hung up, Diane got up and made a cup of herbal tea. Her stomach growled. Deciding she was hungry, she warmed up a small dish of Shelley's chicken and dumplings. It smelled good. It tasted good. She ate a couple of bites, then set it aside. She didn't want to push her luck.

She'd washed her few dishes and made a cup of herbal tea. As she settled back on the couch with her laptop, her phone rang. Jessica.

"Hi, darling."

"Hey, Mom, how are you doing?"

"Not too bad. I just had some of Shelley's chicken and dumplings."

"Yum. And how did it sit?"

"So far, so good. Last night it took awhile to hit me, though, so we'll see."

"You've been nauseated?"

"A couple of times."

"Are you taking something for the nausea?"

"I took some medicine this morning afterward. It seems to be working."

"Good. I was just thinking about Thanksgiving. I told you I'll do all the cooking, so you don't need to be concerned about feeding me. I plan to feed *you*. Did you want to get together with any of your friends?"

"They'll be with their families. It'll just be us and we can keep it really simple."

"What about Leo Spangler? He's alone. Invite him to join us."

"I don't think so. I'd rather have you to myself."

"We'll have plenty of time. I really like him, and I got the impression he thinks a lot of you."

"He's a friend, but that's all."

"Well, friends can get together for a holiday meal. Think about it."

"All right."

"Good."

Diane was sure her answer would be the same. She knew the chemo would affect her in physical ways. By Thanksgiving, her hair would be gone. She'd have dark circles under her eyes. She might have a hard time keeping Thanksgiving dinner down. She did not want Leo to see her that way. Was she being vain? Did it matter?

★ ★ ★

Margaret sat on a stool in the back of the gallery staring at a blank canvas. A picture she'd taken at the limestone quarry was tacked to the easel. But where to begin and how to proceed?

As much as she wanted to start this painting, she lacked inspiration. She felt blah for no reason that she could think of. She should be feeling on top of the world. Her health had improved. The gallery was prospering, even with the tourist season past. Her success with Lighting the Way Greeting Card Company continued. Adelaide loved being a college student and she was doing well in the childhood development class she was taking at Evergreen Community College. But for some reason, Margaret felt a sense of discontentment.

She shook off her melancholy and forced her attention back to the canvas and the photograph. The colors of the onset of winter called for shades of gray and white, shades of brown, ochre—colors that could be drab. She wanted this picture to be vibrant and alive, and yet show the peace and repose of the coming season. Transition and introspection. Those were the emotions the scene evoked. Could she pull it off? Not if she couldn't reach down inside of herself and pull up those moods. As she sat there contemplating her situation, her thoughts called up restlessness and dissatisfaction. Far from the calm, pleasant introspection she thought of for winter.

She loaded the palate with acrylic paint in shades of deep purple, reds, and gold tones, as well as blue, black, and white.

Did she want to wash the background with blue or purple? And why was it so hard to start?

She dipped her brush into the blue and made sweeping brushstrokes, filling the upper half with the background base. She washed the general area of the lake with the blue. Then she stopped and stared again.

The back door opened and Allan came in, toting a small drop-leaf table. He set it down and came over to her.

"What gives? You haven't done much since I left two hours ago. Artist's block?" He rubbed her shoulders, loosening the kinks that she didn't know were there. "You're tense. What's wrong?"

"I don't know. I woke up in a funky mood and I can't shake it."

"Maybe it's the change of seasons. I can feel winter starting to settle in my bones."

"You might be right. I'm sure it will pass." November seemed too early for the winter blahs. If her mood transferred to her painting, it would be a drab landscape. She might as well put up her paints for the day and go take a nap.

CHAPTER EIGHT

Hoar frost covered the trees and lawns Tuesday morning when Diane stepped outside to join her friends. Margaret's car was idling at the curb. Clouds formed above the van's hood from the warmth of the engine. Rays of sunshine pierced through the fog, turning the frosted landscape into a field of diamonds. Diane pulled her stocking cap over her ears. Her nose had to be bright red.

"Good morning," Margaret said as she climbed into the front passenger seat. Beverly, Shelley and Emma were already in the backseat.

"Good morning. Gorgeous day, isn't it?"

"You sound chipper," Shelley said. "How do you feel?"

"Good. Sunday was the worst. Yesterday I felt better. Today I feel almost normal."

"Wonderful! Don't overdo today," Beverly said.

"How do you feel?" Diane asked, turning to look at Beverly. "Are you nervous?"

"Yes. I don't know why. I'll either win or lose. And I have no control over the outcome, so I might as well relax."

"I'd be a nervous wreck," Shelley said. "Dan voted on his way to work. He called and said the polling place was crowded."

"Allan and Adelaide stopped to vote before he dropped her at the bus stop."

"I'm going back this afternoon to take my father and Mrs. Peabody," Beverly said. "I considered waiting to vote with them, but I'm curious to see how it's going. And I didn't want to put it off."

Margaret parked in back of the gallery and they walked to the municipal building annex. As they came up to the building, the line of voters extended out the door. Dennis Calder was near the front of the line with a group of his employees and friends. Two men held up Calder for Mayor signs and loudly proclaimed Dennis would save the town from financial disaster so people should vote for him. Dennis was smiling and shaking hands with everyone around him.

Diane was tempted to yell out a "Vote for Beverly," but knew she'd only provoke the men, and besides, what Dennis was doing was technically illegal and she didn't want any part of that.

Once they got inside they saw tables set up in the front with precinct workers checking names and handing out ballots. Four curtained booths were set to one side of the room.

Augie Jackson was up front. One of the men told him to vote for Dennis. Augie turned toward the friends. For an old man, his voice was strong.

"See that lady back there? That's Beverly Wheeland. She's my choice for mayor. She's one smart lady, and she cares about this town."

A precinct worker asked everyone to settle down.

Dennis and his friends had made their way inside as well. Once they voted they came face to face with the four friends.

"Don't waste your vote. I'm going to win this election. This town needs a strong leader with progressive plans. That's me." He nodded and walked out.

"Don't pay him any attention," Augie said. "He's the one who'll be surprised tonight."

Beverly smiled and thanked him. Diane wanted to hug the old man and punch Dennis Calder. To think she had once considered Dennis a nice guy. He'd wanted to date Beverly. Now he treated her like an enemy.

The mood inside the Municipal Building lightened as soon as Dennis left. Several people greeted Beverly and wished her luck. She smiled and greeted people by name and showed an interest in the people around her. She looked the part of a successful businesswoman in her tailored wool slacks and blazer. Her calm and confidence shined through. What a difference. Surely the townspeople could see that Beverly was the best choice they could make. Diane was glad that she was well enough to participate. She couldn't wait to hear the results of the election.

★ ★ ★

"Are you ready?" Beverly's father was standing by the door, ready to leave. He'd dressed up in his best wool suit.

"Almost. I can't find my leather gloves." Beverly searched her purse a second time.

"Maybe they're in a pocket."

"I looked in my other jacket. Oh, wait. I had my blazer on this morning. Maybe I put them in that pocket." She ran up the stairs to her bedroom.

Sure enough, she found the gloves in the pocket. She glanced in the mirror. Her hair was still in place. She could feel her heart beating. Why was she so nervous? And where was Jeff? She'd been expecting him all day.

She couldn't delay any longer. Her friends would be waiting for her at the Municipal Building. The clerk would run the ballots through the counter at eight o'clock sharp. She went back downstairs.

"I'm ready. Don't you look handsome tonight." She took hold of her father's arm and let him walk her to the car.

"I'm nervous too," he said as he escorted her to the driver's door of her dark Ford Fusion. He squeezed her hand and smiled.

"Yeah." She took a deep breath. "Thanks, Father."

They stopped to pick up Coral Peabody. When they finally walked into the Municipal Building, a crowd had gathered. Their group was clustered to one side. Diane waved at them. Next to her were Margaret, Allan, and Adelaide, Shelley and Augie Jackson. Beverly was pleased to see Gilda Harris, the librarian, and Floyd Carney, the head of the historical society, talking with Diane and Margaret. That didn't mean they were supporters, but it was nice to see them on her side of the room. Dennis and his supporters were the loudest contingent on the far side of the room. The mayor, Evelyn Waters, was busy talking to the town clerk. Her son Lee, the third candidate, stood beside her.

Gerald Kimball stood alone, a camera with a large lens in hand. He snapped pictures of the various groups of people around the room. He gave her a wave, then snapped her picture. She hoped she had smiled at him.

Beverly glanced at her watch. Fifteen minutes until the official count. Her nervous excitement was tempered by disappointment. Jeff wasn't there.

The front door opened, letting in a whoosh of frigid air. She turned, and there stood Jeff, his broad shoulders and handsome face framed in the doorway. Next to him, Edward Maker was removing his hat. No wonder Jeff was late. He'd gone to Augusta to bring his grandfather. She went to greet them. When Jeff saw her, a knockout smile spread across his face. He enveloped her in a big hug and kissed her. His strength gave her a sense of well-being. Looking up into his loving eyes, she knew everything was fine. She turned and hugged Edward and kissed his cheek.

"Hello, young lady. I'm sorry I made Jeffrey late. I insisted on coming to hear the results. This is a big night."

"Thank you for coming. I hope it isn't a disappointment," she said.

"It won't be." Jeff put his arm around her shoulder and together they joined their friends. She suddenly hoped her friends wouldn't be disappointed if she didn't win. They'd all worked hard and supported her in so many ways. She didn't want to let them down.

Someone at the front of the room started a countdown. *10. 9. 8. 7. 6 . . .*

Beverly didn't realize she was squeezing Jeff's hand until he squeezed back. When she looked up, he was smiling down at her. She took a deep breath, then let it out and laughed.

"I think I'm nervous."

"We're all nervous and excited." Shelley held up her hands. Her fingers were crossed.

The elections clerk, the council members, and the mayor crowded into the office where the ballot-counting machine was kept. The crowd grew quiet. Low murmurs replaced the chatter.

"Now I know how all the candidates felt at the State House every election cycle. Someone wins, which means someone has to lose, unless they run unopposed. The campaigning is hard, but this waiting is harder."

"Attention, everyone!" Jules Benton, the town council president, raised his hand high in the air. "I have the results." The crowd became silent.

"Dennis Calder got thirty-one percent of the votes cast. Beverly Wheeland got forty-six percent of the votes cast. Lee Waters got twenty-three percent of the votes cast. Congratulations to our new mayor, Beverly Wheeland!"

The group around Beverly erupted with shouts and applause. For a moment, she stood frozen in place, stunned. She'd hoped, but hadn't dared believe, she would beat Dennis and Lee.

"Congratulations, Beverly!" sounded in unison all around her.

"Smile, darling," Jeff said, leaning down. "That reporter is going to take your picture."

She looked up and smiled just as a flash went off. Then another. *It was true.* She was the mayor-elect of Marble Cove. Amazing how her life had changed in a short year.

Everyone wanted to shake her hand. She smiled and thanked at least a dozen people. Out of the corner of her eye, Beverly saw Dennis Calder leave. He shot a glare her direction that sent a chill down her spine before he stalked out the door.

"Congratulations, Beverly. I look forward to working with you," Jules said, extending his hand.

"Thank you. I'd like to meet with you soon and start learning as much as I can about the town and its operations."

"I'll be happy to help in any way I can," he said, looking pleased that she deferred to him.

Next thing she knew, Beverly was outside, walking down the sidewalk with Jeff and all of her friends. She had no idea where they were going, but she was still in a daze and content to go along.

Allan opened the door to the gallery. It was dark inside, but they all went in. As soon as she stepped through the doorway, the lights came on.

"Surprise!"

She blinked against the light and realized the room was crowded. Shouts of congratulations filled the air. It seemed as if the entire town was there.

Balloons and streamers hung from the ceiling and looped around the walls. In the middle of the room on a table was a beautiful sheet cake with pale aquamarine frosting on top and the words *Embracing Our Heritage: Vote Beverly!* in bright gold and deep-pink lettering, just like her campaign buttons.

Allan took her coat and bag. Shelley handed Beverly and Jeff glasses of foamy pink punch. Next to the cake table, Margaret raised her glass high in the air and yelled for attention. When it quieted down, she said, "I give you our new mayor, Beverly Wheeland. Congratulations, Beverly!"

There were "hip-hip-hoorays," and "hear, hears," and someone yelled, "Cut the cake!" followed by lots of laughter.

"Mayor, please cut the first piece," Shelley said, handing Beverly a knife.

She stepped forward and looked down at the beautiful creation her friend had made for her. Beside the cake were platters of colorful appetizers and a cut-glass punch bowl with frothy pink punch. Her throat tightened with emotion. She looked up at her dear friends, standing behind the table watching her, then at all the people who had come to wish her well. How blessed she was. She stepped to the side.

"It's too beautiful to cut," she said. "Did someone get a picture of all this?"

A flash went off. She looked up and there was another flash. Then she realized it was Jeff. He'd brought a camera and was taking pictures.

"Now cut it. I'm salivating!" Augie Jackson said. "Besides, it's past my bedtime."

Amid the laughter, Beverly cut the cake. She handed Augie a piece. "Thank you, friend. Your support means a lot to me. I'll be coming to you for advice."

"I'll hold you to that," he said, accepting the cake with a twinkle in his eyes.

Shelley, Diane, Margaret, and Adelaide took over serving the cake and punch.

"Go talk to people," Diane said. "I'll save you a piece."

"Thanks." Beverly turned to make the rounds. Mrs. Peabody stood in front of her.

"I'm so proud," she said. She reached up to give Beverly a hug. Surprised and touched by her declaration, Beverly leaned down and hugged the slight elderly lady.

"Thank you. You're an important part of my victory, you know." And it was true. "You've made it possible for me to do this."

Mrs. Peabody was beaming as Beverly turned to greet Rusty Garrison and his wife. Gilda Harris and Charlotte Vincent were there, as were the members of the town council and their spouses. Leo Spangler made a point of congratulating her, then went over to Diane. Beverly noticed he began to help pass out pieces of cake. Leo was such a nice man, and it was obvious he liked Diane more than a little bit. She wished Diane would find love the way she had.

Beverly was surprised to see Rev. Locke standing near the wall, watching the festivities. She made her way to him.

"Good evening, Rev. Locke. So nice to see you here."

"Congratulations, Beverly." He reached out and shook her hand. "I believe it's important to support my parishioners. You'll make a fine mayor."

"Thank you. I'll do my best. I'd appreciate your prayers for wisdom and right motivations as I serve."

He nodded seriously. "It will be my pleasure to pray for you."

"Beverly."

She turned to face Lee Waters and his mother.

"Hello, Lee. Mayor." She wasn't sure what to say to her rival, whom she'd just beaten.

"I wanted to congratulate you on your victory," he said. "You ran a good campaign and you deserved to win."

"Thank you. That's very generous of you."

"To tell you the truth," he said, leaning close so he could speak softly, "I'm relieved. Mother is disappointed, and I would have done my best if I'd won, but being in politics is not my desire."

Evelyn stepped up. "Congratulations, Beverly. I admit I wanted my son to succeed me, but I'm confident you'll put the town above your own interests."

"I appreciate that. I'd like to meet with you next week to map out a plan. I have so much to learn."

"Yes, you do. I'll help you, of course. I'd hate to see my hard work and leadership go for naught. It's already November, so you have less than two months to prepare."

"You're exactly right. I've taken several seminars through the Maine Municipal Association."

"Beverly." Jeff caught her attention. He'd been talking with Augie Jackson and his grandfather and her father.

"I'm going to take Grandpa and your father and Mrs. Peabody to your house, then I'll be back."

"Good idea. Could you take Augie home too? He looks like he's ready to drop."

"Of course. I'll see you later." He leaned down and kissed her cheek.

Beverly watched him walk away. Having him there, giving her moral support and watching out for her father, warmed her heart. She did love that man. She couldn't wait to have some time alone with him. Soon, she hoped.

★ ★ ★

"Wonderful party," Rusty told Shelley as the party wound down. Most of the guests were gone. "I was hoping there'd be one of the beef-and-cheddar wraps left. They were terrific."

"Thanks. I'm glad you liked them. I'm afraid I haven't had time to think about the Cove yet," she said.

"No worries. Take your time. Just come up with the right answer," he said, grinning. Then he raised his hands. "No pressure, you understand. I'm not in a hurry, but it would be nice to know the future is mapped out. Good night, now."

After he left, Shelley went back to cleaning up the food. The platters were nearly empty. Only two pieces of cake remained. She put them in a small plastic container to send home with Beverly.

Jeff had returned and was helping Beverly and Adelaide take down streamers. Leo was helping Diane gather trash, and Margaret and Allan were putting furniture and displays back in place.

Leo left, and soon it was just the friends and Allan, Adelaide, and Jeff.

"This was such a fabulous surprise," Beverly said when they finished and were getting ready to leave. "I can't believe you did this for me. I had no idea."

"You didn't guess with all our sneaking around?" Diane asked.

"No. My mind's been preoccupied, I suppose."

"And it's only the beginning," Margaret said. "Now you have a town to run."

Beverly laughed. "Amazing, isn't it? It hasn't sunk in yet. But the town council makes all the decisions, so I'll be more of a facilitator. I'm sure glad the campaign is over. That's a huge relief."

"Here's a couple of pieces of cake left over," Shelley said, handing the container to Beverly.

"Thank you. I got so busy talking to everyone, I never got a piece."

"Did you get anything to eat?"

"No. Just a glass of punch. I couldn't have eaten anyway. Too nervous and excited."

"It's too late to take you out to eat," Jeff said, "unless you want to ride with me to Augusta to take my grandfather home."

"Not tonight. I bet you haven't eaten, either. I'm sure there are leftovers in the refrigerator at home."

"Let's go stage a raid. I'll take you out tomorrow instead. Are you free?"

"For the entire day. No campaigning. No working."

"Good."

"You two go on. We're finished here for tonight," Margaret said.

"Thank you all again. I still can't believe it." Beverly hugged each of them, and then they left.

"Wow. This turned out great," Margaret said.

"What a turnout," Diane said. "Everyone loved your cake and finger foods, Shelley. I bet you get a lot more orders for the holidays."

"I hadn't thought of that." Shelley wondered if that would be a blessing or not. Could she handle a lot more orders? And Rusty had commented on her beef-and-cheddar wraps. She enjoyed occasional catering, like Beverly's party, but desserts were her forte. For now, she had more than she could handle with the sweets orders, but what did the future hold? What should it hold? Those questions filled her mind. She wished she could see into the future so she would know the right answers.

CHAPTER NINE

Beverly rose early. It was dark outside. The weather forecast called for clear skies and temperatures in the low forties. Picking an outfit took far longer than usual. She wanted to look her best for Jeff, but he hadn't said where they were going. Jeff loved the outdoors, but he hadn't mentioned anything about hiking. She discarded three outfits, then settled on gray wool flannel slacks and a soft lavender merino wool sweater that complemented her dark hair and made her feel feminine. She slipped on a pair of black leather flats, but took a pair of walking shoes downstairs to put in the car, just in case she needed them.

Jeff showed up at eight sharp. When she opened the door, he stepped inside and closed it behind him, then pulled her into his arms and kissed her.

"*Mmm.* What a nice way to start the day," she said, looking up into his warm eyes, which seemed to be sparkling just for her. He wore jeans, an oxford shirt and royal-blue wool sweater that set off his eyes and dark hair. His clothes didn't give away his plans. "You look handsome. I wasn't sure what to wear today."

"You're dressed fine. In fact, you look perfect. Have you had breakfast?"

"No. Would you like me to fix something?"

"No. I want to take you out for breakfast."

"Sounds good. Come say hello to Father before we go. He's in the kitchen."

Beverly kissed her father and made sure he had everything he needed for the day. Mrs. Peabody would fix his lunch and dinner. "I don't know when we'll be back," she said.

"I plan to keep her out all day," Jeff said.

"Don't worry about me. I'll be fine. Have a good time."

"We will." She said that with confidence, though she had no idea where they were going. She didn't care. Just being with Jeff made the day perfect.

"So where are we headed?" she asked as she got into his Subaru Forrester and buckled the seat belt.

"I need to go into Portland today. I went straight from the airport to my grandfather's, then down to Town Hall yesterday, so I haven't stopped by my condo to check messages and get a change of clothes. We'll stop for breakfast on the way." He glanced over at her. "That is, if it's all right with you."

"I have nothing to do and no place I have to go today. I just want to be with you."

He reached over and squeezed her hand and smiled. "My sentiments exactly. I've missed you."

He drove out of town and headed south on Highway 1. "That was quite a party last night. I'm so proud of you."

"Thank you. I was very nervous, but when you walked in the door I knew everything would be fine, whichever way the election went. And my friends were so sweet to give me that wonderful party. I couldn't believe it."

"You're fortunate to have such close friends. I've missed that. All my traveling makes it hard to develop friendships."

Beverly hadn't thought about the isolation of Jeff's career. He seemed so self-assured, she hadn't considered his social circle. But she hadn't met his friends or colleagues. "You must have friends in Portland," she said.

"I know a lot of people." He grinned. "They're happy to see me when I'm home, but they don't miss me when I leave. And vice versa. A lot of them live similar lives."

His offhand comments made her curious to meet his friends. She hadn't had deep friendships in Augusta, so she understood to some extent. Being married to Will had isolated her. Friends had been valuable commodities, chosen for their social or economic standing in society. For networking, not for relationships. The friendships she'd formed in Marble Cove had enriched her life beyond measure. She hoped Jeff would form some valuable friendships when they settled down, but he would still be traveling.

"So tell me what's been happening in your life, other than the election. You mentioned the railroad depot and quarry you found. Are you going to campaign to save it?"

"I hope to. Dennis wants to tear it down and build a strip mall or something like that, but there's a lot of Marble Cove history surrounding that building. It needs work, but I think it's structurally sound."

"And the quarry?"

"We just discovered it. Father read about it in one of his history books. They quarried and processed limestone for building material. Shipping it by boat was too dangerous, so the railroad opened up that industry. I don't know who owns it. It's fenced off."

"Who owns the depot?"

"Don't know that either."

"What about it caught your interest? I'm sure it isn't just that Calder wants to tear it down."

"No. You're going to think I'm crazy, but Margaret and Diane and Shelley and I heard a train whistle and went to investigate. A door was open, so we went inside. It's been abandoned for about sixty years, it seems."

"After your experiences with the lighthouse and the old church, I don't think you're crazy at all. You think the building is worth restoring?"

"Oh yes. The building is traditional Craftsman-style architecture, with the overhanging roofs and large corbels under the eaves. The rails leading down to the quarry are gone, but the roadway is firm and clear. The quarry has filled in with water, which makes it worthwhile to walk there from the depot. The depot could be a museum or a shop of some kind, or perhaps a restaurant, and the quarry would make a beautiful park. The old kilns are still there and might be dangerous, so they'd have to be fenced off."

"Sounds interesting. Maybe I'll take pictures and see if one of my magazines might pick up on it."

"That's a wonderful idea! I'll take you out to see it."

Jeff pulled off the highway and drove down a country road to an inlet where a river emptied into the bay. Next to a boat launch was a blue clapboard house with a white picket fence around it. Berry bushes grew along the fence and several cars were parked in front. A sign by the gate read The Berry Patch Restaurant.

"What a quaint-looking place," Beverly said.

"They've got great food too." Jeff opened the gate for her to go in. Then he took hold of her elbow and escorted her.

Inside, pale green walls with stencils of raspberry and blackberry vines rose above white wainscoting, giving the impression of a garden. They sat next to a window with white eyelet curtains looking out onto the river. Large seagulls waddled around the lawn and patio area outside the restaurant. It was too chilly for dining outdoors.

Jeff ordered sourdough pancakes with berry syrup and fresh berries. Beverly tried the berry *clafouti* with *crème fraîche*. When it came, the *clafouti* looked like an individual quiche, but sweet instead of savory.

"This is delicious. How did you find this place?"

"I stumbled on it during one of my photo explorations. I'll take you with me next time I go exploring. I'd love to have you come on assignment with me. I suppose you'll be too busy with being the mayor."

"I don't know yet what my schedule will be like. Maybe I can go with you on some short assignments. I wouldn't want to get in your way."

Jeff smiled. "You can be my assistant."

Beverly laughed. "I'm not a good photographer."

"You don't have to be. Your organizational skills would be a big asset in my work." Beverly raised her eyebrows. He added, "Of course, you have your own business, and now the town to administrate. But your input would be most welcome."

Beverly liked the idea of helping Jeff. Not as an assistant, but as his wife. They would make a good team, she thought. "And I might need your services. I'm really excited about your idea of doing a piece on the train station and quarry. Do you have another assignment right away, or can you stay around awhile?"

"I have a couple of short assignments. I'll have to spend a few days in Washington, DC, and New York City. Nothing big until after Thanksgiving."

"We'd love to have you and your grandfather join us for Thanksgiving. Celia and Mrs. Peabody too."

"I was hoping for an invitation," he said. "I accept."

They finished and got back on the main road. In a few miles, Jeff turned off the highway and took the road to Boothbay instead of going on to Portland.

"Where are we going now?"

"You'll see." He glanced at her and his eyes twinkled.

Smiling, she settled back. Spending the rest of her life with Jeff promised to be an adventure.

Jeff turned off the road at Boothbay Railway Village. "I thought you might like to see the possibilities with an old railway station."

Beverly sat up and looked around. "This is fabulous. I think I came here on a school field trip many years ago. I'd forgotten it existed."

"Let's go have a look." Jeff took his camera with him.

The village offered a restored steam train, a historical village dating back to the mid-1800s to the early 1900s with houses, stores, a town hall, and an old chapel, as well as a collection of antique cars. Jeff had Beverly pose before the various exhibits.

The buildings in Boothbay Railway Village had been moved to the site from other locations. One of the stations looked almost like a duplicate of the Marble Cove station, which helped Beverly picture the possibilities. The village buildings housed museum collections. She thought a business might be more suited to the Marble Cove station, but any option that would save the building was worth pursuing.

"Can you get some photos of the two depots? They'd be invaluable in a presentation on saving the Marble Cove station. It helps to show people a before-and-after visual."

"Sure. I'll get some shots with tourists and some with just the building features."

Jeff set to work with an intensity that impressed Beverly. She appreciated his thoroughness and the angles and perspectives he shot. She couldn't wait to see the final pictures. She could make a brochure to promote the project and a PowerPoint to present to groups.

They spent time looking at the buildings housing train restoration projects and at the antique cars. The village had developed over thirty years, and was still adding to its exhibits.

Beverly appreciated the development, but had no intention of taking Marble Cove in such a grand direction.

* * *

Rocky's whining woke Diane Wednesday morning. When she opened her eyes, his head was resting on the bed, his sad eyes staring at her. She wondered how long he'd been that way.

"What's the matter, boy? Do you need to go outside? What time is it?" She glanced over at the clock. Nine thirty. "Oh my. You poor thing. I can't believe I slept so long." She pushed to sit up. Every joint in her body ached. Her head ached. Her throat felt dry. She forced herself to get up, glided her feet into slippers, and put on a robe, then let Rocky out in the backyard. Poor dog made a beeline for a bush, then came back inside.

She'd had a grand time at Beverly's victory party, but the excitement and energy had taken a toll on her. She knew the chemo medication was at fault. And that would get worse as the weeks went by.

She opened the refrigerator and stared at its contents. Nothing appealed to her, but she needed to eat. She took out a hard-boiled egg and mashed it with a fork, then spread it on a piece of toast with a little mayonnaise. It tasted like cardboard and stuck in her throat, but she managed to wash it down with apple juice.

After a cup of tea and a couple of over-the-counter pain relievers, she convinced herself to get dressed.

Her image in the mirror looked as tired as she felt. She ran a brush through her hair, then stared in horror. The brush was full of hair. Her hair. Not all of it, but a noticeable chunk.

She had known it was coming. Had known she would lose her hair. But so soon? She hadn't prepared for it yet. She sat down on top of the commode and stared at the brush. Tears filled her eyes. And the doorbell rang.

Maybe she would pretend she wasn't home. But then someone might get concerned. She shuffled to her bedroom and grabbed a scarf and tied it around her head, then went to the door.

"Oh, Margaret. Come in."

"Diane, are you all right? I was starting to worry."

"I'm…" She started to say fine, but that was a lie. She felt lousy. "…kind of under the weather today." She laughed halfheartedly. "I guess I partied too much last night."

"Oh dear. Go sit down. I'll just put this in the refrigerator. Allan made a chicken divan casserole and pineapple carrot muffins."

She went into the kitchen, then came and sat down across from Diane.

"How can I help? Has Rocky been out?"

"Just in the backyard."

"Adelaide and I will take him for a walk later."

"He'd like that. Thanks. I should go out and get some exercise, but I don't have any energy. I kind of ache all over today."

"You seemed fine yesterday, but you probably tried to do too much."

"I'm afraid you're right. I did feel good. This chemo business is like a roller coaster. One day I'm fine, the next, I'm wiped out. I could be writing, but I don't even feel like reading. I think of things I should do, and I just can't make myself do them. Then I think of things I wish I had done, and now I wonder if I'll ever get the chance."

"Oh dear. I understand that feeling. I came across my bucket list that I wrote in college. I had such dreams and ideas, but I never did them. Now I feel like it's too late."

"Really? I suppose we could all say that, but you've accomplished so much. Look at your gallery and your beautiful paintings. I bet they were on your list."

"Yes. I think I've always wanted to be an artist. But look how long it took me to do it."

"But you are doing it, and very successfully. Your paintings are in demand, but more than that, your art touches people spiritually. Most of your paintings give me a sense of serenity and peace. Some of them remind me of God's presence in more powerful ways, like the crashing sea or the glorious sunsets. And you have so many accomplishments. You're a wonderful mother and wife. You're an inspiration to others. You've helped countless people with their finances."

Margaret shook her head. "Here you feel lousy, but you're giving me a pep talk."

"It's all true, and you need to believe it," Diane said, her tone gentle.

"All right. I'll try. So tell me what you haven't done that you want to do."

"Write another book. I suppose no matter how many I write, there will always be that desire. I want to play the piano like Beverly and bake like Shelley and create beauty like you. But I probably wouldn't try to do those things even if I felt terrific. I want to help Jessica plan her wedding someday, if she ever decides to get married, and be there to give her away." She started to mention wanting grandchildren, but realized that was a remote possibility for Margaret. "I want to grow my hair long so I can wear it in one of those lovely upsweep styles that look so elegant." Diane stopped and looked at Margaret. The reality of her condition pushed away any spark of hope.

"You'd think I'd take this cancer thing in stride. After all, I've been through it before. But I'm scared. And my hair is falling out. I know it will come back, but it'll take so long. And...and some men look really good without hair, like Sean Connery or Bruce Willis, but not me. I have a bumpy skull and it's shaped like a lightbulb and I look like an alien when I'm bald."

"Oh, Diane, I'm so sorry." Margaret moved over beside Diane on the couch and gave her a hug. "Of course you're scared. I'm scared for you. We all are. And we're all praying and trusting that God is going to get you through this and heal you again, like He did before. I just know you're going to beat this thing. Do you have a wig?"

Diane shook her head. "I got rid of my wigs. After last time, I didn't want to ever wear one again. I have a baseball cap and some stocking hats and a couple of scarves. Maybe I should get my hair cut really short. Then I won't notice it coming out as much."

"That's a great idea. And I think you'd look great with a short cut."

"I wonder if I can find someone to cut my hair without having to go into a salon."

"Do you know Carlie, who has Cut 'n' Curl? She has a couple of clients who are shut-ins. She goes to their homes. Maybe she'd come here."

"Do you think so? I've never been to her."

"I have her number on my cell phone. Let me call her."

Margaret made the phone call. She talked for a few minutes and hung up. "We're in luck. Carlie said she's had a cancellation and she can come by this afternoon at four."

"Good."

"But you're not happy about it."

"Right. I don't want to cut it, but I'm going to lose it all, so I might as well do it in stages. Maybe then I'll feel a little more in control."

"You'll like Carlie. She's a good stylist, and a sweetheart."

"Thank you, my friend. I'm glad you came by. And thank Allan for the food. I love chicken divan."

"I need to open the gallery in fifteen minutes, but I'll be back for your haircut and then I'll take Rocky for his walk."

"You don't have to come back."

"Yes, I do. I want to see your new haircut. I bet you'll look cute in short hair."

"*Humph.*"

Diane didn't know Carlie, but she'd seen her around town. You couldn't miss her. She was middle-aged and wore her hair in short spikes that had a distinctly purple cast to them. On the short, spunky lady, the hairdo worked. Diane tried to imagine her own hair in spikes. Not that it mattered. In a week or two, it would all be gone. But she wanted to look presentable in the meantime. Otherwise, she might have to hide out in her house and sneak out at night to do errands.

CHAPTER TEN

Emma insisted on walking to get Aiden from pre-K. When Shelley got out the stroller, Emma pointed at it.

"No, Mama. Walk." Her little frown of consternation made Shelley smile. Her daughter was becoming more independent every day.

"I need the stroller for groceries, sweetie. Not for you. You can walk." It was only a few blocks, but Shelley didn't want to end up carrying a sack of food and a toddler.

"Let me tie your hat."

Emma lifted her chin, which put her face right in front of Shelley's as she leaned down to tie the knit hat. Emma stared at her. "Mama got a boo-boo." She pointed, poking the delicate skin beneath Shelley's eye.

Shelley jerked away, startled. Emma reacted to her surprise. Her lips pouted out and her eyes filled with tears. She started to cry.

"Oh, honey, it's all right. You didn't hurt Mama. Just surprised me." She picked Emma up and held her against her shoulder. "It's okay."

"'Kay?" Emma leaned back and looked at her mother, inspecting her face. "Boo-boos."

Shelley felt the skin beneath her eye. Nothing. She felt under the other eye. She didn't know what Emma saw, but she couldn't feel anything.

"Take my hand. Let's go get Aiden."

"'Kay." Emma took her hand and toddled along beside her mother. The sunshine took the edge off the crisp autumn air. With Emma's short legs, the walk took much longer than usual, which suited Shelley. She needed the break to relax. She'd stayed up late baking. Besides three batches of cookies that she'd frozen for Thanksgiving and her usual orders, she'd had an extra order for the Landmark Inn for a small conference they'd booked. She gotten up early, made deliveries, made lunches for Dan and Hailey, and then helped Hailey gather together all the materials she needed for a science project in school. She'd dropped Hailey and Aiden off at their schools, then returned home to make four dozen cupcakes for a bake sale at the community center. Maddie Bancroft had picked those up an hour ago.

Shelley was tired. She hoped Aiden would take a nap later, though he rarely did anymore. He would play quietly in his room while Emma napped, and perhaps she could sneak in a power nap herself then.

Leila Davidson was at the door, making sure children and parents connected. When she saw Shelley, she smiled.

"Can you wait a few minutes? I'd like to talk to you."

"Sure." Shelley and Emma went inside to wait. Aiden ran up to them and waved a picture in the air.

"I drawed a dinosaur. See? Miss Davidson says it's a T. rex. That's a nickname for a ty-rhinoceros."

"I think you mean a Tyrannosaurus rex." Shelley laughed as she stumbled over the name herself. "That's a tongue twister."

"Yeah." Aiden laughed.

The last child left and Miss Davidson came over to them. Shelley wondered if Aiden had done something wrong. But the teacher was smiling.

"You draw well, Aiden. I recognized T. rex right away."

Aiden beamed.

"I was wondering if you would help me with a project for Thanksgiving," she said, turning to Shelley.

"Sure. I'd be glad to." Shelley assumed she was going to ask for cookies or cupcakes or something baked.

"Great. We're going to do a small play. Nothing elaborate, but it helps the children learn when they act out an event. We need costumes. Could you help make them?"

Shelley's eyes must have registered shock. That was not what she'd expected. The teacher quickly elaborated.

"They won't be hard to make. I have patterns and they're cut out of paper. So it takes a stapler, some paint, glue, and scissors. That's about it. We have boy and girl Pilgrims and Native Americans. We'll reenact the hardships, the Indians helping, then a small feast."

"I could be more help with the food," Shelley suggested.

"That's already taken care of. The costumes are simple, I promise you. Your children can help you. Well, Aiden can," she said, looking at Emma.

"All right. When do you need them?"

"We'll do it the day before Thanksgiving, so you have almost two weeks."

Just what she did not need. Another job before the holiday. But she'd said she would help. "All right."

"Great! I'll get you the patterns and supplies."

The teacher gave Shelley a plastic sack filled with construction paper and supplies.

When they got back home, Shelley put Emma down for a nap. She tried to get Aiden to take one, and he finally agreed to lie on his bed with Prize lying next to him and his yellow tractor on the other side.

Shelley decided to chance taking a nap. Before she lay down, she happened to glance in the mirror. Dark shadows marred the delicate skin beneath her eyes. Emma had said she had boo-boos. She did look as if her makeup had slipped. What must Aiden's teacher have thought? She really did need to get more sleep. Aiden's teacher must be desperate for helpers if she asked Shelley. How was she going to make the costumes and fulfill all the Sweet Shoppe Thanksgiving orders and take care of her family and get any rest at all? She had no idea.

★ ★ ★

Jeff parked his Subaru in the underground parking and they took the elevator to his second-floor loft condominium. Beverly loved the old buildings in the historic district of Portland. The city had done an excellent job of maintaining the heritage and architecture of the city while modernizing it for usefulness.

From the outside, Jeff's building was brick, with an ornate arched plaster entryway and a wrought iron gate that led to a recessed portico. Even the sidewalk in front was brick.

Though his condo wasn't big, the two-story ceilings and open floor plan made it seem large. Tall windows and skylights let in lots of light. The old brick walls gave it a sense of tradition, while the modern gas fireplace, the circular wood staircase to the sleeping loft, and the modern kitchen, with state-of-the-art appliances and bronze and copper fixtures, made it contemporary.

"I'll get my things. Be right back." He bounded up the spiral staircase.

Jeff's decor showcased his art. Posters and framed photographs of exotic places and interesting subjects and angles, some in black and white, some in color, and some in sepia tones, dotted the walls. A picture of a child hugging a huge black dog hung next to pictures of his Trans-Siberian Railway trip and an enlarged photograph of an Indonesian wedding with gorgeous native costumes and vibrant tropical flowers.

The furniture was simple wood and leather. Shelves held books and a few art objects that he'd collected around the world, as well as specimens of shells and unusual rocks.

"Will it be hard for you to give this up?" Beverly asked. It wasn't exactly homey, but it had Jeff's life stamped all over it.

He came down with a knapsack and a suit bag. "Give it up? What do you mean?" He set the items on a chair. "Can I get you something to drink? I have mineral water or flavored iced teas."

"No, thank you. I mean when we get married."

"Ah. I hadn't planned to get rid of the condo. I, uh, don't suppose you can move to Portland, now that you're the mayor-elect."

"I have to live within the town limits of Marble Cove, but I moved there for my father, and that wouldn't change, even if I'd lost the election."

Jeff nodded his head, looking thoughtful. "I guess I haven't considered our living arrangements. I've lived here for ten years—had it designed especially for me. I know you want to take care of your father, just as I want to care for my grandfather. We could find someone to live in and be there for his daily needs. I keep pretty close track of Grandpa."

"He's more independent than my father. I doubt if he would let you live with him."

"True." Jeff grinned. "Especially since he and Celia Patterson have reconnected."

"That's something, isn't it? She's so nice, and your grandfather is a sweetheart. I'm happy for them."

"So am I. And I don't want us to drift apart, like they did. Although I'm glad he married my grandmother. Otherwise I wouldn't be here."

"I don't want anything to come between us, either. I just need to know we're on the same page about where we'll live."

Jeff ran a hand through his hair. "Give me some time to think about it, all right? I'm not ready to give up this place. There are so many advantages here. It's close to the airport. Close to the pulse and heartbeat of the city, with the theater, the arts, the history, the water. There's a vibrancy here in the city that Marble Cove doesn't have."

"I understand that. Living in Augusta was similar, although I didn't live downtown. Marble Cove might not offer the excitement, but it has its own charm."

Beverly did understand Jeff's hesitance. She'd felt that way about selling her home in Augusta. It meant saying good-bye to the past and letting go. But what was he thinking? What if he decided he didn't want to go forward? What would she do? She loved Jeff. She wanted to spend the rest of her life with him. If he couldn't move, what would happen? She knew what she wanted. She hoped it was what Jeff wanted too.

★ ★ ★

When Margaret and Carlie arrived, Diane panicked. She nearly changed her mind. She had never liked short hair on herself.

"This is just temporary, you know," Margaret said, as they entered the house.

"Temporary. Right." Diane stood back and let Carlie tote her bag of supplies and equipment inside.

"I could do extensions to keep your length and fill in where your hair's getting thin," Carlie said, "but I'm afraid they'd come out with your hair."

"I know." Diane sighed. "I'm sorry. Thank you for coming. Especially on such short notice. I could have come to your shop, but..."

"Don't give it another thought," Carlie said. Her smile held warmth and compassion. "This is nice and private. Can we wash it in the kitchen sink?"

"Yes, that will be fine."

There was a knock on the door. Diane froze. She didn't want anyone to see what they were doing.

"It's Shelley. I called her," Margaret said. She went to the door and let her in. "We're here for moral support. I didn't call Beverly because she's with Jeff all day. Just ignore us."

"Hey, Diane. I'm glad I got here before you did the deed. Carlie's good. I know it's going to look fabulous. I brought you a turban too. The weather is cold enough you can wear this and no one will think a thing about it." She handed Diane a knit jersey hat. It had a dark blue background and variously sized white and light blue dots and circles.

"I love this. I'll look so fashionable, and it's soft. Thank you, Shelley."

Carlie came out of the kitchen. "Hi, Shelley. Looks like we're going to have a party! Anyone bring balloons?"

"No, but I brought molasses cookies with ginger-and-cream-cheese frosting."

"Yum. I wish all my customers brought treats with them."

"Where are the kids?"

"Adelaide is with them."

"I'll make tea while you get your hair washed," Margaret said. She filled the kettle, then moved out of the way.

Diane leaned over the sink. Carlie had to stand on tiptoes to reach over her head and work up a good lather. Her fingertips were firm but gentle as she massaged Diane's scalp. It felt so good, Diane could have stayed there much longer. Too soon, Carlie was drying her head with a towel, then she wrapped it like a turban.

"There. Do you want to sit at the kitchen table?"

"Sure." Diane sat down and closed her eyes.

Carlie fastened a towel around her neck. "Here's a mirror if you want to watch."

"No, thanks." Diane did not want to see her hair fall away. At least this was by choice, and not because of the chemo.

"All right. Shall I do about two inches all over?"

Diane opened her eyes and swallowed hard. Two inches? She wouldn't have much hair left. "Is that what you have?"

Carlie laughed. "Mine is shorter than that, and I use product on it to make it spike. Is that what you want?"

"No! I'm sorry. It's great on you, but I don't think it would work on me."

"Most people don't want it. I like it because my hair is thin and fine and this gives the appearance of having more hair. And it's outlandish enough to give me personality. Yours will be long enough to curl under or look wispy. I'll use a little mousse on it."

"Okay. Go for it." Diane took a deep breath and held it. Carlie started snipping. The scissors snapped and grated as they cut the hair, which was falling all around her. The enormity of the situation hit Diane. She couldn't stop the tears that sprang to her eyes.

"I'm so sorry," Carlie said. "I know this is traumatic."

"No. It's all right. I didn't mean to blubber."

"You're allowed. Blubber away. Just remember, in a couple of months you can come to me and I'll style your new hair. It will come back."

"Yes. It will." Diane looked at her friends. Margaret's lips were pressed together. Shelley was dabbing away a tear.

Carlie fluffed her hair, then brushed away the loose strands. She filled her hand with foamy white mousse, rubbed her hands together and worked her fingers through Diane's hair. What was left of it. Then she started working the hair with her fingers.

Shelley smiled. "That's cute! I love it."

Margaret stood and walked around her. "I really like it. I think you will too."

"You do?"

Carlie removed the towel. "Ready for the mirror?"

"I'll go look in the bathroom," Diane said. She didn't want to burst out crying in front of them. She went down the hall to the bathroom, stepped in, and flipped on the light.

She didn't recognize herself. But the woman in the mirror looked perky and chic. She looked better than Diane felt.

Okay. She didn't love it, but she didn't hate it, either. She could live with it. At least for a week or two, until it all fell out. She pasted on a smile and went back to the kitchen.

"It's very nice," she said. "Thank you so much, Carlie." She handed Carlie some folded bills, enough to cover the haircut and a generous tip.

"Now let's have those cookies," Margaret said. She had cleared the table and swept away all the hair. Diane was glad she didn't have to look at her locks and tresses all over the floor.

"I wonder how I'd look with short hair," Shelley said.

"Dan would kill you. Don't do it, just because I had to," Diane said.

Shelley smiled. "All right."

Diane still didn't know how she was going to go out and face people. She didn't want to be noticed. She didn't want people commenting. She'd never thought of herself as timid, but she just realized she was a big coward.

CHAPTER ELEVEN

Beverly had all morning Thursday before she would see Jeff. She'd talked to Shelley, so she knew about the haircut. She stopped at Diane's house on the way to her run on the beach. Diane took a few moments to answer the door.

"Hi. Come on in."

"Just for a minute. I'm on my way to run. Wow, I like your hair." She walked around Diane to see the back. "It turned out cute."

Diane looked at her like she was crazy.

"Honest. It looks nice."

Diane sighed. "I hate short hair. When I look in the mirror, it's like looking at a stranger."

"You'll get used to it."

"Well, it'll be gone in a couple of weeks, anyway. Except I'll have to go through having it short again while it grows back in."

"But it will grow back. How are you feeling?"

"Better. Today's a good day so far."

"I want to go to the library and see if there's anything about the railroad station. Want to come with me?"

"Yes. When?"

"Give me an hour and a half to run and then clean up. About nine forty-five?"

"All right. I'll meet you at your house."

Beverly noticed Rocky standing behind Diane, looking longingly at the door. "Shall I take Rocky for a run?"

"He'd love it, if you don't mind."

"Of course not."

Diane got Rocky's leash and clipped it to his collar.

"We'll see you later. Come on, Rocky."

Rocky didn't hesitate. He kept up with Beverly as she took off at a jog toward the beach. She reached the boardwalk and released Rocky to let him run, then she settled into an even stride. A gentle breeze nipped at her face and teased her hair. A colony of seagulls swooped and dived at the deep-emerald, plankton-rich water, then rose into the air in unison, making a great racket. Must be a school of herring in the area. Down the beach, Rocky ran full tilt, his ears flopping in the breeze. She looked around. She was alone for as far as she could see.

Slowing, taking a deep breath, Beverly inhaled the damp, salty air. She'd discovered home. Marble Cove was the home of her heart.

Now Jeff held her heart. He loved her. She believed that. And she loved him. Was his love large enough to include Marble Cove? Could he let go of his beautiful condo and his life in the city for her? Did he want to?

If circumstances were different, she would move to Portland into his life. But he'd known her circumstances when he asked her to marry him. He'd encouraged her to run for mayor. That meant he wanted to move to Marble Cove, didn't it?

She remembered how hard it had been for her to give up her house and her life in Augusta. She was glad she'd finally taken the plunge. Was he going through a sort of withdrawal, as she had?

She suddenly felt vulnerable. Would she be enough for Jeff? In some ways, she hadn't been enough for Will. He'd needed approval and recognition that she couldn't provide. Jeff had enough self-assurance for both of them, but he loved adventure and travel and challenge. Would he suffocate in Marble Cove, or would he find the freedom and belonging she'd discovered? She hoped—prayed—he would find it too.

★ ★ ★

"Aunt Shelley, do you have to bake today?" Hailey was sitting at the table, playing with her breakfast cereal, twiddling her spoon around and around, but she hadn't taken a bite. Aiden was almost finished with his cereal.

"Yes, I do. What's up? Aiden, run upstairs and get dressed for school now."

"But, Mom, I need to take Prize out."

"I'll let Prize outside. You go on. Now."

"Oh, all right." His lower lip stuck out as he shuffled off toward the stairs.

"Now what's on your mind, Hailey? Emma, don't throw your cereal." She grabbed a rag and cleaned the milk off the mat. She wiped Emma's hands and face and put her down.

"Sorry." She turned her attention to Hailey.

Hailey shrugged her shoulders. "Nothing."

Something was bothering Hailey. Shelley sat down at the table across from her and ignored the sticky mess Aiden had left. "Is something wrong? Something bothering you?"

"No." She put her spoon down as if she'd finished, but she hadn't even started. "I'd better get ready for school."

"Wait, honey. Are you having problems at school? Maybe I can help."

"No, school's fine. It's just...there's an assembly today. The teacher said we should invite our parents. It's no big deal."

"Ah." Shelley racked her brain trying to remember if she'd seen a notice. Maybe they'd sent an e-mail. "What time is it?"

"This morning at ten. If you're too busy..."

"No, sweetie. I'm not too busy. I want to come. I just didn't remember seeing a notice. Emma and I will be there. Okay? Why don't you finish your cereal and go get dressed? I washed your red outfit. It would look nice today."

Hailey's face lit up. "Yeah. Thank you, Aunt Shelley." She started wolfing down her cereal.

Shelley mentally chewed out her sister as she went upstairs to check on Aiden and get Emma dressed. Hailey needed her own mother, not a poor substitute, which is what she was turning out to be. She'd never had a child in school before. She needed to be more aware of Hailey's world and what was going on. Hailey needed to know she could count on her for support and attendance.

Aiden was dressed in the clothes she'd laid at the end of his bed. "Now can I go play with Prize?"

"Brush your teeth first." Shelley realized she hadn't put the dog outside. She put Emma in her playpen, then hurried back downstairs. Emma's protests followed her down. Oh, how she wished she could clone herself.

★ ★ ★

Diane rang the doorbell at the Wheeland house. Beverly answered the door.

"Come in. I'm just about ready. Cute hat. Why don't you say hello to my father while I get my notebook."

"All right." Diane went down the hall to the study. "Good morning, Harold."

He looked up from his newspaper, then set it in his lap. "Good morning, Diane. How are you this morning?"

It was a casual social question that held extra meaning for Diane. He knew about her cancer and her treatments. He was a friend and he cared. But she hated being an object of concern and even pity to everyone. "I couldn't be better. How about you?"

"I'm in fine fettle," he replied, giving her an impish smile. "Where are you off to this morning? Not a treatment, are you? This is Thursday, right?"

"We're going to the library. You started us on a path of discovery. Now we have to search it out."

"Oh. The railroad and the quarry. Take good notes. I want to hear all about it."

"We will."

"Shall we take my car?" Beverly asked, coming into the room.

"Let's walk. It's nice out, and I need the exercise."

"All right. Father, I'll be back by lunchtime."

"Is Jeff coming for lunch?"

"He should be here by then."

"I'll have Mrs. Peabody make something special."

Harold went back to reading his paper as they left.

"Jeff took me to see the Boothbay Railway Village yesterday. Have you been there?"

"Not in years. We took Jessica and Justin there when he was in junior high. Eric and Justin loved the old cars. I was more interested in the old buildings. In fact, I did a piece for the newspaper on the village based on that trip."

"So you reported on the restorations?"

"Yes. They moved those buildings to the site to recreate a historic village. It was quite an undertaking. Have they kept it up?"

"Yes. It's wonderful. They have two restored railway stations. One of them looks like our station."

"*Hmm.* I'd forgotten that. Their buildings are all museums, aren't they?"

"They sell gift items and food in some of them, but the village itself is a museum. I don't see us doing anything so grand. However, the depots are wonderful. I could envision ours restored and functioning as a store or restaurant or visitors' center. Any interesting facts we can find about its history, we can use to get support to save it."

They reached the library. Gilda Harris was behind the desk and smiled and gestured for them to come over.

"Morning, Diane. Beverly, I wanted to congratulate you again. I'm so pleased that you won the election. You're going to be a great mayor."

"Thank you, Gilda. I'll do my best. It's good to know I'll have you to turn to for advice and perspective on things."

The librarian beamed. Her blue eyes twinkled as she gazed at them over the top of her glasses. "You know I'll help any way I can. So how may I help you today?"

"We're looking for information on the railroad that came to Marble Cove until the mid-twentieth century. I don't know if the info is old enough to be housed with the historical society, or if you'd have it in the main library."

"Look in the section on local history. I believe the railroad came in here in the late 1800s, so they might have information upstairs also."

"We'll look down here first. Thanks, Gilda," Diane said.

"You're welcome. I like your hat, Diane. Looks warm."

"It is." Diane turned and walked down through the stacks to the local history section. Beverly followed her.

"You do look good in hats. And she didn't notice that your hair is short."

"At least she didn't say anything." She scanned the shelves. "*Hmm.* Here's a book on mining in Maine. It might have something about the quarry and railroad," Diane said, pulling out a book.

"I have one on coastal railroads. Let's find a table and see what we can dig out."

They sat at a table near the front window, where the light was good. Diane checked the table of contents, then flipped to the section on limestone quarries and began reading. She was surprised how old and widespread the industry had been. The first lime kiln was erected in Thomaston in 1733. Some quarries were still in operation when the book was written, which was in—she flicked back to the copyright page—1993. Two hundred and sixty years after the first quarry. She doubted Marble Cove's quarry was that old. She looked for Marble Cove, but couldn't find any references. She wondered if it had gone by a different name. "I can't find our quarry. There's no mention of Marble Cove, so it had to have a different name. Are you having any luck?"

"Yes. The coastal railroads are spurs off the Maine Central Railroad. The Marble Cove branch opened in 1884. Oh, here's our quarry name. It says a short spur was added two years later out to the Burr Oak Limestone Quarry. That's the BO on the padlock. I bet burr oaks are the trees along the creek. And later, in the early 1900s, they ran a spur to the Cannery. That's long gone too."

"Does it say when it closed? That would give us a recent history to work on."

"No. That's all it says here. That doesn't tell us much. Maybe we need to check the *Courier* archives. They must have covered the event."

"We might find something if they still have those papers. Remember the mess we had looking for information about the lighthouse."

"I remember. They need someone to organize their attic storage. But I don't know where else to go."

"We should check there. Then we could talk to Augie. He would remember something about the railroad if it was still open when he worked for the *Courier.*"

"Good idea. Tomorrow is your chemo treatment. Maybe we can check the newspaper archives and talk to him Monday or Tuesday if you feel up to it."

"That sounds good. I always enjoy talking with him. And it helps, you know, to have something to look forward to. Thank you for keeping me involved."

"We all need goals," Beverly said. "As long as we're reaching for the right ends, and our goals don't keep us from gaining the real prize."

Beverly's thoughtful, far-off gaze caught Diane's attention. "Are you talking about Jeff?"

Beverly's eyes met Diane's. "Yes, I guess I am. I didn't expect to fall in love again. Moving here, caring for my father, and starting my own business all made sense. So many things have happened that I believe God guided me here. Jeff even encouraged me to run for mayor."

"So what's wrong?"

"He isn't ready to move away from Portland. He loves to travel. Loves having adventures. Loves the ambiance of Old Portland, where he lives. I'm not in a place where I can uproot and go with him." She shook her head. "I don't know where that leaves us."

"Oh dear. Jeff loves you. He pursued you. I don't believe he'll choose the city over you. Give him time."

She let out a short laugh. "I have no choice. And I'm not in a hurry. I won't push him. He can have all the time he needs. I just don't want to lose him."

Diane smiled and reached out to cover Beverly's hand. "You won't. Remember, he didn't give up when you were hesitant."

Beverly smiled. "I wish I had your confidence."

Chapter Twelve

Diane rolled over and glanced at the lighted clock next to her bed. Ten thirty. She'd been tossing and turning for two hours. Her body ached. Her head ached. Her legs tingled with a restlessness that refused to quiet down. On a normal day, she would be thinking about turning in for the night at this hour, but she'd nodded off in her chair two hours ago, then dragged herself to bed.

Her second chemo treatment that morning had gone quickly. She and Beverly had gotten out of the treatment center in time for lunch. Her appetite had held. The pepperoni pizza had tasted good. She was glad for that. But now the acid from the sauce was kicking back.

Diane popped another antacid tablet into her mouth and rolled over on her side. She closed her eyes and began to pray silently. Praying took her thoughts off herself and helped her relax. She wondered if that was a selfish reason to pray, but decided God wanted her prayers, no matter what the reason. After all, praying was just having a conversation with God. And she knew He would listen.

She prayed for Jessica and Justin and each of her friends. She prayed for patience and a good attitude. She didn't want to feel sorry for herself, but clouds of doubt and hopelessness gathered at the edges of her consciousness, pressing toward her. In the dark of night when she couldn't sleep, when the rest of the world slumbered, she felt the most alone, and she prayed for the strength to reject discouragement. She visualized the medicine that was causing her aches and pains attacking the cancer cells. She was so tired. If she could only sleep for a few hours.

Her thoughts drifting, Diane imagined seeing Marble Cove a hundred years ago. The entire town was crowded around the train station, waiting for the train. The women were dressed in their Sunday-best outfits. The men were wearing suits and hats. Children ran around, playing tag and leapfrog and laughing. She knew someone important was coming, but she couldn't remember who. She strained on tiptoe to see down the tracks. Then she heard it. Over the cheers of the crowd, the sound of the train whistle pierced the air.

Diane woke. She peered into the darkness, broken only by the lighted clock dial. The whistle caught her attention. It sounded close by. But she wasn't dreaming anymore.

Getting up, Diane went to the corner window that faced southwest toward the train station. Parting the curtain, she looked out. No light marred the black velvet night. As her eyes adjusted, thousands of stars appeared in the sky. The sound had stopped. She listened for a few moments, but heard nothing.

Rocky nuzzled her hand and whimpered, as if to give her comfort.

"Hey, boy. Did you hear that sound?" She wondered if he could hear the train whistle, but he hadn't gotten up until she went to the window, so probably not. "Do you need to go outside?"

They went through the kitchen and she let him out the back door. The tinny taste of acid sat on her tongue. She ate a couple of saltine crackers, then let Rocky in again and went back to bed. Had she heard the train whistle or only dreamt about it? She couldn't help wondering if the sound had been a warning, like the ringing of the old bell at Old First or the light at the lighthouse.

Lying in bed, she listened. Soft snores came from Rocky's corner as he settled in to sleep. The soothing sounds relaxed her. The edges of sleep crept close.

A siren split the air. Diane sat straight up in bed. Rocky lifted his head and whined. The siren went on and on. Definitely real. Diane got up and put on her robe, then went to the back door. The sound came from the direction of the train station. She couldn't see anything, but someone was in trouble. *Please, Lord, let them be safe.*

★ ★ ★

Beverly yawned. The numbers on her computer were beginning to blur. Time to quit for the night. She needed to run one more column of figures in the budget spreadsheet on the Mountford Hotel's Christmas promotion. So far, everything looked reasonable, but she was a stickler for accuracy. She began a complicated formula to calculate the return on investment when a shrill sound grabbed her attention. A train. The same whistle she'd heard outside the newspaper office the week before.

Beverly jumped to her feet and hurried to the window of her upstairs office. She peered out in the direction of the train station. A bright orange glow danced above the dark outline of pine trees.

Fire!

Grabbing her cell phone, she dialed 911 and reported the fire, then rushed to put on her shoes and a sweater. She thought to tell her father she was going out, but she could hear him snoring. She doubted he would wake up while she was gone. Her heart beating fast, she hurried downstairs, slipped on a down parka and gloves, grabbed her keys, and rushed out to her car. The glow of the fire illuminated the western sky, guiding her way. She could hear sirens behind her. She reached the parking lot for the park near the train station in a few minutes. From there she couldn't see the fire, but sparks danced in the air above the thicket of trees beyond. They weren't coming from the direction of the train station. It was safe.

A pumper truck, sirens blaring, passed the parking lot and turned down a road through the trees. Beverly followed the truck to the edge of a field. The truck went out into the field. She parked along the road and walked in. Though no clouds blocked her view of the stars, gusts of wind propelled her along. Wind was the enemy in a fire.

Beverly crossed her arms over her chest and shivered, partly from the cold, and partly from the realization of the impending danger. Her back felt the cold of the night and the wind. Her front absorbed the intense heat of the fire. Mist from the high-pressure streams of water cooled her face. The fire could spread easily to adjacent trees and beyond. At the end of the stand of trees, Beverly saw buildings, lit by a yard light. It looked like a barn and farmhouse. If the trees all caught fire, the railroad station was vulnerable too. She heard more sirens coming in their direction. They drove out onto the field and parked near the other truck.

Standing back out of the way, Beverly watched crews work to keep the fire from spreading. Two pumper trucks shot streams of water onto the burning trees. In a wide circle around the trees, crews cut down trees to slow the spread. Two lights bobbed across the field toward them from the direction of the farmhouse. A tractor appeared and began dragging cut trees out of the forest into the field.

She lost track of time. The fire crews finally contained the blaze and the localized area of burning timber began to shrink, like a spent bonfire. She walked toward the fire trucks.

"It's a muddy, sooty mess over hee-ah, miss," a man said, approaching her. "You'd best leave."

"I don't mean to get in the way. I just wanted to thank you all for such a fast response and hard work."

"'Preciate that. These guys are pros." He looked tired and dirty, but she sensed his pride in his crew.

"I'm Beverly Wheeland. I called in the fire."

"Ya don't say. The new may-ah checking up on her employees? That's dedication, coming out in the pit of the night."

"It's not like that. I saw the fire and wanted to make sure no one was hurt. I'm glad I got to see you in action. You all did a fine job."

"Well, thank ya, ma'am. I'm Joe Tillman, your fire chief." He doffed his helmet in her direction. "Say you turned it in? How did ya see it?"

She wasn't sure how to answer. With the truth, she decided. "I heard a train whistle. When I looked out my window, I saw the glow of the fire, so I called it in."

He'd removed his helmet and was scratching his head with dirty, blackened hands. His face was covered in soot. "Heard a whistle, you say? That's impossible. No trains around hee-ah."

"I know. It doesn't make sense, but that's the truth."

"Well, don't know how it happened, but I'd say ya saved that family down at the end of the trees. Wind's a-blowing that direction. Doubt they'da seen it comin'."

"It might have burned the old train station too," she said.

"Ay-yup. Well, wouldn'ta been no loss they-ah, as I see it. Old building might be good for fire practice one of these days."

"I hope not. It's a historic building. I would hope, if it were in danger, your crews would make every attempt to save it."

Joe's eyebrows rose. He gave her a short nod. "Yes, ma'am. I'll make note of that."

"Thank you. I'll leave now and let you get back to your crew. Please pass on my appreciation to them."

"Ayuh." He gave her a wave and set off toward the fire crew.

As Beverly walked back to her car, the cold seeped in, chilling her to the bone. She yawned and remembered she'd been tired before she heard the train whistle. Now she was exhausted. But at least she would sleep well, knowing that farm, and the train station, were safe.

She wondered if the fire chief was one of Dennis Calder's friends. Whether he was or not, he discounted the value of the old train station. Saving it might prove to be an uphill battle. She was all the more determined to win that fight.

★ ★ ★

Shelley poured a second cup of coffee and sat at the table with her Bible. She'd intended to do her daily devotions before everyone got up. Usually on Saturday, she managed some quiet time while the family slept in, but not this morning. Emma had come downstairs first. They had fifteen minutes of snuggle time on the couch before Aiden joined them. He wanted to cuddle too, so she tucked a blanket around the three of them and read them a story. Most mornings were hectic, with bakery orders to deliver and getting Hailey and Aiden ready for school and Dan out the door to work, so she relished a free Saturday. She'd made deliveries Friday night.

Dan and Hailey came downstairs at the same time. The cozy group squeezed over and made room, with Aiden climbing on his daddy's lap. Shelley's heart sang as she continued reading the story. These special family moments became more rare as the kids grew older. Having Dan join them was the cherry on top of the ice cream sundae.

Shelley finished and closed the book. She hated to break the spell, but this called for a celebration.

"So what shall I make for breakfast this morning? Gruel or chipped beef on toast?" She managed to keep a straight face.

"Mom!" Aiden made a yucky face. "I don't like that stuff, whatever you said."

"Make some of those slimy eggs with the green sauce," Dan said, winking at Shelley.

"No, Daddy," Emma said, her lower lip pouting out.

Hailey looked dismayed at first, but she caught Dan's wink. "I vote for chocolate chip pancakes."

"Yeah! Me too!" Aiden yelled.

"Me, me, me."

Shelley laughed. "We've been outvoted, Dan."

"Looks like. I'll change Emma while you work on breakfast."

"I'll help cook," Hailey offered.

Breakfast was one of those memory-making family occasions that Shelley loved so much. They made a sticky, gooey mess, with homemade syrup that Shelley had made from wild blackberries on their pancakes. The chocolate chips had melted and smeared on the table, on the children, even on Dan's cheek. Emma finger-painted the dark red and the chocolate brown on her tray. Aiden tried to confine his food art to his plate, but he overshot his target. Shelley gave the kids damp cloths to wipe their faces, then she couldn't resist teasing Dan. "You're as messy as the kids. You have chocolate on your cheek."

"I was saving it for later." He wiped at his cheek, smearing it more, making the children giggle at his antics.

Shelley was still laughing when he took the children to the living room to watch Saturday morning cartoons—a treat—while she cleaned up the kitchen.

Hearing the TV and the children's laughter, she sighed happily as she sat at the dining room table and read from the Psalms. She thanked God for her family and her many blessings. She had just finished when she heard a tap on the back door and it swung open.

"Hello? I'm here to see my grandkids," Francis Bauer announced in a voice loud enough to be heard down the block. "Where is everyone?" She spotted Shelley at the table. "Goodness, Shelley, are you still in your robe at this hour?"

Shelley glanced at the clock. Nine fifteen. "We had breakfast first," she said. "The kids and Dan are in the living room."

"Meemaw!" Aiden came running with Emma on his heels. He launched himself against his grandmother, hugging her around her waist. She hugged him and leaned over to kiss his check just as Emma reached them with a big hug. Hailey came too, but held back. Frances kissed the top of Emma's head, then looked up. Seeing Hailey, she extended one arm. Hailey smiled and went over to give her a hug. Shelley wanted to hug Frances herself for accepting her niece as one of her own, even though they weren't related. Hailey became more a part of their family every day.

"Would you like a cup of coffee, Frances?"

"Yes. I don't suppose you have any of those blackberry scones like you made for the Cove."

"I'm afraid not, but I have blackberry jam you could put on an orange almond scone."

"That will have to do." Frances sat at the table. Shelley set a cup of coffee and a scone in front of her, then got the jam out of the refrigerator. She sat across from her mother-in-law, where her Bible still lay open to the Psalms.

"How nice that you can take time to read the Bible," Frances said. "I always had my devotion time early, before the family got up."

Shelley held back a sigh. "I try to, but they got up early this morning. We had snuggle time instead."

"Well, I'm glad to see you have free time. I don't feel so bad asking for a favor."

Shelley's heart sank. Had Frances changed her mind about hosting Thanksgiving? The Bauer family overflowed Shelley's small home, and the extra time of preparing the house and the meal would cut into her baking time, but they would manage. "What is it, Frances?"

"The Ladies' Auxiliary is doing a dinner for seniors at the community center. I promised to ask if you would make pies for it." Her eyes pleaded.

"When is it?"

"The day before Thanksgiving at noon."

Shelley knew classes at the center were canceled for that holiday week, but she didn't think Adelaide's classes at the college were out. How would she fulfill all of her Thanksgiving orders, help with Aiden's play at pre-K, prepare for their own family dinner, *and* make pies for the community center? But how could she say no to her mother-in-law? It was a worthy cause.

"How many pies do you need?"

"Only eight. Four pumpkin and four apple. They wanted ten, but I said that was too much."

She had eight apple pies in the freezer, but they were promised. Between now and then, she could add more. She couldn't make the pumpkin ahead, but she had made and frozen a dozen crusts. "I'm sure I can squeeze it in," she said, drawing out her words.

Frances smiled. "If you're sure. I realize you have extra business on the holidays, but I knew you'd want to help. Have you given any thought to postponing your business until the children are grown?" Frances glanced up at the clock, saving Shelley from having to answer. "Oh dear. I must scoot. I have a million errands to run."

After Frances left, Shelley sat staring at her Bible. The beauty and glory she'd read in the Psalms had lost their joy. Strong hands gripped her shoulders, massaging her muscles.

"I heard. Why didn't you tell her no?"

"I can't do that. As she said, it's for a worthy cause."

"I'm sure it is. My mother is always involved in a worthy cause."

"And it's wonderful that she has the heart and the time to do that."

"Yes. The time is the key, in your case. I hate to see you overextend yourself. You have a full plate as it is. And I'm not able to help, with my work and classes."

Shelley took Dan's hand and tugged, so he sat down in a chair next to her. It was time for a serious talk. She needed to know what he thought, to get his perspective. She turned to him. "Dan, Rusty asked me to take over managing the Cove when he retires."

Dan looked stunned. Just like she'd felt when Rusty proposed it. "Wow. That's a big responsibility. Does he want you to manage it for him or buy him out?"

"I don't know. He didn't go into detail. Just that he's looking for someone to take his place when he retires."

"I'm making decent money and it will get better when I become a journeyman, but I doubt we can afford to buy the business, even with your extra income."

"I've thought of that. The bigger question in my mind is whether I should even consider it. It's a great opportunity. One I might never get again. And Rusty isn't in there baking or making coffee. He just manages the business."

"But you're already doing the baking for him, so you'd being doing both. That's a stretch."

It was a stretch. Especially since she was questioning whether she should keep her home business going. If Dan objected, as Frances hinted…"Tell me the truth. Do you think I should quit my business?"

He looked surprised. "The Lighthouse Sweet Shoppe? Do you want to quit?"

"No. But I admit it makes it hard to participate in things at school and church for Aiden and Hailey. In a couple of years, Emma will be in pre-K, and the kids' activities will keep increasing."

"And I can't help unless it's in the evenings or weekends."

"When you were out of work, I got a little spoiled," Shelley admitted. "But I'm so glad you found work that you enjoy and you can utilize all your talents."

"Yeah. Shelley, I know you love to bake, and you're a great cook. But I know it's hard on you. If you want to stop baking for people, we'll be able to get by on my salary, and that will get better, so don't let the income make you feel like you have to keep working. I want you to be happy. I will support you and do what I can to help, whatever you decide. Just make sure it's your decision, and not pressure from someone else. Not even pressure from yourself to perform. You don't have anything to prove. You've already established that you can be successful at whatever you do."

"I don't want to stop. Thinking about Rusty's offer got me questioning everything, I guess. It's a great opportunity. He said it wouldn't be right away, but he's thinking about his future. And it wouldn't mean being there every day. He has great employees."

"*Hmm*. That's a lot to think about, Shell. I hate to see you take on too much."

"I know, and right now, I just need to take it one day at a time and get through Thanksgiving, then Christmas."

"I promised Dad I'd give him a hand this afternoon, but I've got the rest of the morning. Want me to help with the dishes or get the kids dressed?"

"If you'll take charge of the kids, I'll handle the kitchen and do some planning. I need to add eight pies to my schedule."

She just had to figure out how she would get everything done for Thanksgiving, then she could start thinking about making a decision about the future of her business.

Chapter Thirteen

It was three o'clock Saturday afternoon before Beverly could round up the friends. Shelley was the last to arrive at the gallery. Beverly thought she looked tired. She knew this was a busy time for Shelley with her baking business. "I hope I didn't mess up your schedule, asking you to come down here."

"Oh no. I need some groceries, and Dan took the kids with him to see his father, so it's a good time to get out. Since Frances came by unexpectedly this morning, I've been playing catch-up all day," she said, pulling off her gloves and stocking hat. "She wants me to make eight pies for the seniors dinner at the community center."

"Yikes! As if you're not busy enough," Diane said. "I suppose you said yes."

"How could I turn her down? It's a good cause."

Margaret shook her head. "Surely there are other people in town who can bake pies."

"You'd think. I suppose it will be good advertising for my business. I just don't know how I'm going to get it all done." Shelley sighed. "But I will."

"Let us know if we can help," Diane said.

"Thanks. I'll keep that in mind. So what's up?" Shelley said, looking at Beverly.

"Well, did any of you hear a train whistle last night?"

Margaret and Shelley shook their heads.

"I did," Diane said. "I thought I'd dreamed it."

"It was real. I looked out the upstairs window and saw the glow of a fire out near the train station, so I called the fire department, then I drove out there. It was in the woods past the station."

"Really? I got up and looked out the back, but I couldn't see anything," Diane said. "Is the station all right?"

"Yes. I don't know how it started, but it burned part of a field and some trees. I talked to the fire chief after they got it under control. I don't think he believed me when I said I heard a train whistle, but when I voiced concern about the station, he said it wouldn't be a great loss if it burned down. If it had caught fire, I doubt they'd have tried to save it."

"Oh dear. That was a close call. Doesn't anyone think the station is worth saving? Thank goodness you saw the fire!" Margaret said.

"I wouldn't have if I hadn't heard the whistle," Beverly said.

"Another warning," Diane said, frowning thoughtfully. "I can't help wondering about the train station's history. It had to be important to Marble Cove at one time."

"It's weird that I feel an attachment," Shelley said, "since it's been out of use for so long, but if we lose the train station, we'll lose part of the town's heritage. I want to preserve it for Aiden and Emma. I think we're supposed to save the station."

"I agree. It's a link between the past and the present. We just have to make people see that," Margaret said.

"I'll try to reason with the town council," Beverly said. "But we'll need more evidence of the station's value and its possibilities. People need to see it's worth more to the town as a historical building than as a mini-mall."

* * *

Diane felt good Monday morning. She'd given up on coffee temporarily, preferring the sweet, spicy taste of chai tea. She ate a poached egg on a bed of potato pancake and had one of Shelley's blackberry scones. Her stomach seemed to take it well. Then she took a shower.

Working shampoo into her hair, she massaged up a good lather. When she pulled her hand away, a big chunk of hair came with it. She stared at it as warm water sluiced over her back and tears streamed down her cheeks. As she rinsed off, the rest of her hair washed down the drain, leaving only a few strands. This was the moment she'd dreaded. Her short haircut hadn't lasted a week. She scooped up the remaining hair on the tub floor to keep it from clogging the drain, and set it on the counter. She tried to ignore it as she dried off and got dressed. She avoided the mirror too.

The pile of hair kept drawing her gaze. She couldn't throw it away. Symbolically, that would mean giving up, which she admitted was silly, but it seemed important to keep her hair. She rinsed out the shampoo and patted it dry, then wrapped it in a tissue and set it aside.

She pulled Shelley's turban over her short, thin hair and considered calling Carlie to come shave her head. At least that would be a positive move. But she hated to do anything that drastic. She would have to do something soon, however. She could limit going out, but she had to get groceries on occasion. She knew her friends would be happy to run errands for her, but she hated to ask. They didn't need to become her caregivers. She didn't need someone coddling her anyway. She would hate that. Unless it was Eric, and that was impossible. Oh, how she missed him.

Her cell phone rang. She picked it up and looked at the caller ID. Leo. She ignored it and let it go to voice mail. She didn't want to have to refuse him, but she couldn't let him see her like this.

★ ★ ★

Monday afternoon, Shearwater Gallery was empty except for Margaret, who was working on her quarry painting. She scraped her palette knife through the burnt umber and sienna paints, then pressed the edge of it against the vague splotch of sand-colored rocks on the canvas, delineating the sharp edges of quarried stone. She stepped back and looked at the effect. The rocks needed more texture. She mixed modeling paste with the sand color and sculpted the rocks. Standing back, she looked at her progress with a critical eye. She wasn't satisfied. Even with the texture, it didn't have the spark of life she was trying to create. It needed something. Of course, it wasn't finished. She cleaned her knives and covered her palette with plastic wrap to keep the paint from drying out. When the rocks dried, she would add color to give depth and contour.

As she was cleaning her brushes, Adelaide came in, followed by Allan.

"Mom, guess what I get to do?"

Adelaide's cheeks were a rosy pink and her eyes alight with excitement.

"I can't imagine, but it must be good."

"I get to be a student helper at the community center d-day care. I'm gonna help children Emma's age. I'll help them learn the a-alphabet."

"Sweetheart, that's wonderful! You're so good with children."

"Yes. My teacher says I could work at a day... day care center someday. But I have to take more classes to get my certificate."

"Is that what you want to do?"

"Oh yes! I want to take care of little children like Emma and Aiden. They like me to play with them."

"They do. They love being with you. I think you'd make a wonderful day care helper."

"Thanks, Mom. That's what Dad said too."

Allan was standing back, listening. "I certainly did," he said. "Now we need to get home and let your mother work on her painting. I like what you've done so far with your mixture of textures. It's different from your usual landscapes, but not like your impressionist paintings, either."

"I'm trying to portray realism with an extra vibrancy. I have a long way to go on this, so we'll have to wait to see if I can make it work."

"I have no doubt that if you can see it in your mind's eye, you can paint it."

"I hope you're right." She didn't want to expound on that subject and was glad when Adelaide continued her thoughts.

"I'm gonna ask Shelley if I can practice with Emma and Aiden, so I can get really good."

"I'm sure she'd love to have your help. She has a lot of baking to do before Thanksgiving."

"We're going to get groceries," Allan said, "then we'll go home and fix dinner. Do you need anything?"

"Not that I can think of. You go on. I'll close up here soon."

After they left and she finished cleaning up, Margaret sat down at her computer. When she wrote her bucket list all those years ago, she'd wanted to study the Impressionist period, but now that didn't appeal to her. She wanted to broaden her horizons and develop as an artist. She wanted something new. She wanted a challenge. Just like Adelaide.

Margaret couldn't believe the changes in her daughter. The new confidence. Her excitement for the future. She'd been so protective of Adelaide and her feelings that she had failed to imagine how far her daughter could stretch and grow. In a way, it was sad to think of her little girl becoming an independent adult, and yet it was a thrill to see her blossom. Realizing she and Allan had played a part in their daughter's success gave Margaret a glow of satisfaction. They'd done a pretty good job raising a special-needs child. They'd learned how to parent as she'd grown and matured, and they'd made some mistakes along the way. But by God's grace, she'd become a beautiful, gentle, loving young woman. That was worth every sacrifice, every item on a college girl's bucket list.

Margaret pulled the journal out of her desk and opened it to the list. *Hike the Appalachian Trail. Visit Mayan ruins. Sail to Tahiti.* Oh my. She laughed, imagining herself shimmying up a mast. She would need a ladder and a hoist. Not a pretty picture. *Go on an archeological dig.* Twenty years ago, she would have enjoyed that, but she didn't want to spend a summer digging in the dirt or living in a tent now, though that was an activity she and Allan could do if they wanted to. Puttering in her garden satisfied her desire to get her hands dirty. She reasoned that all those items might have been fun and challenging in the short run, but none compared to the life she'd lived.

She took a pencil and crossed off all the items that she no longer wanted to do. Then she looked at what was left. She put a star next to the numbers she'd accomplished. Getting her degree. Having a successful career. She'd married a wonderful man. She'd become a mother to a very special child. She'd pursued her art, though not in the order on her list.

Now the list was shorter, but what remained still seemed impossible. With the gallery to run and Adelaide living at home, she was tied down. Would she ever be able to do the items that remained? In college, she'd been single and carefree with life ahead of her. Now she had responsibilities. Not that she'd trade her family for any adventures. But it wasn't just the responsibilities. In a few years, she might not have the energy or the health. In fact, she didn't have the energy now.

★ ★ ★

Shelley knocked on Diane's door. She heard movement inside, but Diane didn't come to the door. Shelley knocked again. Rocky barked. Maybe that was all she'd heard, but Diane's car was out front, and she wouldn't have gone walking without Rocky. She tried the door. It was locked. Then she caught a movement of curtains.

"Diane? Are you all right?" She was about to go around and try the back door when the front door opened. Diane was dressed and wearing the turban she'd given her.

"Hi, Shelley. Come on in."

"Are you all right? I was getting worried."

"I feel fine today."

"But? Something's wrong. How can I help?" Diane's face looked a little puffy from the chemo, but otherwise she looked all right.

"I, well, I lost some of my hair this morning. I was washing my hair and it just came out in my hand."

Shelley couldn't miss Diane's distress as her chin quivered.

"Oh, I'm so sorry. I know I'd hate it if I lost my hair. I have some more scarves. I can tie great turbans. I'll be happy to come over every day and tie one on your head for you." Shelley held out the dish and bag she was carrying, hoping it would cheer Diane. "Here. I brought some maple custard and bran muffins. They're full of good things, like eggs and protein powder and carrots and walnuts. I'll put them in the kitchen."

"That's so sweet of you. I've lost my appetite for a lot of foods, but yours always taste good to me."

"I'm glad. You have to keep your strength up."

"I suppose you're right."

Shelley heard anguish in Diane's lukewarm response. She missed Diane's upbeat, adventurous attitude. She wanted to cheer up her friend but didn't know what she could do to make her smile. She hadn't had any experience with someone going through cancer before. Just hearing the *C* word was enough to instill fear. And yet Shelley had read of so many people who had fought the disease and won. Diane was a fighter. She would win this battle again. She'd gotten a miracle before. *Please, God, give Diane another miracle*, Shelley silently prayed. *And encourage her.* It was time to call in the troops. Maybe Beverly and Margaret would have some ideas on how to cheer up their friend.

On her way back across the street, she took out her cell phone and called Beverly.

"Hi, Shelley, what's up?" Beverly asked when she answered.

"Hi. I just left Diane's. I'm concerned about her."

"Oh? Is she all right?"

"She said she feels good today, but she's depressed. She lost a bunch of hair today. We need to cheer her up, but I don't know what to do. Do you have any ideas?"

"As a matter of fact, I do. There's a great wig shop in Augusta. I think we should take her there. Maybe if we go together, we can help her get through that step."

"That's a great idea! We can all try on wigs so she won't feel alone. When do you want to go? Maybe I can get someone to watch the kids for a day."

"Can you take the time out of your schedule?"

"For Diane, I'll make the time. This is important."

"Okay. I'll call Margaret and see if she can go. Diane should still feel good tomorrow. Can you get someone on such short notice?"

Shelley didn't like to ask her mother-in-law to babysit, but Frances owed her a favor for sticking her with making pies. Shelley didn't mind helping out, but the timing stunk. "I think I can. I'll make a call and let you know later."

★ ★ ★

"So what do you think?" Beverly asked Jeff as they picked their way through the tangled bushes around the outside of the old train station later that day.

"It looks sound. I'd say it has every bit as much promise as the restored stations we saw at Boothbay Railway Village. But it needs a lot of work, and it might be expensive."

"I know. And I doubt the town has that kind of money. If we can prove it has historical value, perhaps we can get some grants or find donors. We haven't learned much about the railroad history in Marble Cove, but we do know there was a spur to the limestone quarry. It was called the Burr Oak Quarry, but we haven't discovered who owns it or much of its history."

"Let's walk down to the quarry," Jeff suggested. "Sounds like there's quite a history there. As far as I know, it hasn't been documented recently. That's another story angle I can pitch and see if there's any interest."

"That'd be wonderful! If you can, it would help show the value of saving the landmarks." Beverly could hardly contain her excitement. With Jeff's help, she could make a case for preservation.

"The light is good right now. I'll take a few shots." Jeff got his camera and took a series of pictures from various angles around the outside of the station. He tried the doors. They were locked.

"Didn't you say you looked inside?"

"Yes. Someone locked the doors after we were here. They were locked last week when we came by. We'll have to find out who owns it and get permission to go inside."

Jeff tried the windows. Some were boarded up and others were stuck tight. "Guess I'll have to wait to get inside. Let's go look at the quarry."

He took a few snapshots of the station from the pathway until it disappeared from view.

When they reached the fenced blockade, Jeff started up along the perimeter to the west, in the opposite direction Diane had gone. Beverly followed him. They climbed over rocks and skirted trees, looking for a way around the fence. When it angled north, they followed it for another fifty yards until it ended at a rock embankment that plummeted twenty feet into the creek.

"We could climb down with ropes, but I don't want you going down without safeguards," he said.

Looking down, Beverly appreciated his concern. The rocks looked unstable and the descent was steep. She wondered if he would have gone down if she hadn't been with him. She guessed he would. Some of the pictures she'd seen had to have been taken under precarious circumstances.

"We'll find out who owns the property and get permission to go in. Maybe we can get access to a key."

"Sounds like a good idea. We've lost the best light for today anyway."

Beverly looked out across the cove. A bank of fog was moving in. A damp, chill breeze preceded it. Soon it would obscure the entire area. "We'd better head back before we get socked in by the fog." They both had on windbreakers, but the damp cold could cut through.

Jeff took a few more pictures, then put his camera away. He gave her a smile that melted her heart and took hold of her hand. "Shall we go?"

She looked down at their clasped hands. Jeff's hand enveloped hers in warmth and tenderness, making her feel loved and protected.

"Jeff, what do you see yourself doing in ten years?"

"Ten years is a long time. Let's see." He looked down at her with a serious expression. "I see *us* pursuing interests together, even if they aren't the same interests. I imagine I'll still be doing photography, and I'll try to convince you to go with me on some expeditions. I want to show you all the fascinating places and things I've discovered. I want to discover new ones with you. But I want to help you achieve your passions, like saving the railroad station and uncovering the stories behind things. Ten years? I hope I'll still be selling photographs. Someday I'd like to have a showing of my work.

What about you? What do you want our life to look like in ten years?"

"I expect my father will still be alive, but needing even more care. I don't want to be away from him if he needs me. And then there's Marble Cove. I don't know if I'll still be mayor. Perhaps not. But I'll still have a passion to help the town."

Jeff stopped and turned to face her. "That's two of the things I love about you. Your love and concern for your father and your passion to help people. I feel the same way about my grandfather. I want to be there for him when he needs me. I don't know how much I can help with your town projects if I have to travel for assignments, but I support your involvement."

"So you see us living in Marble Cove?"

"In ten years? I don't know. I can't see that far into the future. Is it important?"

"Yes. It is." Beverly searched his face for clues to his thoughts. She didn't want him to agree with her just to appease her, but she didn't want them to move ahead, then discover they had different goals and interests. She'd been down that road before, and she didn't want a replay.

She could see distress in his eyes. She was afraid to hear his answer. She steeled herself against the pain she felt coming.

"I wish I could say I'm ready to sell my place and give up all of my life in Portland, but I'm not. I'm sure you understand that. You went through a lot of emotional doubt and turmoil when you had to sell your house in Augusta."

"Yes, but that was a turning point for me. I needed to let go in order to move on with my life." She wanted to tell him he also needed to let go if they were going to get married and make a success of their relationship. But she couldn't tell him that any more than he could have told her. He had to discover that for himself. He had to make that decision. And she had to be patient and let him. She didn't know what to say, so she said nothing. She looked into his eyes and smiled. She needed to exercise patience. She just hoped that when Jeff made his decision, he would choose her.

Chapter Fourteen

Shelley knocked on Diane's door at nine o'clock Tuesday morning. Aiden and Hailey were in school. Frances had arrived and picked up Emma. She would pick up Aiden from pre-K and Hailey after school. Shelley had the entire day free, and it felt wonderful. But the reason for her free time might not feel so great. She hoped Diane would be up to their surprise.

The door opened. Diane still had on her pajamas and a robe and slippers. The blue knit turban covered her head.

"Good morning. How do you feel this morning?"

"Not too bad. Come on in. I haven't gotten dressed yet." Diane looked down at her attire and laughed. "I guess that's obvious."

Shelley smiled. "That's all right. I'll come in and wait while you get dressed. I'm glad you're feeling good. We're going to kidnap you today."

"What? Oh no. I don't want to go out." Diane looked past her to where Beverly and Margaret were coming up the walk. She frowned. "What have you cooked up?"

"Just a little outing. Why don't you go get dressed? We're taking you to Augusta for some shopping and lunch."

"Do I have a choice?"

"No."

"All right. Come on in. All of you. I'll go get decent. I guess no one will know me in Augusta."

"That's the spirit," Margaret said. The three friends sat in the living room, chatting softly while Diane got dressed.

"I hope this is going to cheer her up," Shelley said. "Maybe we should have given her more warning."

"She would have turned us down. This is the best way," Beverly said.

Diane came back out wearing dark-blue corduroy pants and a matching sweater with the blue turban. She'd dabbed on a little makeup and lipstick. She looked ready for a day on the town. Shelley felt relieved that she had joined into the spirit of the friends' abduction. Shelley couldn't help wondering if she would be as brave and upbeat if she had to endure a battle with cancer.

★ ★ ★

Diane did not feel like going out with her friends, but she didn't want to hurt their feelings. They were trying so hard to cheer her up. At least Shelley's turban hid her balding head and they were going out of town, so she wouldn't see anyone she knew. She put on a smile, determined to go along with her friends' surprise. Surely it was better than sitting home alone feeling sorry for herself. Beverly drove. Diane sat in the front seat.

"Where's Emma?" she asked.

"She's spending the day with Frances."

"Oh." Diane knew Shelley didn't like to ask her mother-in-law to babysit. She'd gone to a lot of trouble for her. "So what are we doing today?"

Beverly laughed. "We're going shopping, and you're going to love it."

Beverly knew Diane did not love to shop. If she had to go shopping, perhaps she could find some pretty head scarves.

"Let me catch you all up on the train station," Beverly said.

Smooth change of subject, Diane thought, but she did want to know about the station.

"Jeff and I went out there yesterday. He thinks it looks sound enough to restore and he's going to take photos of our station and quarry and others along the coast and see if someone will do a story on it. That should get some people interested."

"That's wonderful. I'm doing a painting of the quarry from pictures I took. It's coming along all right. If it turns out well, I plan to display it in the window. That might get some attention too."

"I can't wait to see it," Diane said. "Are you going to paint the train station?"

"I might. But I don't want to show it as run-down and abandoned. I'll have to think about that."

"If you painted it as if it's restored, that would get positive attention," Beverly said. "Maybe with some plants and flowers around it. Or people. That museum Jeff took me to see had antique cars and people in period costume. That would make a great painting. Jeff took pictures. I'll see if I can get one for you."

"I like the idea of doing an old-fashioned picture. Maybe from the 1920s or even the 1950s. Isn't that when the train stopped coming to Marble Cove?"

"Yes. And that's a great idea!"

Diane was pleased to hear her friends' enthusiasm about the train project. She'd missed getting together with them recently. She didn't want to socialize or see a lot of people, and she didn't want to go out in public, but she felt safe and comfortable with Margaret and Beverly and Shelley. Amazing how they had come to seem like family to her.

In Augusta, Beverly parked in front of a hair salon. Diane couldn't imagine why she'd stopped there, unless her friends thought she should get her head shaved. That might be a good idea. Then she wouldn't have to watch her hair come out in clumps. When they entered the shop, Beverly talked to a salesperson, who took them to a back room.

The room had a comfortable couch and chairs, but what caught Diane's eyes were shelves with mannequin heads sporting wigs. Dozens of them. Every imaginable style, length, and color. And on tables in front of each seat were mirrors on stands.

"We're all going to try on wigs," Shelley said, grinning.

Diane looked at her smiling friends. She wanted to cry and to hug each of them. They'd planned this just for her, to help her through this tough time. She didn't like wigs, but what options did she have? It could be months before she had a presentable head of hair again.

"All right. I guess it's time for me to buy a wig. What style should I get?"

"Let me bring you several to try on," the saleswoman said. "You're all welcome to try on any of the wigs in here. Have you worn wigs before?"

"I have," Diane said. She was the only one.

"First pin your hair up and back out of the way, then put on the wig cap."

Beverly twisted and pinned Shelley's long hair out of the way. The saleswoman helped each of them make sure their hair was securely pinned up and the cap in place.

"Good. Now there are two tabs on the front sides of the wigs," the attendant said. "Position them so they are right in front of your ears. Don't bend over. Watch yourself in the mirror."

Diane watched her friends. Margaret picked a brunette shoulder-length straight style. She had quite a time putting it on. The attendant went to help her.

"Model for us, Margaret," Diane said.

Margaret watched in the mirror while the attendant adjusted the wig. Then she stood and faced them, posing as if for a picture.

Margaret's face looked thinner and her neck longer in the sleek style. The dark color and her exaggerated pose made her look years younger.

"Oh, wait. I have my camera." Beverly rummaged in her bag and found it. "Okay. Smile for me."

Margaret posed and batted her eyelashes while Beverly took her picture.

"You look good in dark hair," Shelley said.

"You think so?" Margaret looked in one of the mirrors on the wall. "I always wanted dark hair. I wonder if Allan would like it?"

"You'll never know unless you try it," Diane said, enjoying her friend's antics.

"Now it's my turn," Shelley said, putting on a short henna wig. She had to push strands of her long blond hair under the wig. She stood and modeled the wig, looking at herself in the big mirror that covered the wall. "I always wanted to be a redhead. What do you think?"

"Wow, does it change your looks!" Diane said. Her young friend looked impish and daring. "That looks great on you."

"*Hmm.* I kind of like it. I wonder what Dan would think?"

"I think he'd like it," Beverly said. "But he'd adore you no matter what style or color you do your hair."

"I don't know. He likes my hair long."

Beverly tried on a blonde wig with a long updo. She looked very sophisticated, but the blonde didn't match her complexion. She looked in the mirror and made a face showing her dislike. "I always envied the blondes in school. My mother wouldn't let me bleach my hair, and in truth, I didn't have the nerve after one of my friends tried it and her hair turned orange."

Diane opted for a wig that looked just like the hairstyle and color she'd had before her haircut. It looked good on her. She didn't care for the feel of the wig, but she had to admit, no one would know it wasn't her own hair.

"That looks great, but try this one, just for fun," Shelley said, giving her a short, spiky auburn wig.

"Okay, but I want to look natural." Diane tried it on.

"I love that on you," Beverly said. "It really brings out your blue eyes."

She had to admit, it looked good. It made her look younger. But it would draw attention to her, and she did not want attention. She removed it.

"Here's one made for you," Margaret said, handing her a wig with long, ash-blonde hair that curled softly.

Diane put it on. She loved the feel of the soft, real hair curling around her shoulders and down her back. She looked at the back of it in the big mirror.

"Wow, you look like a movie star," Shelley said.

Diane laughed. "Hardly. I like long hair on other people, but it's so much work. I always get frustrated and cut it off before it gets very long."

"It's no work at all," Shelley said. "I just pull it up in a ponytail."

"Which is great on you, but not on a fifty-five-year-old woman," Diane said.

"Not true. I think it's lovely," Margaret said.

"I agree. If you like it, you should get it," Beverly said.

"*Hmm.* I'll think about it." She removed it and set it aside.

They tried on wigs of every imaginable color and style, even purple and pink-tipped spikes, until they were all giggling and laughing at each other.

Margaret tried on a short, sleek, capped style that was longer in the front and sides. The warm brown wig had hints of magenta and gold.

"That's a perfect artist's do," Diane said.

"Do you think so?" She picked up a mirror and looked at the back.

"You look glamorous," Shelley said.

Margaret laughed. "You must need glasses. But I could be incognito when people come in the gallery. If they don't like my paintings, I can pretend I'm not the artist."

"Silly. Everyone likes your paintings," Shelley said.

Diane tried on the short wig again. It did make her look younger. And she felt a bit daring in it, as if she could take on the world, or that nasty villain cancer.

After they tried on nearly every wig, they made their choices. Shelley found an inexpensive synthetic curly blond hairpiece that fit over her own hair when she pulled it up in a ponytail and twisted it into a bun. It had strands of red, giving it a stylish, sophisticated look. Beverly bought hair extensions and thin braids with feathers woven in, and had the attendant put them in her hair. She looked chic. And Margaret went with the funky artist's wig she had tried on. Beverly took pictures and had the attendant take several poses of all of them in their wigs and hairpieces.

Diane felt like she'd been given a strong dose of vitamins and mood elevators by the time they left. She'd bought the short, dark, spiky wig and the wig that matched her natural hair. She'd also picked out two soft turbans. One was the blue of the sea, and the other was Christmas red. She wore the spiky wig. She didn't know if she would have the nerve to wear it again, but it made her feel adventurous and lighthearted.

They all wore their new purchases to go out to lunch. At the juice bar, where they all ordered healthy fruit smoothies, the waitress took a picture of all of them sipping their drinks.

By the end of lunch, Diane was exhausted, but she didn't let on. She wanted to store up every moment of the special day. She couldn't believe her friends gave up an entire day of their precious time to bolster her spirits. With her new wig on her head, and her friends' encouragement, she silently resolved to overcome her distress and get out as much as possible. She could take a nap when she got home.

★ ★ ★

Wednesday morning Beverly stepped inside the Municipal building annex in the lovely converted Victorian home next to the police department. She stopped and looked around. She had been there several times before, but now she viewed the building with new eyes. The foyer had been opened up to give it more of an office appearance. The walls were pale blue with maple wainscoting around the bottom. Framed photographs of local points of interest and an old map decorated the walls. The business office was on the right, and the reception office was on the left. The French doors were open, giving a view of the counter.

"Good morning, Beverly." The receptionist greeted her with a big smile when she walked into the reception room. Beverly wondered if she was always so cheerful and perky.

"Good morning, Angela. I have an appointment with the mayor."

"She just went up to her office. I'll page her. You can wait in the foyer if you'd like. There's a coffeepot by the tourist brochures if you want some coffee."

"Thank you." Beverly read the notices on the bulletin board while she waited. Several meetings were listed. The water board. The planning commission. The port commission. The town council. The school board. She could keep busy attending local meetings, although that was not required. She jotted down dates and times. Attending meetings was a great way to gain insight into the various departments and get to know people, but she didn't want anyone to feel she was interfering with their jurisdiction, either. She'd attended a few meetings while she was campaigning and she'd felt welcome. Now she had a vested interest in learning how each department operated and how they worked together. She decided she would space them out so that she attended each one quarterly.

She was looking at a photograph of the Cannery in its heyday, when she heard footsteps on the stairs. Evelyn Waters came through the doorway from the stairs.

"Morning, Beverly."

"Good morning, Mayor. I appreciate your taking time to talk to me." Beverly shook hands with Evelyn.

"Would you like a cup of coffee? I usually get mine from the pot down here. That way I don't drink too many cups."

"No, thanks."

"All right. Come on up. I'll show you around." Evelyn led the way up the stairs to a hallway. Shiny green-and-cream textured wallpaper covered the walls. Two bronze chandeliers lighted the hallway.

"The council's offices are there on the right. They're rarely used. Most of the time, I'm up here alone. We did some major renovations to the plumbing twenty years ago. There's a men's lavatory down the hall, and a powder room up close to my...the mayor's office. I insisted on it." She gave Beverly a wink.

"I got to pick my office too. I hope you'll appreciate that." She led the way to the room in the front corner. Beverly's heart skipped a beat.

"I like purple. If you don't like it, you can have it painted whatever color you want. I hope you don't pick something garish, though. Keep the Victorian ambiance if you can."

They stepped into a large room that was round in the front with tall sash windows. Beverly blinked. The decor brought to mind a Victorian gilded birdcage. Lavender and white vertical stripes covered the walls. Wallpaper trim with nosegays of violets and gold cherubs bordered the walls at the ceiling and the base. Lace curtains hung on the windows, letting in natural light. All it needed was a pair of canaries or an old-fashioned opera singer. She would definitely make some changes. She smiled at the mayor, who was watching her for a reaction.

"This is certainly unique," she said, hoping she didn't sound critical.

"All of the furnishings are mine except the desk and file cabinet, so you'll have to do your own decorating. I was going to paint it all off-white for Lee, but that won't be done now."

"I have a few office pieces that will do fine," Beverly said. "I've met the town councilmen, but there's a new councilwoman. I haven't met her yet."

"Martha Goodman is visiting her daughter in Des Moines and wasn't here for the election results. She's a Mainer. She and her husband ran a fishing operation. He died a couple of years ago. She still runs the business and goes out on the boats."

"I look forward to meeting her."

Beverly asked about the mayor's duties, and Evelyn gave her a long discourse on the job of running the town. She was a hands-on leader and filled the hats of mayor, city manager, and ambassador full-time. Beverly wasn't sure it needed to be such a demanding position, but she kept that to herself.

"This is off topic, but does the town own the old train station at the west end of town?"

"No. What makes you ask?"

"I was out walking with friends and we came across it. I hadn't paid any attention to it before. I've seen some old train stations restored, and they're beautiful buildings. It's too bad it's been let go. You would have been very young when the railroad closed. Do you remember anything about it?"

Evelyn laughed. "Not that young. I rode the train from Marble Cove to Boston with my mother once. We had to change trains a couple of times. I loved it."

"Do you happen to remember the stationmaster?"

"I remember him very well. He was rich and very proper. He always had a hat on and he had a gold pocket watch. I thought he looked like he belonged in the previous century. He was a bachelor, I believe, though I suppose he might have been divorced or a widower. He had a cook, which was a big deal around here. He put on fancy dinners. Since my father was the mayor, my parents were often invited to his dinner parties. I never got to go, but mother would tell me all the details. They always had at least four courses and he used to hire a soloist to play the piano and sing for the guests. She would come on the train and she looked like a movie star. She had blonde hair and dressed classy. She reminded me of Doris Day."

"Really? He sounds like an interesting character. Does he still live around here?"

"He must have moved away soon after the railroad shut down. At least I don't remember seeing him after that."

"*Hmm.* Do you know who owns the old railroad station now?"

"The railroad deeded it to the town years ago, when my father was mayor. Odd. No one has cared about that building in years. Now you're the second person to ask me about it recently."

"You mean Dennis Calder? He wants the property. He would tear down the old station and put up a new building. Do you think it could benefit the town?"

"His brand of progress only benefits Dennis Calder. Just because he lost the election doesn't mean he'll stop trying to get what he wants," Evelyn continued. "He's an opportunist and doesn't mind bending the truth to get his way. Watch out for him."

"Yes, I will. So you won't approve his plan if he tries to tear down the train station?"

"Not a chance. He won't get approval from the town while I'm mayor. I'm glad to hear you don't like his ideas either. Just watch your back. I suppose it's a good thing you were elected mayor. I had hopes that Lee would succeed me, but he doesn't have the passion for the job, and he hates stress."

"I'm not thrilled about stress either. But I think I can handle it. Lee's young. Perhaps in a few years he'll want to lead the town. I don't plan to be the mayor forever."

"I said that too. And here I am, a lifetime later. I'll miss it, but I have things I'd like to do before I'm too old to do them."

"I hope you have a wonderful time in your new endeavors. And I hope I'll be able to call on you for advice from time to time."

"Happy to help out anytime if I'm around, but I plan to be gone as much as possible. I've always wanted to travel. I'm going to start in January, right after I turn the gavel over to you."

After Beverly said good-bye, she ran errands. Mrs. Peabody had left a list of foods they needed from the grocery store. As she shopped, Beverly thought about what she'd learned from the mayor. She wouldn't have to worry about Evelyn looking over her shoulder or telling her how to run the town. That could be a good thing. She expected there would be plenty of people trying to tell her what to do. But what she'd learned about the train stationmaster piqued her interest. So he was a bachelor and he liked to put on fancy dinner parties. The history of the railway station was becoming more colorful. She couldn't wait to see if Diane felt good enough to go digging through the newspaper archives with her. There must be articles about the stationmaster and the pianist who came to play for his parties in the society section, if nothing else.

CHAPTER FIFTEEN

Shelley would have loved to take a short nap Wednesday afternoon. Emma was asleep and Aiden was playing quietly in his room, his version of nap time these days. Shelley sliced the long loaf of baked biscotti into thin, individual pieces and put them back into the oven to crisp.

The morning had been hectic, so Shelley had missed her usual quiet time. She loved having a few moments alone to read her Bible and pray. The day went better when she started with her focus on God, instead of on the rush and demands of it.

She took a cup of reheated coffee to the table and opened her Bible to the Proverbs and started where she'd left off, at the fifth and sixth verses of chapter three: "Trust in the Lord with all your heart and lean not on your own understanding; in all your ways acknowledge him, and he will make your paths straight." The verses didn't give her insight into her current dilemma. It said to trust in the Lord. She did trust Him. But she'd prayed, and so far, she didn't have an answer.

Shelley thought about Margaret and her art gallery. She had retired from her career in accounting before she pursued her art. Should she wait until her children were grown and gone to pursue her dream? But she was already doing it. Should she stop, as Frances suggested? If only someone could make the decision for her.

As she started to close her Bible, the phone rang. She picked it up. The number wasn't local. A phone order? She took mail orders over the Internet, not the telephone.

"Hello?"

"Is this Shelley Bauer?"

"Yes, it is. Can I help you?"

"This is Melissa Boardman, Darlene Kearns' daughter."

"Hi, Melissa. Goodness, it's been years since I've talked to you. How are you?"

"I'm fine. But I have sad news. My mother..." There was a pause. Shelley thought she heard a choking sound. "My mother passed away two weeks ago."

"Oh no!" Tears sprang to Shelley's eyes. "Melissa, I'm so sorry. What happened?"

"She had a heart attack. It was sudden. We didn't know she had any kind of heart problem."

"You and your mother were so close. How are you doing? Is there anything I can do to help?"

"No. But thanks for offering. I should have thought to call you sooner. We had a memorial service last week. I guess I wasn't thinking clearly."

"Of course not. It's all right." Shelley would have dropped everything and gone to the service. An image of her high school youth group leader flashed into her mind. She was so kind and supportive. When her own family was falling apart and her parents were divorcing, Darlene gave Shelley the safe harbor she needed. Shelley owed much of her faith to the woman who had been mentor and surrogate mother to her in those turbulent days. Seeing Darlene's rock-solid marriage and trusting relationship with her husband had given Shelley the courage to give her heart to Dan and take a chance on marriage.

"I've been going through her things," Melissa continued.

"That must be hard."

"Yes, and yet there are many, many good memories. I found an old devotional book with your wedding invitation tucked inside. I know you were close to Mom and she cared so much about you. I think she'd want you to have the book. It isn't in great shape. It's a yearly devotional book, but it looks like she read back through it and marked in it several times. I suspect she kept your invitation with your picture on it so she'd remember to pray for you."

Shelley clamped her lips together to keep from crying out loud. Darlene had promised to pray for her and for her marriage. Shelley realized she had kept that promise. All her prayers had covered Shelley and Dan and the children through the years. What a special legacy she'd left. "Thank you. That means the world to me. I'd love to have her book. Your mother was a special angel to me and to many others. I'll be praying for you, for comfort. I know you're going to miss having her in your life."

"Thank you." Melissa's voice cracked. She cleared her throat. "I need your address so I can mail this to you."

"Of course." Shelley gave Melissa her address, then they said good-bye.

After she disconnected the call, she stood staring at her kitchen. She'd just prayed for an answer from God. Instead, she'd gotten bad news. What was God trying to tell her? She was reminded of Darlene and how she had hugged and held Shelley while she cried over her parents' divorce. She'd encouraged Shelley to follow her dreams and cling to her faith. At a time when she'd needed a good role model, Darlene had been there for her.

Shelley remembered the earrings Darlene had given her when she'd graduated from high school. She went up to her bedroom and rummaged through her jewelry box. There they were. She pulled them out and put them on, then looked in the mirror. The bright-orange-and-black enameled Baltimore oriole earrings dangled from her ears. Darlene's favorite bird. She'd told Shelley that she loved seeing the beautiful birds because they brightened every day and reminded her that the Lord was with her.

"Mama, Mama, Mama."

Emma was awake. Shelley left the earrings on and went to pick up her daughter. She hugged her and held her close. Sweet Emma. Soft and warm from sleep. If not for Darlene, Shelley might not have had the courage to take a chance on a relationship. How empty her life would be without Dan and Emma and Aiden.

"Pretty, Mama. Birdie." Emma reached out with one finger and touched the bright earring.

"Yes, sweetheart. It's a birdie. An oriole."

"Oreo?" Emma looked confused for a moment. Then she smiled. "Cookie?"

Shelley laughed. "No, not the cookie. A Baltimore oriole," she said, enunciating each syllable. "It's a special bird."

"Ball and more Oreo," Emma said.

"No Oreos, but I think we can find a treat."

"I want a treat," Aiden said, rushing out of his bedroom.

"All right. Let's go downstairs. I'll get milk and cookies for all of us."

Shelley could imagine Darlene smiling down on her. The thought left a lump in Shelley's throat. She hadn't seen her friend in several years, but knowing she was gone left an empty spot in Shelley's heart. Her own sorrow gave her a glimpse of the pain Melissa must be feeling. Thinking about her friend made her wonder what advice Darlene would have given to her about her business dilemma. Like Dan, she would have supported Shelley in her decision, but would she have had some words of wisdom? Shelley would never know.

★ ★ ★

Since she and Jeff had toured the Boothbay Railway Village and revisited the Marble Cove train station and the quarry, Beverly's desire to save the remnants of the past had become a compelling passion. Sleepy little Marble Cove teemed with stories going back to the first settlers of Maine. They'd learned much of that history when she and her friends had investigated the lighthouse and Old First and its founder, Jeremiah Thorpe.

How did the railroad and quarry fit into that history? She couldn't wait to find out and was glad Diane wanted to dive into the research with her Thursday morning.

Diane had a nose for uncovering a story. Her experience as a journalist and her natural curiosity and imagination made doing research with her fascinating. She wouldn't give up. So Beverly was excited Thursday morning to climb the stairs to the *Marble Cove Courier*'s morgue with Diane.

They picked their way across the second floor, which had housed a corset factory and was littered with old sewing machines and debris. The only light came from windows obscured by many years of dust on the inside and weather on the outside. They crossed the room to the stairs leading to the third-floor attic. The stairs seemed even more narrow and precarious than Beverly remembered from their previous foray into the dusty newspaper archives, but they'd made it before, so she sallied forth, with Diane right behind her.

"It's cold up here," Diane said. "This wig is warm, though. It'll keep my head from freezing." She'd worn her new wig that matched her natural hair.

"That's a plus, but it may need shampooing when we're finished here." Beverly pushed a cobweb out of the way and tried not to think about the spider that had spun it. "I think I'll leave my stocking cap on." She took a high-powered flashlight out of her pocket and flipped it on. She found the single lightbulb in the ceiling and pulled the chain. It came on, but cast a dim light.

Another light came on. "I brought a flashlight too," Diane said. "If I remember right, you found the books from the 1950s over here." She shined the light on a bank of shelves. "There are the ones you saw last time: 1952, 1942, and 1921. There's 1951. That's the year Mrs. Peabody's letter was postmarked. I'll start with it."

"And I'll look for early history. I remember seeing old papers from the 1890s last time we were here." Beverly flashed the light against the far wall, looking for dates on the spines. "There's the book I saw before. 1896. The railroad came through to Marble Cove in 1884. There might be some mention of it. I wonder if there are any earlier records. Too bad these are out of order."

"Putting this room in order would be a great project for a history buff," Diane said. She sneezed.

"Maybe you shouldn't be up here. Your chemo treatments lower your immune system. I don't want you catching a cold."

"I don't want that either. I'll take a hot shower and drink some herbal tea when I get home." She had opened a book and was looking through it by the light of her flashlight.

Beverly went around the shelves looking for an earlier book. She found one halfway around the room from 1887. Very carefully, so the pages wouldn't fall apart, she opened the book. The pages were yellowed and the print faint.

"This first headline mentions the railroad," Beverly said. She read the article out loud. "'The *Mary Frances* Meets Her Death in Marble Cove. The whaling vessel, the *Mary Frances* out of Portland, limped into port Tuesday with damage to hull and rudder. After a disappointing whale harvest, ship owner George Hennesey announced the ship will be salvaged at the Marble Cove shipyard, as return to Portland would be too costly. Cargo and stores were transferred to the Marble Cove arm of the Maine Central Railroad for shipment to Portland. Hennesey rues the demise of the glory days of whaling. The demand for whale oil and baleen has dropped, and the trade is no longer profitable, says Hennesey.' That shows how the railroad was replacing shipping." Beverly laid the large book of newspaper pages open and took a picture with her digital camera. "Something like this might help publicize the historical significance of the railroad."

"Anything about the quarry?" Diane asked.

"Not yet. I'll keep looking."

"Nothing yet in this book," Diane said. She turned a few more pages. "Here's something. Layoffs at the quarry. This says orders for lime had dwindled so much that they were going to close the quarry. They would fulfill open orders, but take no new orders. This is from August 1951. So that might have carried them through that fall." She turned a few more pages. "Here it is. 'Historic Burr Oak Limestone Quarry Ceases Operation.' The quarry opened in 1778 and ran continuously until the last shipment went out November 29, 1951. It must be a lot larger than the lake we saw. There must be other pits or lakes. I'd love to get inside and see it all."

"With the quarry shut down, commercial shipping out of Marble Cove would have been limited. The only other large enterprise was the Cannery."

"Right. I don't see anything in these newspapers about the railroad closing. There's an article here that the president of the Maine Central Railroad visited here December tenth. A formal dinner was held at the home of the stationmaster…" Diane stopped and stared at the faded newspaper.

"What?" Beverly moved closer to look over her shoulder.

"The stationmaster, Elias Thorpe. He must be related to Jeremiah Thorpe!"

"Wow. I didn't think there were any more Thorpes. He must have lived in Marble Cove."

"He did, according to Evelyn Waters. This says the mayor and the owner of the quarry and the town council all attended. Oh, and entertainment was provided by Belle Marie, from the Maine State Music Theater."

"She must be the pianist-soloist Evelyn Waters told me about. She said she looked like Doris Day."

"There's a picture, but it isn't very good quality. She looks blonde and she's dressed in a fur coat. Try taking a picture of it. Maybe we can enhance it."

Beverly took a picture of the article.

"There's nothing more in 1951. There must be other articles about Elias Thorpe, though. I'll check the next book." Diane sneezed again.

"I think we should leave. I don't want you getting sick now. We found some early history and more recent information. I'll put together a timeline and see if that gives us a better picture of the railroad history. Maybe we can learn more about Elias Thorpe. Did you ever try calling Augie?"

"No. I felt so crummy Monday, I didn't want to talk to anyone. I'm sorry."

"Don't be. I'm thankful you're having a few good days every week. You have a treatment tomorrow, and I don't want you getting a cold that could delay your treatments."

"I suppose you're right. We can come back later if we need to do more research. You could talk to Augie without me."

"I wouldn't think of it." Though Beverly wanted to find out about Elias Thorpe, she couldn't leave Diane out of the investigation. She was equally excited about this mystery. "You're much better than I am at ferreting out the whole story. We'll wait and see how you feel next week. We can talk to Augie then."

"All right. If you insist. I don't want to hold you back," Diane said, but she smiled, and Beverly knew she was pleased to be part of the research into the train mystery.

★ ★ ★

Shelley delivered an assortment of pastries to the Cannery for their Thanksgiving promotion. The sardine-factory-turned-specialty-mall was running promotional events all week to get people in the holiday mood. She had a half hour before she needed to pick up Aiden from pre-K, so she and Emma stopped at the gallery to see Margaret.

"Well, hello. Come on in out of the cold. It must be near freezing out there."

Emma clapped her mittened hands. "Fweezing," she proclaimed.

Just then the door opened and Diane and Beverly came in and quickly shut the door.

"Brrr. It's cold out there," Beverly said.

"Fweezing!" Emma squealed, giggling and dancing around in a circle, making them all laugh.

"What brings you all out on such a blustery day?" Margaret asked.

"I just made a delivery and we're hanging around town until Aiden gets out of school. I hope you don't mind us busting in on you," Shelley said.

"No. I'm happy for the company. Everyone else is at home by the fire, I suspect. I haven't had a soul come in today. Come on back. I just heated some water for tea."

They went back to Margaret's work area. She filled cups with hot water and set out tea bags.

"How's your painting coming?" Beverly asked.

"Not as well as I'd like. I'm trying to put some vibrancy into the fall scene, but so far it's looking pretty dull." She laughed, but without humor. "Like me."

"What's wrong?" Diane asked.

"I don't know. Allan thinks I have the onset of winter blahs. I know I should count my blessings, but I feel like life has passed me by. There's so much I haven't done."

Margaret's distress made Shelley wonder if she should grab at her opportunities now, before it was too late. If she didn't, would she end up like Margaret, regretting the things she hadn't done? Yet she admired all that Margaret had accomplished. It was very confusing.

"I understand how you feel, but you didn't give up on your dream to paint and open a gallery. Just look at it," Diane said, waving her arm around. "Not many people can make a business successful, and you've done that, even after having a successful career."

"I know. Don't mind me. I'll get over it. What brought you and Beverly to town?"

"We just came from the newspaper office," Diane said, taking a sip of hot tea. "We braved the morgue, looking for articles about the railroad and the quarry. We found a couple of things that might help us put together a timeline."

"And collected a lot of dust. Diane got the sneezes, so we decided we'd found enough and it was time to leave," Beverly said. "You'll never guess who the stationmaster was."

"Who? Does he still live in Marble Cove? He must be pretty old," Shelley said.

"At least in his eighties, I'd guess," Diane said. "And I've never heard of him around here. But he is probably related to our Jeremiah Thorpe."

"Really?" Margaret's eyes widened. "A Thorpe?"

"Yes. His name is Elias Thorpe," Beverly said. "Has to be a descendant of Jeremiah Thorpe. It's not exactly a common name."

"Maybe he's the one who took Jeremiah's treasure," Shelley said, her eyes sparkling.

"I thought of that too," Beverly said. "We need to talk to some eyewitnesses. Diane and I will try to go see Augie Jackson next week. If anyone knows the details of the railroad and the quarry, it'll be Augie."

"I hope so. I'm really getting curious." Shelley looked around as she sipped her tea. Printouts of the Eiffel Tower and a huge stone arch were taped up on the wall. "Those are pictures of France, aren't they? Are you going to paint them?"

"They're in Paris. The arch is the Arc de Triomphe." Margaret sighed. "I'm just dreaming. That's probably as close to Paris as I'll ever get."

"You could take a trip there. It's supposed to be really pretty in the springtime."

"Maybe." Margaret sighed. "It was on my bucket list. I wanted to go study art in Paris after college."

"You made a bucket list in college? I thought that was something for old—er—older people."

Margaret smiled. "We didn't call it that then. It was a dream list when I was young and single. I dreamed of lots of things I wanted to do."

"Wouldn't that be cool!" Shelley said. "They have some great culinary schools there, but I'd be lucky to find time to take a baking class in Augusta." She laughed, then glanced at her watch. "Oh. Speaking of time . . . I've got to run. Aiden gets out in a few minutes." Shelley put Emma's hat and gloves back on her, then put on her own gloves.

"We need to get going too. I think I've worn Diane out this morning," Beverly said. "We just wanted to say hi. I like the idea of a bucket list, Margaret. We're never too old to dream."

They followed Shelley out the door.

"I'll bring over something for your dinner tomorrow night," Shelley told Diane. "I'm praying you don't get sick from your treatment."

"Thank you. Your prayers and your delicious cooking mean a lot to me, but I know you're swamped with the holidays coming up. Please don't feel obligated to cook for me too."

"Oh no. You could never be an obligation to me. I'm glad there's something I can do to help. It isn't much, really."

"It's a lot, Shelley. More than you can imagine. I'm blessed and humbled that my friends care so much."

They went separate ways. Shelley watched her two friends get into Beverly's car and drive away. As the youngest in their group of friends, Shelley felt like she was the one who was blessed. She thought about what she could fix that would give Diane a boost of vitamins. They were all trying to protect Diane from catching a cold while her immune system was down. Maybe some creamy fresh broccoli and cauliflower soup spiced with rosemary and thyme and some lemon pepper. She could make crusty French bread to go with it.

Shelley thought about her three friends. They were all following their dreams. Margaret with her art and gallery. Maybe she had never made it to Paris, but her paintings were beautiful and famous. She'd reached her goal without going to Paris to study. Diane was following her dream with her writing, although the cancer had sidetracked her temporarily. And Beverly had started a business, and now was putting her talents to work serving their community. But they were all older than she was and they didn't have a young family at home.

They'd known what they wanted, though. That was a first step to achieving a dream. She'd dreamed of having a baking business for a long time, and she'd thought she'd reached her goal. It was going pretty well. But was this the right time? Or should she put it on hold until the future, when her family was grown? If she followed her friends' examples, she would wait. Margaret had even given up her dream to study in Paris. She had sacrificed her dream for her family.

CHAPTER SIXTEEN

Diane checked her hair and makeup for the third time. The wig was in place. At close examination, it looked like her own hair, but it felt fake. She hoped Leo wouldn't be able to tell the difference. Her skin looked pasty, even with makeup giving her some color and covering the dark circles under her eyes. Why had she agreed to let him come over?

Then she recalled the care and sacrifice of her friends to help her through her hair loss and distress. They'd given up a valuable day to spend with her picking out wigs so she would feel comfortable around people. And this wasn't even going out in public. Just Leo coming over, bringing pizza, which she loved, and a funny movie to cheer her up.

She knew she was being vain. Eric would have told her she looked fine and that men didn't notice those things, but he'd been color-blind and sweetly partial when it came to her and her appearance.

Why she cared what Leo thought, she didn't know. They were just friends.

The doorbell rang. She went to answer it, smoothing her skirt as she went. Now she felt overdressed, though it was a casual skirt and sweater. The scarf around her neck covered the bump under her skin where the port was. She took a deep breath, smiled, and opened the door.

All she could see was a big, flat box. She stood aside. "Hi. Come in out of the cold. Brrr. It's cold enough to snow."

"Almost," he said. "But the pizza is hot. Shall I put it in the kitchen?"

"Yes. I've got plates and Caesar salad on the table." She was glad he was carrying the pizza. The look in his eyes warmed her enough to make her blush and she could see he wanted to give her a hug, but he set the box down, then turned away to remove his coat.

"You look wonderful," he said when he turned back to her. "The chemo doesn't seem to have affected you too much, although I'm sure it's been tough."

Diane felt guilty for her cover-up. She'd wanted to impress him rather than be honest about the effects of the treatments. She trusted Leo, but she couldn't stand the thought of him imagining her with a bald head, so she just smiled. "Thank you. I'm having a good day and I'm celebrating. I'll pass the halfway point in my treatments tomorrow. So far, so good."

The caring look he gave her melted her heart. "That *is* cause for a party! Thank you for letting me celebrate with you. I've been praying these treatments wouldn't be too hard on you, but that the new drug will zap that cancer for good."

"I appreciate your prayers. I think they're working." She did not want to discuss her cancer. "Now let's have some of that pizza while it's hot. It's one food that still tastes good to me."

She opened the box, letting out a puff of steam and the aroma that was spicy enough for her to smell. The chemo had affected her senses of taste and smell, making most food seem bland and unappealing.

Diane enjoyed the pizza, but could only eat one piece. Leo ate several pieces, then insisted she freeze the rest so she could have a piece whenever she wanted one.

After dinner, Diane made popcorn. She carried two bowls of buttered popcorn to the living room while Leo set up the movie.

"I hope you like this. It was recommended as a must-see funny movie." He joined her on the couch and picked up the remote to start it. "Oh, wait. I almost forgot."

"What?"

"No movie is complete without theater candy." He got up and went to his coat. He took two boxes out of his pockets and came back to the couch.

"I seem to remember these are your favorites. Voilà!" He handed her the boxes. Dots and Hot Tamales.

"I love these. Oh, you sweet man." She gave him a big smile. "This is perfect. Roll that movie."

He put his arm across the couch in back of her. She leaned against him and enjoyed the feel of having a special friend who understood her need to feel normal.

Diane laughed so hard at the movie she had tears in her eyes. The deep chuckles made her relax and forget her troubles for a couple of hours. Leo laughed along with her. They didn't talk. Didn't need to. The shared companionship was enough.

When the movie finished, he got up to leave. "I don't want to keep you up too late," he said. "I want you to invite me back."

He put on his coat. Diane followed him to the door. He turned to her. "Good night, Diane. Thanks for a lovely evening."

"Leo. Thank you. I'm so glad you came over."

"You are? Good. I was afraid you didn't want to see me anymore."

"No, it's not that. I've been acting like a hermit since my diagnosis, but I don't want to keep doing that. Do you have plans for Thanksgiving? Would you like to come have dinner with us? Jessica will be here and she'd love to see you."

"And I'd like to see her. Are you sure *you* want me to come?"

She knew his question was personal. She didn't even hesitate, as she would have done last week. "Yes, *I* want you to come."

"Then I'd love to. May I bring something?"

"Jessica said she is doing the cooking. She'll be here Monday night. She's taking a few days off to spend here. You can ask her then."

"Okay, I'll check with her. Good night, Diane." He leaned down and kissed her cheek. She smiled and gave him a hug, being careful to avoid hitting the port.

As she got ready for bed, she realized she felt better than she'd felt in a long time. A good laugh and a good friend were the best of medicines. Why had she hesitated to have Leo come over? She hadn't thought her appearance mattered to her, but she didn't want Leo to see her without hair and looking like lukewarm dishwater. She wanted him to see her at her best. She had to wonder if her feelings for the good-looking veterinarian went deeper than friendship. But she wasn't about to explore that train of thought. At least Jessica would be happy that Leo was coming for Thanksgiving dinner. Diane frowned, wondering if Jessica knew how to cook a turkey and stuffing.

* * *

At the Bauer household, the dinner dishes were done. Emma and Aiden were bathed and ready for bed. Dan sat at the dining table with Hailey, helping her with her math homework. Shelley was so glad he understood it the way the schools taught it now. Besides, he had to work math equations with his electrical classes that were way over her head.

Taking up the far end of the table, Shelley stapled and taped Pilgrim hats out of black and white construction paper for Aiden's pre-K class play. She had seven hats to go, then she needed to piece together the Pilgrim collars. A batch of cranberry orange crumb cake baked in the oven, sending a sweet scent throughout the house. Another batch waited to go into the oven along with a pumpkin sponge cake in a jelly roll pan for cream-filled pumpkin pinwheels.

Hailey closed up her math workbook and went upstairs to get ready for bed. Shelley and Dan followed her up and tucked all three children into their beds and said prayers with them. On the way back downstairs, Dan put his arm around Shelley's shoulders.

"What were you working so hard on while Hailey and I were solving the math problems?"

"Costumes for Aiden's class. They're doing a play next Wednesday. I don't suppose you could get an hour off work in the morning to come see it?"

"I doubt it, but I'll see what the schedule looks like. If we're working in town, I'll see if I can take a short break. Maybe I could take an early lunch."

"That'd be great. Aiden would be very pleased." Shelley leaned against Dan's side and thanked God for giving her a math-savvy, helpful husband.

Dan followed her to the kitchen. "What smells so good in here? Is there a sample in there for the math whiz?"

Shelley laughed. "You deserve a treat. I'm sure I can spare a piece for you."

Dan settled at his laptop and Shelley cut him a slice of the warm cranberry cake. "I had a call from an old friend from high school."

Dan looked up.

"Darlene Kearns died."

Dan frowned. "Do I know her?"

"She was at our wedding, but I haven't seen her in several years. She was my youth group leader at church when I was in high school." Shelley's eyes filled with tears.

"I'm sorry, Shell. That's tough news."

"Yeah. Her daughter is going to send me a book she had with my name in it as a memento."

"That's nice."

Dan clearly didn't understand the significance of the book from Darlene. She sighed, then sat down with her notebook and opened to a blank page. She stared at it for a moment.

"Dan?"

"*Hmm?*" He didn't look up from his laptop.

"Do you have a bucket list?"

He looked up. "Say what?"

"A bucket list. You know, a dream list. Things you want to do or have in your life."

"Never gave it much thought. Why?"

"Margaret found one she'd made in college and I think she regrets that she hasn't done some of the things on her list. She wanted to go to Paris to take art classes and paint over there."

"No kidding? Why would she want to go halfway around the world when there are great things to paint right here?"

"I don't know. Because it was her dream. You must have some dreams?"

"Right now, I dream of finishing these classes and becoming a full journeyman electrician. That's enough."

"Yeah, I guess."

He looked at her, his brow furrowed. "You're serious about this, aren't you? I want to support my family and be a good father and husband. I want to help Aiden play Little League baseball and maybe he and Emma could play soccer. I want to fish and hunt and maybe get a boat someday. I'd like to do more woodworking. Maybe teach Aiden how to build things someday. That's about it. Simple dreams. Nothing fancy, like going to France. Do you want to go to Paris too?"

Shelley smiled. "No. I don't care about going to Paris, unless I went to take culinary classes, like Margaret wanted to take art classes."

"You don't need culinary classes. You're already the best baker in Marble Cove. Maybe in Maine."

"Thank you. But I have a lot to learn. I don't have any dreams of going to France, though, so you can relax on that score."

"Good." He nodded and turned his concentration on his computer screen. Shelley knew he had work to do on his college classes and left him alone.

She wrote "Bucket List" at the top of her blank page. What did she want? *To be a good wife and mother. To manage my household well. To raise Aiden and Emma and Hailey to be responsible, compassionate people. To help the children discover their dreams and talents. To take family vacations. To pay off the mortgage and become debt free.*

Her list was pretty short. What was wrong with her? She didn't have big dreams. She didn't want to run marathons or go on fancy cruises. She should write down to expand her business, but she didn't want to be selfish. Besides, she didn't want to regret it, like Margaret, if she never realized her dream. If she didn't write it down, maybe she'd forget about it by the time she was Margaret's age. She put down her pen and closed the notebook. That was enough for one night. She might add to it later. After she prayed about it. That's what she would do. Like the verse she'd read in Proverbs. She would pray and wait to find out what path God wanted her to take.

★ ★ ★

Margaret picked up a dish to dry and set it on the kitchen table. Her thoughts went back to the conversation with her friends earlier. Shelley had suggested maybe she could take a trip to Paris. It might be nice, but visiting art museums and galleries wouldn't be the same as her dream. It might even be depressing, knowing she was settling for a substitute. She turned around and picked up another dish and set it on the table.

"Aren't you going to dry those?" Allan asked.

"What?" She looked up at him, puzzled, then looked at the wet dishes on the table. "Oops. I guess my mind was elsewhere." She dried the dish.

"You've been off in another world for two weeks, and it doesn't seem like a very pleasant world. What's wrong?"

Allan was so perceptive. Poor man must think she was getting senile. "I went through an old box of photos, looking for some sketches of the quarries we visited in Minnesota a long time ago. I found an old journal from college in the box. I'd written a bucket list in it of all the things I wanted to accomplish in my life. Reading through it, I realized I haven't done most of the things I dreamed of doing. I guess I'm disappointed in myself."

"Really?" He put down the dish he was washing and dried his hands, then turned to face her, leaning back against the sink. "Things like what? Name one."

"I wanted to take a trip to Paris and spend time painting and studying the masterpieces at the art museums and live in a garret."

"Ah. A long trip?"

"A couple of months, at least. But that's impossible now."

"Why?"

"Why?" Was he being funny? "Adelaide. The gallery. Your furniture orders. Money. To name a few obstacles."

"Ah. We could work around all of those objections. The gallery is doing well. You could hire someone to run it while we're gone. Maybe even one of your artists. You're already set up with a studio area for painting."

"Yes, but Adelaide. We can't leave her."

"I see two options. We could take her with us. Or she might love a chance to be more independent for a while. We could arrange for her to stay with someone or have someone come stay with her at the house."

Leave Adelaide behind? Her chest tightened at the thought. But Allan was right. Adelaide grew more capable every day as she stretched her limits and took on more classes and responsibilities. And Margaret could rely on Diane and Beverly and Shelley to keep a watch over Adelaide, just in case she needed something.

"But the cost. It would take a fortune to spend two months abroad."

"Would it? Have you checked? With your royalties and sales and my furniture orders, I think we could swing it."

"Really? You think we could? And you'd go with me?"

"Absolutely. I'm not going to miss out on your grand adventure. Drag out that bucket list and let's see if we can chip away at it."

Margaret put down the dish and hugged her husband. "I knew there was a good reason I married you. Who else would indulge me the way you do?"

Allan smiled and held her tight. "You've started something, you know. I might have to come up with my own bucket list. We'll be busy for years, checking off our dreams.

"It sounds like I'd better spend some more time in my workshop. I need to crank out additional stock for the Christmas season so we can afford to chase those dreams."

"Good idea. I'll do some new paintings for the Christmas season. And I'll look into the trip possibilities. It might still be beyond our reach. I think we'd better plan for a least a year to make all the arrangements and save up. I have no desire to be a starving artist or stay in a youth hostel. I want a few more creature comforts than I needed when I made that list."

"Yes, my love." He gave her a kiss on the cheek, then returned to washing the dishes.

Margaret picked up a wet dish and dried it. She could feel the wide grin on her face. She laughed out loud, gaining a look from Allan. His eyes were twinkling. The cloud of gloom had lifted off her shoulders. The bucket list might still need to be scrapped, but not without further study. Just the possibility of chasing some dreams brightened the future.

She thought about letting the dishes air dry and doing a computer search about Paris, but she would wait. Then she thought about the picture she'd tried to finish of the quarry. She had the basics on the canvas, but it needed a lot of work.

Now she couldn't wait to get at it. She could see the scene in her mind's eye. From old, scarred rock quarry and kilns to nature's reclamation. From the glory of autumn into the tranquility of winter. It would be the first of her Christmas stock. First thing in the morning, she would paint her picture to commemorate a new season filled with promise.

CHAPTER SEVENTEEN

After Margaret opened the gallery Friday morning, she put on some forties dance music, then got out her palette and went to work on her painting. It had texture, but it needed more color. Jewel tones. To the jazzy beat of the music, she dabbed and swirled on touches of vivid blues and silver, ochre and gold and royal purple. Several customers came in to browse. She sold two small paintings and a pottery cornucopia and one of Allan's knickknack shelves. She was glad for the business, but she couldn't wait to get back to her painting. On the canvas, autumn came to life. At the end of the day, she was pleased with the painting, but it wasn't finished. The transition was still missing. She had Saturday to work. She wanted to display it on Monday, the beginning of Thanksgiving week. With an hour before closing time, she logged on to the Internet and began searching. She was amazed at all the art class opportunities in France, and the costs surprised her. They weren't cheap, but more reasonable than she'd expected. Maybe this dream could come true after all.

★ ★ ★

After church on Sunday, the Bauer family gathered at Dan's parents' home for Sunday dinner. It was tradition. But this Sunday, Shelley sent Dan and the children so she could have a quiet afternoon for her baking marathon. She had forty-two orders to pack and ship Monday morning so they would be delivered before Thanksgiving.

Baker's boxes and waxed tissue paper covered the table. The stack of orders was piled on the counter. She'd compiled a spreadsheet of the types of cookies needed and the total. Once these were shipped, she could concentrate on her local orders. This year she had more than ever before.

Twenty dozen pumpkin spice biscotti and twenty-four dozen apple pie biscotti sat in large popcorn tins that she'd repurposed for cookie storage.

The sink was filled with apples. Canisters of oatmeal, flour, and sugar sat on the counter, their contents liberally dusting the counter surface. The air smelled rich and sweet with cinnamon, nutmeg, and maple syrup. Shelley ran apples through the manual apple peeler-corer and hummed along with a country song on her MP3 player. The maple apple pie bars were new, and they packed well for shipping.

Her bar cookies were as close to a pie dessert as she could ship and know they would arrive intact. Besides her standard brownie varieties and the apple bars, she'd advertised pecan praline bars. She'd gotten lots of orders. People were willing to give up their standard pies.

It was the perfect afternoon. Her family was having fun and eating well. She had her orders under control. She would have to bake long hours all week, but she could make it. Even with the pies for the community center and the pies for their family Thanksgiving.

She was chopping the apples when the phone rang. She was tempted to ignore it, but it might be Dan, so she picked it up.

"Hello?"

"Hello, is this the Lighthouse Sweet Shoppe?"

"Yes, it is. Can I help you?"

"I sure do hope so. I'm calling from the Willow's Corner Assisted Living Center. We have an emergency. You see, our cook had a stroke and we've got kitchen helpers that can put together meals till we can find a new cook, but we've got Thanksgiving coming up and none of them know how to make the pies. We've got thirty-two residents plus staff of six, and no pies for Thanksgiving. Can you make seven pies for us? We can have someone pick them up."

"Oh dear. I'm booked up solid. I don't think I can squeeze in any more." Shelley tried to think of how she could help. She hated to turn them down. Adelaide was out of school all week. She could take care of Emma. Shelley couldn't miss Aiden's play, but that wouldn't take long. If she worked a little later every night. There had to be a way. Only seven more pies. She'd need more pie tins. More ingredients. "What kind of pies do you want?"

"Anything you can make. Apple and pumpkin would be great, but we'll take anything."

If she started right away, she could make and freeze a couple of large apple crisps. She had enough apples and oatmeal.

Pumpkin dump cake tasted great and was easy to make. "What if I make apple crisps and pumpkin desserts? They aren't pies, but they have similar flavor. You can serve them with ice cream or whipped cream. Would that work?"

"Oh yes. That'd be wonderful. When can we pick them up?"

"How about Wednesday evening?"

"Perfect. I can't tell you what a relief this is. Our residents would be so disappointed if they didn't have a Thanksgiving dessert."

Shelley gave directions to her house, then hung up. She sagged against the counter for a moment, then took a deep breath and jumped back into her cooking. She had several large disposable aluminum roasting pans. Perfect for large apple crisps. She went back to the bar cookies. She still had to get all of her shipments ready.

Oh, to be able to hire an extra pair of hands at the holidays! What a luxury that would be. But she didn't need anyone full-time, and she preferred to work alone. What would it be like to run the Cove? Could she hire extra part-time help to keep the coffee shop and her own bakery business going and still make money? Would her family suffer? It always came back to that. To fit in this new order would require several hours of work. That was a couple of hours her family would have to do without her. She knew her mother-in-law was against her working while the children were young. But Dan promised to support her, whatever she decided.

And thinking about it was slowing her down. She shoved aside thoughts of the future and her business and started packing bakery boxes with orders.

Dan and the kids came home and separated to their own activities. Aiden started an army encampment in the middle of the living room floor. Emma came into the kitchen to bake in her toddler's kitchen set just like her mama. Hailey curled up with a book, and Dan sat at his computer, working on schoolwork. They all seemed oblivious to her. For one day, they didn't need her constant attention. But she knew it wouldn't last. In an hour, it would be bedtime for the children, and her services would be required.

She tried to time her work so she would have an hour free to settle the kids down for the night. If she put something in the oven, she would have to take it out in thirty minutes at the longest. She would mix up a batch of cranberry orange sugar cookies and put them in the refrigerator to chill while the children bathed and she dried Hailey and Emma's hair and got them all tucked in and prayers said. She still had to make a delivery to the Cove, but that wouldn't take long. She found the recipe and set out all the ingredients. Into a large bowl, she measured out the flour and sugar. Using her time wisely, she could get out twelve dozen cookies before she shut down the kitchen for the night.

★ ★ ★

Later into the night, Shelley couldn't sleep. The house was quiet. The clock next to her bed ticked loudly in counterrhythm to Dan's breathing, deep and regular in peaceful slumber. Branches from the barberry bush below their bedroom window scratched the side of the house as it writhed in the wind.

Thoughts of the Cove and the Lighthouse Sweet Shoppe rolled around and around in her head. She'd seen Rusty that evening when she'd delivered the muffins, Danishes, and crumb cake for Monday morning. He hadn't asked for a yea or nay, but he'd asked if she'd had time to think about his offer. He was serious. *What should I do? I need to give Rusty an answer. He could ask anyone. Surely there are people more qualified than I am, but he asked me. This is the chance of a lifetime. But is it the right thing for me to do now? If I turn it down, will I ever get another chance like this?*

Shelley turned over, punched her pillow, and snuggled under the covers. Sleep didn't come. She lay still, saying silent prayers for Dan, the children, her friends, her in-laws, her church, the town. Even that didn't put her to sleep. She started listing all the things she had to do that week, starting with express-mailing the cookie orders as soon as she dropped Hailey and Aiden off at school. The last time she looked at the digital readout on the clock, it was two thirty. She closed her eyes and refused to open them again.

When the alarm blared at 6:00 AM, she tried to ignore it, but it would not shut up. Groggy and unresolved, she groped her way to the bathroom to hold a warm washcloth over her puffy, sleep-deprived eyes. Day one of a busy week stretched before her. Time to hit the ground running. Or crawling.

★ ★ ★

Margaret set the painting of the Burr Oak Limestone Quarry in the window on display. She had put the final touches on it

Saturday afternoon. Inspired by thoughts of Paris, her brush had danced effortlessly across the canvas, lightly glazing the scene with touches of frost, to herald winter. The colors and textures had turned out well, she thought.

Stepping down from the display window, she opened the gallery and went back to her studio, where she had started work on a new angle of the lighthouse, from across the cove on a low bluff, looking out at the tall, white bastion of hope, with the sea in the background. She'd snapped the picture when they were out at the quarry, so it was a distance perspective that captured some of the town, with the lighthouse visible out on its point, and an expanse of water.

This painting was for the Lighting the Way Greeting Card Company. She hoped Matt Beauregard would like it. The style was the same, but the view was a departure from the usual lighthouse scenes that he bought to use on cards and calendars.

She had painted the basic shapes and colors in. Now she worked on filling in details. In the foreground, swooping over the water of the cove, she sketched in a flock of laughing gulls. She hoped birders would be able to pick out the species from common gulls.

She heard the bell on the front door and looked up. It took her a moment to recognize the couple in their winter coats and hats. Their faces were red from the cold.

"Beverly, Jeff, how nice to see you this morning."

"We're out for a walk and saw your new painting," Beverly said. "Jeff saw it first from across the street. He pointed it out to me. I love it! You captured the quarry beautifully."

"Do you think so?"

"Anyone who's been to the quarry will recognize it," Jeff said. "You've done a masterly job expressing the tone and texture, and I like the effect of frost on everything. It makes it look restful."

"Good. That's exactly the mood I tried to portray. A transition from the vibrant fall colors to a peaceful winter landscape. If you can see that, maybe others can too. It'll be interesting to see what kind of response I get. You're brave to be out walking this morning. It's gotten awfully cold out there."

"The wind has picked up off the ocean. We aren't going far. We're headed to the Cove for coffee and some of Shelley's coffee cake, if they haven't sold out," Beverly said.

"They may be slow today. Not many people braving the cold."

"We'll see you later."

Margaret felt the whoosh of frigid air as they went out. Such a handsome couple. Watching them, she could see the spark of magic between them. Though Beverly didn't share a lot, Margaret knew that her first marriage had lacked the kind of close relationship she had with Allan. She was happy that Beverly had found her heart's companion.

★ ★ ★

"Good mornin'," Brenna McTavish called out as Beverly and Jeff entered the Cove. "Nice to see someone bravin' tha cold. I was getting lonesome in hee-ah."

"Morning, Brenna. No customers today?"

"Had a few regulahs earlier. What'll ya have? I've still got a piece of Shelley's bluebear-rah crumb cake."

"I'll just have a latte," Beverly said.

"Make that two, and I'll have the crumb cake," Jeff said.

They carried their lattes to a table in the back corner. It was warm so they removed their coats. Beverly picked up her cup and held it between her hands to warm them.

"I picked up an extra fork. Want a bite?" Jeff asked. He held up a bite toward her. Brenna had heated it. Steam rose from the cake, carrying the delicious aroma of berries and vanilla.

"Just one." Beverly took the bite he offered and closed her eyes. "Umm. So good. I'll have to be careful when I start working here in town, or I'll turn into a butterball."

"That, I can't imagine. But I love butter." Jeff gave her a warm smile. He raised his cup to his mouth and took a long drink.

"I loved Margaret's picture of the quarry. Do you think anyone will recognize the location?"

"No one has been out there for a long time," Jeff said. "Maybe I'll get Margaret's permission to photograph her picture and include it with the pictures I took. I've gotten a positive response from *Maine Treasures* magazine. They put out a coffee table book every year too. We might get in that."

"Really? That's exciting. If we could just get inside the quarry… Have you had any luck there?"

"Not yet. Haven't found out who owns it. Seems to be some kind of trust."

"Thank you for taking an interest in this. It means a lot to me," Beverly said, reaching for his hand. He took her hand, but she sensed a hesitation. His grip was usually firm and assuring.

"I want to share your interests," he said. He glanced at her, then looked down at his coffee cup. She realized he hadn't said much since he arrived at her house that morning and they walked to town. Something was bothering him, and she wasn't sure she wanted to know what it was.

"Is everything all right?" she asked.

He cleared his throat. "I've been thinking about our situation. Your obligations here. My career and living in Portland. I know you want me to move to Marble Cove, but it isn't that simple. My loft is also my studio. It's set up so I can work out of it. In Portland, I'm close to some of the publishers and writers I work with. I just don't see how it can work out to move right now."

The look he gave her pleaded with her to understand. Beverly's heart sank. They could wait to get married, but for how long? Jeff was comfortable in his nomadic life, with his condo that served as a place to sleep and a studio. Could their relationship survive such an arrangement?

Chapter Eighteen

Shelley carted the last of the boxes of cookies into the post office. She'd timed it just right, arriving as the doors opened. Her business helped keep the financially strapped postal system operating, Dan had told her. Still, she hated holding up a line of people trying to get mail or send a package. This time, the line was empty.

The clerk's eyes grew wide as she piled boxes on the counter. "How many you got there?"

"Forty-two. It's the biggest bunch of orders I've had at one time," Shelley said, smiling, but trying to convey her apologies for all the work of shipping them.

"Ayuh. Let me get some help. I've got to be free to take care of other customers if they come in."

Shelley looked around as he disappeared into the back. No one else was in the post office. Not even by the bank of post office boxes. She shrugged. She was happy to get the orders mailed in time to arrive by the holiday on Thursday.

When the clerk returned, he had a package in his hand. "This just came in for you. Today's mail is already out for delivery, so you might as well take it now, instead of waiting until tomorrow." He handed Shelley a small package wrapped in brown paper. The return address showed it was from Melissa Boardman. Shelley was tempted to open it right then, but tucked it into her bag instead. She wanted to be alone when she looked at the precious reminder of her mentor.

She headed to the grocery store, where she picked out several small, meaty-looking pumpkins. She would make her pies out of a mixture of canned and fresh pumpkin, for extra flavor. She found the other ingredients she needed for her local orders, then piled the sacks in the back of her Subaru.

At home, she unloaded the groceries and set the precious package on the table. As much as she wanted to tear into it, she decided to wait until she'd picked up Aiden from pre-K and gotten the children fed and down for quiet time. Then she would be alone to savor the contents. She headed across the street to get Emma. The mail orders on their way, she mentally ran through her to-do list of local orders and family responsibilities. She had a busy week ahead. She hoped nothing more would pop up to hinder the tight schedule she'd set for herself.

★ ★ ★

Diane had a slight fever and little energy on Monday, but she refused to let that slow her down. She was so grateful for caring friends, but wished she could do more giving and less receiving. Today she'd insisted on watching Emma while Shelley ran errands. The toddler had played quietly with Rocky, who lay still and sighed with forbearance as Emma brushed him with the finesse of a two-year-old, then lay on top of him and hugged him. He wasted no time retreating when Diane gave him a treat and let him go outside. Emma had shown Diane how to put together the puzzles Shelley had brought over, then pointed and asked why and repeated words as Diane had read two storybooks that she'd saved from Jessica and Justin's childhoods.

Diane was exhausted but happy with a sense of accomplishment by the time Shelley collected her daughter. She managed to down a protein shake and take a catnap before Beverly picked her up at one o'clock.

"You look tired," Beverly said when Diane got into her car.

"A little. I had a busy morning with the delightful Miss Emma." She chuckled. "But I managed a quick nap after she left."

"That's good. And here I am dragging you out when you should be home resting."

"Nonsense. Spending time with you and Augie is great relaxation. I haven't seen him since election night, so it'll be good to talk to him."

Beverly pulled up in front of Augie Jackson's cottage. His yard was still a riot of color. Though many of the flowers that filled his front yard had died back from the autumn frosts, the tenacious purple, red, and orange chrysanthemums held tight to their stems, and the yellow and gold strawflowers looked as pretty as the first day they bloomed. Large puffs of red sedum and spikes of purple Russian sage and pink coneflowers stood out among the golds and browns of dead stalks.

Beverly rang the doorbell. Augie took a few moments to get to the door.

"Come in out of the cold," he said, waving them in. "Winter is coming on fast. We'll have snow before December, if my lumbago is accurate, and it usually is. The cold sets into these old bones, you know." He stood a bit hunched over and moved a little slower than usual, but the twinkle was still in his eyes. He had on a green cardigan sweater, and a cheery fire burned in his small fireplace, keeping the room warm. Diane went over and stood in front of the fireplace for a moment to warm her hands, then she sat on the dark-blue-and-burgundy couch.

"Can I get you ladies something to drink. Tea or water?"

"Nothing for me," Diane said. Beverly declined a drink also. She waited until Augie moved toward his big burgundy recliner, then she sat on the couch next to Diane.

Always the perfect gentleman, Augie waited to sit down until they were both seated.

"To what do I owe the honor of this visit?" he asked. "Have you ladies uncovered a new mystery?" His eyes sparkled with curiosity. He loved a good mystery.

"I don't know that we have a mystery, but we need information about the old train station, and you are the best source of that in town," Diane said.

"Why, that station has been closed for at least sixty years. It must be pretty run-down. What do you want to know about it?"

"Anything you can tell us," Beverly said. "Dennis Calder wants to tear it down and put in a mini-mall. We think it'd be a shame to demolish it. It's part of the town history."

"Indeed it is. They hauled a lot of fish and lime out of here on that train, and carried many a passenger between here and everywhere else that connected through Brunswick. I took the train to Portsmouth and Boston myself back in the day."

"So the train station was a center of commerce and travel for Marble Cove?" Beverly asked.

"And communication. The telegraph office was in the station before we got telephone service in town. During World War II, it was part of the emergency communications system. Someone manned the phone lines around the clock for alerts that had to go out and for sightings from the port of any enemy activity. We had fishermen and pleasure schooners out looking for German U-boats all the time."

"Did they ever spot one?" Diane asked.

"Oh yes. The wooden hulled boats could sneak up on them because they didn't have the mechanisms that make a lot of racket. The U-boats would sit on the bottom during the day, then come up at night and find merchant ships to sink. Our civilians would be waiting for them and report their position. We didn't have the activity they had down in Boston and New York Harbor and the Chesapeake, but they'd make runs up here looking for supplies. We'd run boats of supplies out to the navy ships and the lighthouses and any strategic posts." Augie shook his head and looked off, as if seeing that distant time past.

"So the railroad station was an emergency post in the 1940s."

"Before that, during the Great War too," Augie said. "There wasn't a town that wasn't affected by the wars. Everyone had to do his, or her, part. The quarry sent lime to the army. They used it in the trenches to stave off infection and also used it to whitewash tanks and trucks as camouflage. The Cannery sent canned sardines, which was good nutrition. So Marble Cove did its part for the war effort."

"I didn't realize all that," Diane said as she scribbled notes on a pad.

"Did you know the quarry owners or the stationmaster?" Beverly asked.

"I knew who they were. The stationmaster was Elias J. Thorpe." Augie laughed. "He was a pompous man. Didn't have time for a lowly reporter like me, unless he wanted his picture in the paper."

"Do you know what happened to him?"

Shaking his head, Augie said, "The day the last train pulled out of Marble Cove, he up and disappeared. That was in early 1952. Strangest thing. Most folks thought he went on vacation, but he never came back. Left his big house with everything in it, near as I could tell. I did a story on the demise of the railroad."

"That was in 1952? We didn't look in that year's papers," Diane said. "We went through some of the archives, but we left when I started sneezing."

"That morgue must have two inches of dust on everything by now," Augie said. "I thought about cleaning it up and organizing it after the fire, but I never got around to it. Back in the day, I wanted to interview Thorpe, so I tried to track him down. Because he never paid his taxes on the house, the county sold it at auction, lock, stock and barrel, as they say. Fancy furniture, a grand piano, sets of fine china, silk linens, a brand-new silver Jaguar coupe. He had the best of everything, and he left it behind." Augie rubbed his chin. "I did wonder if he met with foul play. No one ever reported finding a body. He just disappeared off the face of the earth."

"Was he married? Did he have any children or relatives?" Beverly asked.

"None that I ever discovered." Augie grinned. "Now there's a real mystery for you. And I wouldn't be surprised if you and your friends figure it out. If you do, I want to be the first to hear about it."

Diane grinned. "You can be sure we'll keep you posted on our progress. What about the quarry? Who owned it?"

"A pair of brothers. Last name was Gentry. We called them the Marble Cove Gentry. They kept to themselves, like they were royalty, but they treated their workers well. My father worked for them during the Depression, until he got a job in a munitions factory. He learned machinery and welding. After the war he opened a machine shop. The quarry was hard work. Breathing that lime dust all day wasn't good, but it was a job. There were plenty out of work during the Depression. People were happy to work an honest day for honest pay."

"Are the Gentrys still around?" Beverly asked.

"No. They moved away after the quarry shut down. That was in 1951, if I recall correctly. The railroad didn't last much beyond that. The Cannery started shipping by truck. Passenger trains weren't enough to keep the railroad alive."

"So the railroad just dried up," Beverly said. "Still, there's a rich history attached to the train station. We should be able to compile a good case to preserve it."

"I wish you luck. If I can help, let me know. There's little enough of preserving our heritage these days. Like that Dennis Calder. I'm sure glad the people of Marble Cove had the good sense to elect you mayor, Beverly. If you need me to write an article about the station and our history, I'll be happy to do it."

"Would you? I accept. I'm going to need all the ammunition I can muster. Thank you, Augie. With supporters like you, we'll find a way to save the station. I sure wish I could talk to Elias Thorpe. Do you know if he was related to Jeremiah Thorpe?"

"Can't say I've given it any thought," he said, scratching his chin. "There's a good probability that he is, or was. That's too big a coincidence for a small town like Marble Cove."

"That's what we think too," Beverly said. "I hope we can prove it."

★ ★ ★

Shelley thought her children would never go down for their naps. Aiden was excited about the play he was in. They'd been practicing at pre-K. Emma followed his lead. The children were wound up like two tops. After a half hour trying, she finally got them to settle down so she could have some private time.

Emma was tired. When she finally lay still for a few minutes, she fell asleep. Aiden wouldn't sleep, but he lay on his bed with a book. Shelley crept down the stairs, careful not to disturb them.

The brown package sat on the kitchen table waiting for her. She picked it up and looked around, half expecting an interruption. No sounds marred her peace. With a sigh, she sat at the table and carefully unwrapped the brown paper. Inside, the book was protected by a plastic bag. She could see creases in the faded cover of the paperback book. With great care, she unzipped the bag and removed the book.

As books went, there was nothing attractive about it. No fancy cover art. She opened the cover. The book was inscribed *To Darlene with love from Mother, Christmas 1999.*

She turned the page. *Devotions for Daily Living,* the page announced. It was a one-year daily devotional book. Considering the dog-eared condition of the pages, Darlene had loved this book and read through it many times. As Shelley leafed through the pages, she saw the dates that Darlene had entered after each reading. *January 1, 2000. A new millennium. A new century. A new decade. A new chance to see God's grace and provision,* she'd written. Remembering back, it hadn't seemed that way to Shelley. After that date, there was just the year.

There were notations of prayers. Names Shelley didn't recognize. References of Bible verses next to some of the names, most in the Psalms. There were a few notations of birthdays, a baby's birth, a death. Shelley got to January 21. Her name appeared at the bottom. *2000. Shelley Becker came to youth group tonight. Such a pretty girl, but she seems sad. Prayed for her. I hope she comes back.*

Wow. Darlene prayed for her the first time they met. And the book had been new. That had been her junior year of high school. Her parents were fighting and withdrawn. Shelley stayed away from home as much as possible. The next week, Darlene had prayed for her again. And the next. Then Darlene began praying for her and for her parents' marriage daily. In May, under the year 2001, she'd written, *Shelley's father left today. Shelley is devastated. Lord, please give me words to comfort her and to help her know it's not her fault.*

It was true. Shelley had felt guilty, like she must have done something to drive her father away. Otherwise, he would have taken her with him or at least explained to her. But he didn't. Her mother hadn't helped either. She'd snapped at Shelley and at her sister, as if it were their fault. She'd blamed her husband and her circumstances and everything except herself. If it hadn't been for Darlene, Shelley would have run away. But Darlene had hugged her and wiped her tears and prayed with her.

Three days later, on her birthday, Darlene had written Shelley's name and a Bible verse, Jeremiah 29:11. She'd given Shelley a Bible for her birthday that year, Shelley remembered. That passage was one of several Darlene had highlighted before she gave the Bible to her. Shelley still had it. Both of her parents had forgotten her birthday that year. Looking back, Shelley didn't know how she would have made it through those days without Darlene's encouragement and prayers and her steadfast faith.

Shelley flipped through pages until she came to the devotional on July 14, the summer before her senior year in high school. At the bottom of the page was written, *Shelley helped me make six pies for the church picnic. We had such fun. She has a gift for baking.* There was a Bible verse. Shelley got out her Bible and looked it up. Deuteronomy 16:15: "For the Lord your God will bless you in all your harvest and in all the work of your hands, and your joy will be complete."

Shelley stared at the verse, reading it again. She did find joy in her work. She loved creating delicious food. She loved making it beautiful. It gave her pleasure, and she knew it pleased others too. God had blessed her harvest of baked goods with more orders and more local customers. She filled a need. And that filled her with joy. She smiled. It was good to be needed and wanted. People wanted to eat her food.

Shelley closed the devotional book and held it between her hands. She didn't have time to read through the entire book, but it was meant to be read daily. She would add it to her daily devotional readings. Right now she needed to get busy baking, or she wouldn't have all the pies and desserts ready for her customers for Thanksgiving. Thinking about her baking business filled her with a sense of anticipation and excitement. That was a good thing. Wasn't it?

CHAPTER NINETEEN

Tired though she was, Diane ran the vacuum cleaner and dusted. She didn't want Jessica seeing her house in disarray. When she finished, she glanced at the clock. Jessica wouldn't get here for another hour. The premade pizza was ready to go into the oven. She'd made a salad. There was nothing to do but wait. She took Rocky out for a short jaunt, then sat on the couch to rest a few moments.

Sharp banging on the door woke her. Startled, she jumped up, then had to steady herself as a wave of dizziness hit her. "Coming," she yelled. Rocky jumped up and barked. Diane made it to the door and opened it. Jessica stared at her with a frown.

"Mom, are you all right? I was about to call Margaret or Shelley."

Diane smiled and opened her arms. "I'm fine. And I'm so happy to see you. I just fell asleep for a moment, and I didn't hear you knocking. Come in."

Jessica came inside and shut the door, then she hugged her mother, but gently, as if she were made of fragile china. She held her at arm's length and studied her. "You look tired, but good." She seemed surprised and relieved. "I'm so glad to be here. Traffic was awful. I thought I'd never arrive."

"Well, you're here now. Put your suitcase in the bedroom. I'll pop the pizza in the oven."

"Pizza? That's the one food you always liked before. I'm glad you still do."

Diane turned on the oven to preheat. The table was set. She put on a kettle of water for tea. Jessica came into the kitchen.

"Mom, why don't you go rest on the couch? I can do this."

"I had a catnap. Let's sit in here and talk. I'm making tea."

"Herbal?"

"Of course." The kettle whistled. Diane poured hot water in the mugs with the tea bags and set them on the table. They sat down to drink their tea while the oven heated.

"So tell me what's happening in Boston. What have you been up to?" Diane asked.

Jessica talked about her cases and how she was getting involved in a downtown teen ministry through her church. Diane noticed Martin's name came up several times. So they were still spending a lot of time together. She'd wondered but didn't want to come right out and ask.

"So how about you?" Jessica asked. "Are you writing?"

"Not much right now. My editor and my agent advised me to concentrate on getting well and not worry about book deadlines. I really need to get back to work, though. I don't want to lose my momentum." She already had lost it, but she didn't want to admit that out loud.

"I agree with them. You'll get back into the groove soon enough. I really like your wig. If I didn't know better, I'd think it was your real hair."

Diane smiled. "Beverly, Shelley, and Margaret took me wig shopping. I think we tried on every wig in the place and modeled them for each other. We all got wigs or hairpieces and wore them to lunch." A tear worked its way into the corner of her eye. She dabbed it away. "I miss you and your father so much. But my friends have been wonderful, checking up on me and feeding me and running errands. I don't know what I'd do without them."

Jessica reached over and took her mother's hand. "I'm glad. I hate that I can't be here to take care of you. All I can do is pray. And I do that every day. My care group from church is praying too."

"I can tell. It helps to know I'm surrounded by your prayers. And I'm a big girl. I'm doing fine." She squeezed Jessica's hand to reassure her, then let it go. It was time to change the subject. Dwelling on her illness did not help. "How is Martin?"

"Martin is fine. How's Leo?"

Diane laughed. "Leo is doing fine. And yes, I invited him for Thanksgiving dinner, per your request."

"Oh, good. I like Leo. And I imagine you've kept him at arm's length, not letting him help you or comfort you."

"Not true. He's been over for dinner and brought movies." Once. But she didn't tell Jessica that detail. "He's been very attentive."

"As much as you'd let him be, I'm sure." Jessica gave her a knowing look. Her daughter knew her well. She *had* tried to keep Leo at a safe distance.

"Okay, so I don't want him to see me at my worst. You wouldn't either."

Jessica's smile faded. "Oh, Mom, I hate it that you have to go through this. And you're right. I don't like Martin seeing me when I'm a mess. I had the flu, and he practically broke down my door, insisting on bringing me chicken soup and herbal tea and a big stuffed bunny to cheer me up. He was so sweet."

"I like your Martin. He seems like a real jewel."

"Yes. He is." Jessica was quiet for a moment. Diane knew her daughter well enough to know she had something on her mind. Diane was curious but didn't push her.

"Mom, did you ever question whether Dad was the right man for you? Before you got married, I mean. How did you know he was the one?"

"Yes, I had questions and doubts. Not about your father so much as about myself. Was I ready to make such a life-changing commitment? Would I be able to give him the love he deserved? Was I ready to share every aspect of my life? I was pretty independent, you know."

"But you decided the answer was yes to all your questions."

"Yes. As far as knowing he was the right one for me—my heart, my spirit told me he was. But being in love and loving are not the same thing. Is that what you're asking?"

"Yeah. I guess it is. Martin proposed to me. I—"

"What? When?"

Jessica looked startled. "A-about a week ago."

"And you're just now telling me? How could you keep it a secret?"

"I wanted to tell you in person. You're the first. I haven't told anyone else. I haven't given him my answer. I'm just not sure."

Diane frowned. Why wasn't her daughter bubbling over with her news and dancing with excitement? "Do you love him?"

"Oh yes. There's no doubt about the chemistry between us." She got a dreamy smile on her face. "He's so sweet and thoughtful and gallant. Such a gentleman. He reminds me a lot of Dad."

"Is that part of your doubts?"

"I suppose it is. Like, am I attracted to him because he's like Dad? 'Cause if that's my reason, eventually he won't be like Dad and I'll be disappointed. Does that make sense?"

Diane chuckled. "Yes, in a convoluted way. You want to love him for himself."

"Exactly."

"Can you separate the two?"

"I think so."

"What about you? Do you want to be married?"

"Yes. But I see so many people who get married and then they're not happy. People from church, even. I want to be happy like you and Dad were. How did you do it?"

"The million-dollar question. Well, how did you make it through college, then law school? Lots of people want to be a lawyer but never make it, you know."

"I see what you're getting at. It takes commitment and perseverance. I wanted to quit many times, but I wanted the prize more than I wanted to quit. So marriage is making a commitment and sticking to it?"

Diane chuckled. "In a nutshell, I suppose, but you're dealing with people, not law books. You have an advantage over me from the start, though."

"I do? What's that?"

"Your faith. You are deeply grounded. Your faith, when I went through this cancer before, was a rock that I held onto. Your faith helped me seek and find God in my circumstances. It helped me rediscover my own faith. It will help you find your answer."

"I have been praying about it."

"Keep praying and listen to your heart. Trust yourself. When the time is right, you'll know. And I'll be praying for you too."

Jessica released a big sigh. "Thanks, Mom." She got up and gave Diane a hug. "I always know I can talk to you and things start making sense. Now I'd better put that pizza in the oven. I'm starving."

Diane's heart swelled with love and gratitude for her children. What a blessing from God they were. It meant a great deal to Diane that they still came to her to talk through their problems, even though they were both adults with good, strong character and wisdom. Even so, the world could be a challenging, difficult place. She was glad she had the assurance that they were safe in God's hands.

★ ★ ★

The house was quiet. No one was up yet. Shelley loved the days when she had early-morning time to herself. She poured a cup of coffee and took her Bible and Darlene's devotional book to the table. She thanked the Lord for the beautiful day, for her family and friends and her many blessings. She asked for the strength and patience and love and energy she would need for this day. Then, instead of her usual devotional, she opened Darlene's book to a page marked with an insert. It was May 19, Shelley's wedding day. Tucked into that date was her wedding announcement with a picture of her and Dan on it. They looked so young. So much had happened since then.

The title of the day was "God's Workmanship." Beneath the title was the verse of the day, Ephesians 2:10: "For we are God's workmanship, created in Christ Jesus to do good works, which God prepared in advance for us to do."

Shelley read the short devotional. Her name was written in at the bottom. Darlene hadn't written the devotional, but Shelley could almost hear her saying the words—*Shelley, you were created for a unique purpose that God prepared for you and planted in your heart. No one else can fulfill your purpose like you can.* Shelley thanked the Lord for the devotional and her mentor, then closed the book and went upstairs to get ready for her day.

Dan was up. She could hear the water running in the shower. The children hadn't stirred yet. Shelley took the bright-orange-and-black enameled earrings out of her jewelry box and put them on, then chose a bright-orange scoop-neck shirt with a design of blues and greens and purple on the front. It had a few sparkly rhinestones to give it bling, and the earrings went perfectly with it. Shelley wore a pair of brown denim jeans. She had a busy day ahead. The earrings and pretty top made her feel perky and ready to tackle anything the day offered up. She hummed as she went downstairs to prepare breakfast and lunches.

"Going somewhere special today?" Dan asked, coming into the kitchen.

"No. Just the usual. I have a lot of baking to do."

"Oh. I thought maybe you were going out with your friends. You don't usually get all dressed up to bake." He came over and gave Shelley a good-morning kiss. "You look great."

"Thanks. I thought it might boost my spirits and my energy."

"Yeah? Maybe I should dress up to go to work."

She looked up at him and smiled. "You are dressed up. In your uniform. And your hair is clean and trimmed. Your face is smooth," she said, rubbing her hand over his clean-shaven chin. "You look neat and professional and completely competent."

He smiled. "Well, now I feel ready to conquer the world. Or at least a few wiring jobs."

"Good. I think we're both going to have a great day!"

He laughed. "With that kind of an attitude, we're bound to."

Shelley gave Dan his breakfast, then went to round up the children and get them ready for school. The next hour went quickly with a flurry of activity. Shelley enjoyed it. She didn't worry about the long list of tasks ahead of her. They would get done in their turn. Dan left. Shelley went out the door to the car with Hailey, Aiden, and Emma in tow.

After she dropped Hailey off at the elementary school, she took Aiden to pre-K. She and Emma went inside with him to deliver the costume hats and collars she'd made for the Thanksgiving program. She talked with the teacher about arrangements for the next day, when the children would perform the play. Then she and Emma left. She had pies and desserts to make.

As they stepped outside, a merry whistle drew her attention to the tall maple tree in the yard. Most of the leaves had fallen. There, near the top, barely visible amidst the yellow and red leaves, a spot of bright orange caught her eye. She looked, stunned. It was a Baltimore oriole, singing a happy song. Just as Darlene had said, it filled Shelley with joy and hope. She looked around, half expecting to see Darlene or Jesus or an angel. She laughed. Of course she couldn't see them, but she had the strangest sensation that they were all there, watching her, willing her to smile.

Not that sighting an oriole was unusual, although they were shy birds and hid in the thick foliage of trees, but it was late. They'd flown south earlier in the fall. Why was this one still hanging around? Could it be there as a sign, just for her? It seemed unlikely, but stranger things had happened. Shelley believed in miracles. She'd experienced a miracle that spared her children's lives. Remembering that day, Shelley peered up at the bright-orange-and-black bird. She leaned down to Emma. "Look, sweetie. Can you see the pretty bird?"

"Purty birdie?" Emma pointed at the top of the tree. The bird let out a long, sweet song.

"You're here just for me, aren't you, pretty bird?"

"Here for me," Emma said and laughed with delight.

"Yes. It's here just for us." Shelley hugged her daughter. Someday, when her daughter needed encouragement, she would remind her of the bird they saw that day, when Darlene or an angel or God Himself sent her a sign.

CHAPTER TWENTY

Jessica put two prepared piecrusts into the shopping cart. "I hope you don't mind if I don't make pies from scratch," she said.

"Since I'm not making them, I'll be happy with whatever you fix," Diane said. She'd never been able to get her own crusts to come out as flaky and buttery as Shelley's anyway. "We're doing a leftovers potluck Friday with just the gals, so we might get some of Shelley's pie then."

"You seriously believe Shelley will have leftovers? I doubt it."

Diane chuckled. "You're probably right. Well, we won't go hungry." She hoped she would have an appetite and be able to eat the meal Jessica planned to prepare. She'd picked out a fresh turkey, large enough that there would be plenty left with just three of them eating it. The cart held stuffing mix, potatoes, yams, brown sugar, whipping cream, rolls, jam and butter, cranberry sauce, green beans and cream of mushroom soup for the green bean casserole, and fruit for the whipped cream salad that was traditional. "We have enough food here to feed an army."

"I wish the army could join us," Jessica said. "I miss Justin. I hope he has a good Thanksgiving."

"I hope so too. He said a family from church had invited him over."

"Good. Can you think of anything I've missed?" Jessica looked at her list, rechecking each item.

"Can't think of a thing. This will be a feast."

"Yeah. That's the idea."

"There's Allan and Adelaide. Their cart looks as full as ours." Diane waved and Adelaide waved back.

"Between us, we have enough food for the entire winter," Allan said. "Hello, Jessica. It's nice to see you again."

"Hi, Diane. Hi, Jessica," Adelaide said, a big smile on her face. "I'm going to help Dad cook Thanksgiving dinner."

"It looks like you're going to have a feast too," Diane said.

Adelaide looked at her father.

"It'll be a feast for sure," Allan said. "Adelaide is making sweet rolls and pies that she learned from Shelley."

"I bet she won't cheat, like me," Jessica said.

"Oh no. I never cheat," Adelaide said.

"Of course not," Jessica said. "But you'll use real ingredients and make it all from scratch, won't you? Instead of getting ready-made pie shells and pie filling."

Adelaide looked confused until Jessica held up a can and a pie shell. Her eyes got big. "Shelley uses flour and butter and rolls out the dough. I like to roll it out," she said. "It's fun. That won't be so fun." She pointed to the piecrust.

"You're right. I think your way is much more fun. I'll have fun stuffing the turkey and mixing up our special salad instead."

"Oh, good. Cooking should be fun. That's what Dad and Shelley say."

Jessica smiled. "They're absolutely right."

"What a sweetheart she is," Jessica said after they parted ways. "She was really concerned that I need to have fun. I can't say I've had much fun lately. Too much work, which I love, but work is a challenge. It's not fun. Maybe I need to lighten up and be more relaxed. I wonder what Martin would think of that?"

"Life hasn't been much fun for me, either," Diane said. "Even my writing isn't fun anymore. Neither is cooking." She looked at her daughter and grinned. "Now there's a challenge for both of us. Let's have some fun."

"Starting now, but I refuse to make the piecrusts from scratch."

"I'm with you on that. I hope Leo won't notice."

"Unless I'm wrong about him, he won't admit it even if he does notice. He's too much of a gentleman. That's one of the things I like about him and about Martin."

"Do you miss him?"

"Yes."

"You should have brought him with you for Thanksgiving."

"He didn't want to cause any extra burden for you. He went to see his dad and stepmom."

"Bring him next time. If you want to."

"Okay. Maybe I will. If I want to. And I probably will." She grinned. "Let's get these groceries home. Then you can take a nap while I have fun making the pies."

★ ★ ★

Piecrusts covered every inch of the dining room table. Fresh pumpkin cooled on the counter. Four apple pies baked in the oven with four more ready to go in when they came out. Emma sat at her own little table with a lump of pie dough and a small rolling pin. Her little brow was furrowed in concentration as she rolled the dough, like her mother. The results didn't look anything like piecrust, but she didn't seem to notice. She looked up.

"See, Mama?"

"Good job. Shall we bake it?"

Emma nodded.

"Let's put some butter and cinnamon sugar on it first." She handed Emma a small butter spreader. Emma glopped it on. Then Shelley let her shake on the cinnamon-sugar mixture. It went everywhere. Shelley ignored it. She would clean it up later. She wanted Emma to have fun learning to cook, even as a two-year-old. She put the sugary bits of dough on a pie tin. "Now we'll bake it."

Before the next batch of pies, Shelley baked Emma's creation. It only took a few minutes, which was good, as Emma kept asking if it was ready.

"It's hot," Shelley said, taking it out of the oven. "Let's have some milk with it." She poured two small glasses of milk and put Emma's globs on a fancy small dessert plate.

"It's ready," Shelley said, squatting down next to Emma at the little table.

"Weddy." Emma gave her mother a toothy grin, then picked up a piece and stuffed it in her mouth. Shelley took a small bite.

"Yum! This is good, Emma."

Emma clapped her sugar-crusted hands with glee. Shelley's heart surged with delight. Her mother had been too absorbed in her own life to let Shelley make a mess in the kitchen and share a sweet moment when she was young.

"Shall we save some for Daddy?"

"Daddy?" Emma looked around.

"Not yet. He'll be home for dinner."

"'Kay." She turned toward the living room. "Aiden! Hay-wee! Cookie!" Emma yelled, running into the living room. She grabbed a doll and began playing with it. Her attention was gone.

Aiden and Hailey came into the kitchen, looking hopeful. "Emma said there's cookies," Aiden said.

"I didn't make cookies today, but there's some piecrust." Shelley always baked the scraps with cinnamon sugar.

"Goodie. I love crust." Aiden reached for some.

"Wash your hands first. I'll pour some milk to go with it."

The two children raced for the bathroom to wash up as she set a plate of crust scraps on the table with two glasses of milk.

"You can eat that in here, then wipe your hands on a washcloth before you go back out to play."

"Okay. Thanks, Mom."

"Yes. Thanks, Aunt Shelley. I love these. My mom never makes pies."

"You're welcome." Shelley wished her sister would be able to spend time with her daughter, but that wouldn't be anytime soon. At least she and Dan were able to help Hailey collect some good memories to help her later in life.

She put the rest of the pies in the oven and turned to puree the cooked pumpkin. It was crunch time, and Shelley felt energized and excited. The next two days would be crazy, but she loved the creative process and the joy of knowing people would enjoy the results of her labors.

★ ★ ★

Wednesday morning, Shelley dropped the pies off at the community center, then hurried to the pre-K. Her in-laws had taken Emma with them to free her for the delivery. When she got there, Frances and Ralph were talking to another set of grandparents. The room was filled with families of the students. Emma sat next to her grandpa. They'd saved Shelley a seat. She made her way through the rows of folding chairs.

"This is quite an audience," she told Ralph as she sat down next to Emma.

"Well, it's a big deal," he said. "We've been through this with all of his cousins." He chuckled. "They're so uninhibited at this age, it's always interesting."

"Hey, got room to squeeze in one more?"

Shelley looked up. Dan had come. She was so pleased. "Come sit next to me. Emma can sit on my lap."

"Daddy!" Emma reached for him. She was a daddy's girl. If he was around, Shelley was second choice. Dan encouraged it. He adored his daughter. Shelley was glad they had such a close relationship.

"Come here, pumpkin." He reached for Emma and picked her up, then sat down and steadied her as she stood on his leg so she would be tall enough to see. She mussed his hair and giggled.

Shelley gave him a you-asked-for-it smile. "I'm glad Mr. Stover let you off to see this."

"Yeah. He said I could have an extra half hour if I need it. He's a family man."

The children played their parts with enthusiasm. Aiden announced his lines, as Captain John Smith, with authority, enunciating his words well. He got carried away thanking the Indians and thanking God for making sure they had lots to eat, especially pumpkin pie and ice cream. That got a chuckle from the audience. Dan leaned over and whispered to Shelley, "He has his priorities in the right place. Add some apple pie and pecan pie to that."

Frances offered to take Aiden and Emma home with her after the play. Shelley knew she was grateful for the eight pies that Shelley had delivered to the community center. She accepted the offer. She still had a lot of pies and desserts to make for delivery that night.

★ ★ ★

Beverly handed Jeff an apron. He tied it around his waist, then scrubbed his hands like a surgeon would scrub for surgery.

"You're going to rub the skin off your hands," Beverly said.

"Can't be too clean." He dried his hands. "Now where's a good knife?"

"At least you didn't say scalpel. I hope Mrs. Peabody doesn't get too upset at us for messing up the kitchen."

"It's your kitchen."

"Well, not so much. Not since she started cooking for Father. And I really appreciate her cooking. She's worked hard to make sure he gets the right nutrition for his diabetes. He's been so much better since she started fixing our meals. She runs a tight kitchen. When I told her we would cook the turkey, she seemed skeptical. She knows I'm not much of a cook."

"But I am. At least on certain things. Like turkey and stuffing. My grandfather taught me, and we always make it this way."

"How can I help?"

"How are you at cleaning the bird?"

Beverly made a face. "Not my favorite job, but I can do it. Don't you have something I can chop up?"

"Sure. You can chop the pecans, but not too small. Then there's celery and onions and apples to cut up."

"I can do that."

"All right. We'll trade places."

They worked together well. By eight o'clock, the bird was ready to be stuffed and go in the oven. Beverly started washing the bowls and utensils.

"It's a little early yet. What else can we make ahead?" Jeff asked.

"We're doing the mashed potatoes and gravy and condiments. Mrs. Peabody was going to come over and make them here. She is also making rolls and sweet potatoes and her famous chocolate cream pie. I told her that was too much, but she insisted. Celia is making a salad and two other pies. Can you think of something else we need?"

"Corn casserole. My favorite vegetable. I bought all the ingredients. We can make it tomorrow."

"Can we make it tonight? It'd be best if we're not in the kitchen tomorrow while Mrs. Peabody is cooking."

Jeff frowned. "That's all right for now, but what about after we're married? I like to cook. We don't have to cook big meals every day, but we'll want to sometimes."

Beverly turned to face him. "Are you saying we will live here after we're married? But I thought you said you—or you meant…or are you thinking way in the future?" She wasn't making much sense.

Jeff took hold of her wet, soapy hand. "I know I confused you the other day. I'm still trying to wrap my mind around all the changes ahead of us. I guess I've gotten too comfortable at my place in Portland. I spent some time thinking and praying and really looking at my life. It's pretty empty without you in it. I remember the night I ran into you at the lighthouse—it was the best day of my life. I'm grateful that my grandfather's history here brought me to you. I don't take that for granted."

"I'm glad." Beverly gazed at him and dared to hope she meant more to him than Portland.

"I've been thinking about the changes we'll both have to make when we get married. You'll have to put up with my crazy schedule. It hasn't mattered to anyone before. I've come and gone without thinking about anyone else. The last few assignments, I've missed you. I wanted to hurry and finish so I could get back here. I've never had that constraint before."

"Did you resend it?"

"No. I wanted to get back. But I can see you coming with me and showing you all the wonders I get to see."

"I'd love that. But..."

"But you have your father to think of, and now the town. I realize I'm going to have to share you. When I thought about that, I got jealous. That surprised me. I want to share your life. But I want to share my life with you too. Does that make sense?"

"Perfect sense. I want to be part of your life. How do we find a balance?" Beverly gazed into his eyes and waited for his answer.

"For now, we need to live in Marble Cove. I've been thinking, though, that there's no reason we can't keep the condo in Portland. We can use it as a weekend getaway. We can go into the city for plays or concerts or just a break from the pressures you're going to face as mayor. If I need to work on an assignment, I can run down there for a day, but I want home to be with you."

Beverly hadn't considered the possibility of a compromise. She hadn't seen how they could keep both worlds. Of course they could. And Jeff wanted to be with her, above all. She couldn't hide the wide smile that spread across her face. "I think that's a marvelous plan. And that leaves our options open for the future. As long as my father is alive, I want to be close to him. As long as I'm mayor, I have to live in town. But I won't be mayor forever. I've committed to four years. After that we can both decide whether I'll run for another term. I want us to make decisions together."

Jeff leaned over and kissed her. She closed her eyes and kissed him back, sealing their agreement. She felt such relief, she wanted to shout and dance around.

"I'm not much of a cook, but I love the idea of our cooking together. If we can find someone to come in several times a week to check on my father, and if Mrs. Peabody will keep cooking for him, then maybe we could find a place nearby. He's told me many times that he doesn't need someone watching him all the time. But he has had spells, so I hate to have him live alone."

. Jeff took her in his arms. "Having elderly parents and grandparents is a concern. We'll work it out."

She leaned her head against his chest and wrapped her arms around him. "Thank you. I know you're concerned about your grandfather too."

"I was. He seems like a new man since he started seeing Celia Patterson. Between Coral and Celia, the Patterson women are a real blessing to us."

"Yes, they are. I hope that remains true for a long time to come."

CHAPTER TWENTY-ONE

Diane woke late Thanksgiving morning, but it was still dark. She heard the back door close and movement in the kitchen. When she put on her robe and got up to investigate, Jessica had been out for a run with Rocky. Both of them were wet. Jessica rubbed Rocky down with an old towel.

"The fog is so thick and cold, Rocky and I became popsicles," Jessica said. "But we've had our exercise for the day."

"Thank you for taking him out. I can't believe I slept this late."

"We tiptoed around so we wouldn't wake you up. What would you like for breakfast?"

"Something light. We're going to have a big, early meal. Do we need to start working on the turkey?"

"It's all done and in the oven. I'm doing all the cooking today, remember. I want you to relax."

"I don't do much of anything else these days," Diane said. "Margaret and Shelley and Beverly and people from church keep bringing me food. Besides, I haven't had much of an appetite."

"I hope you are hungry today, or you'll be eating leftovers for a week."

"You can take some home with you so you can have turkey sandwiches. And we can send some home with Leo."

"That's why I bought such a large turkey," Jessica said. "Shelley sent over some sweet rolls for our breakfast. I'll warm them up. We can eat them while we watch the Thanksgiving Day Parade. I just hope it's not this foggy in New York City."

"We try to keep our fog to ourselves," Diane said. "I'll get dressed while you warm the rolls."

She remembered cuddling with Jessica and Justin when they were little, watching the parade on Thanksgiving morning. Eric would bring in wood and build a fire in the fireplace and they'd have cocoa and sweet rolls. It seemed like yesterday in her memories, but so much had changed, and her little ones were all grown up. What a comfort it was to have Jessica waiting on her and cooking the meal. Diane put on warm slacks and a soft green merino wool sweater over her oxford shirt. She fixed her wig on her head and applied some makeup. Not that it mattered what she looked like, but she thought she should make an effort to look nice for the holiday.

★ ★ ★

Flour covered every surface in the Hoskins kitchen. Margaret made Allan and Adelaide pose for a picture. Their aprons and hands were white. Allan had a smear of flour on his cheek. Adelaide had some in her hair. Margaret wished she were a portrait artist, like Norman Rockwell, so she could capture the scene on canvas. They were grinning and having a grand time making dinner rolls from scratch. She'd have been just as happy with store-bought rolls, but the memory they were creating was priceless.

"Show me again how to tie it," Allan said.

"It's easy. Like this." Adelaide rolled a chunk of dough between her hands to make a long rope. Then she tied it into a knot. "Shelley said not to tie it too tight or it won't rise."

Allan copied his daughter's actions. "Relax, Dad. That's what Shelley said. Relax and have fun with the dough."

Margaret was tempted to join them, but they were having such a special time, she was content to watch. Allan had always included Adelaide in working in the kitchen, and they made a great team. But she'd really blossomed since she began helping Shelley last year. Adelaide was a natural with the children and had discovered her interest in child care. But she'd also learned how to handle food in a greater capacity, because Shelley had needed a helper and had accepted her as a peer and had the patience to show and explain the steps to baking. Shelley had no idea what a great teacher and motivator she was to Adelaide. This Thanksgiving Day, Margaret's heart filled with gratefulness for Shelley and her influence on Adelaide, and for Diane and Beverly, who treated Adelaide as the exceptional and talented young woman that she was. Adelaide had special needs and limitations, but she'd progressed this year far beyond Margaret's dreams for her.

Allan looked up and caught her eye. He gave her a smile that said he understood her thoughts and shared her appreciation.

They had much to be thankful for. And to think, a few weeks ago, she'd been depressed about what she hadn't done in her life. How silly she'd been! But no more. From now on, she would be grateful for each day and look forward with anticipation to all the adventures life still held for her.

★ ★ ★

"Come in, come in out of the cold." Beverly held the door open as Jeff's grandfather and Celia Patterson came in carrying dishes. "I'm glad you made it all right. I was concerned about the fog. It was so thick. It looks like it's lifting, though."

"It's only foggy in Marble Cove. It's hanging low over the cove and the bay. The sun is shining up above and starting to burn it off here," Celia said. "We had a pleasant drive, didn't we, Edward?" She looked up at him and smiled. He smiled back. Beverly couldn't miss the affection between them.

Jeff came to help. "Let me take the food while you hang up your coats." He managed to carry the two pies and balance the salad bowl between his arms.

"I'll take your coats," Beverly said. "Go on into the study and visit with my father. Mrs. Peabody is in the kitchen. We'll join you in a few minutes."

When Beverly went back into the kitchen, she had to stop in the doorway and watch Jeff charming Mrs. Peabody. He had lifted the turkey roaster out of the oven to make room for her to warm the rolls and sweet potatoes that she'd prepared. Jeff had gone across the street earlier to carry them for her and help her, though she always insisted she did not need help.

Jeff was a natural with the old folks. His deep love for his grandfather had given him a special interest and fondness for the older generation. Coral Peabody was not immune to his spell. She peeked at the turkey and declared it a beauty. She asked about the stuffing. When Jeff said it had apples and sausage and oysters, she nodded with approval. He'd won her over. She didn't even mind sharing the kitchen with him and had allowed him to peel the potatoes for her. When he apologized for getting in her way, she shrugged it off.

Beverly was floored. Perhaps it was a female thing. Mrs. Peabody didn't like sharing the kitchen with another woman, but didn't mind having a man there. But that wasn't true either. She'd shooed Beverly's father out on many occasions.

Beverly smiled as she watched the interaction. What did she expect? Jeff had that same effect on her. He genuinely liked people and they responded in kind. His openness and kindness, his respect and interest in others shone out from him. Each time she was with him, she fell deeper in love. She thanked God for bringing them together. Although she hadn't believed their meeting at the lighthouse had been part of a miracle at first, she knew now that it was all woven together. She relished the thought of all the Thanksgivings and all the special days they had ahead of them. A lifetime of memories to make.

★ ★ ★

The fog had lifted, leaving behind crystal-studded trees and bushes surrounding the drive to Ralph and Frances Bauer's house. The sun shining on the hoarfrost left by the fog sparkled like brilliant diamonds. Shelley loved the icy wonderland. It set the stage for winter and the special times that came with the season. She'd become more comfortable around Dan's noisy family. She'd met all her obligations and filled all her Thanksgiving orders. Today she was relaxed and ready to have a good time.

The children were excited to see their cousins. Everyone accepted Hailey as family and she had become friends with a couple of the cousins who were close to her age.

When they pulled to a stop in the driveway, children in coats and hats and mittens poured out of the house to greet them.

"Let me carry in the desserts," Dan said. "You go on inside. I'll come back out and get the rest."

"I'm so thankful for such a sweet, helpful husband," Shelley said, kissing his cheek.

"And I'm thankful for such a great baker," he said, grinning at her as he took two big pans of desserts.

"I'll get the diaper bag." Shelley grabbed the bag and a blanket for Emma's nap, though she wasn't confident she would get her to lie down with all the activity.

The men were all huddled around the television, watching a football game. The women had congregated in the dining room and kitchen, talking while Frances folded whipped cream and minimarshmallows into a huge bowl of fruit salad. Dan looked for a spot to set the desserts.

"Put the pies in the dining room on the buffet," Frances said, turning toward him. "Oh. Those aren't pies. Where are the pies?" A look of distress clouded her face. "Oh dear, I hope you didn't misunderstand me, Shelley. I specifically asked you to bring pies and rolls."

"I brought desserts and rolls. I had so many pies to make this week, I decided to bring something different today. They're similar, but easier to serve. I brought maple apple crisp, pumpkin dump cake, and pecan pie bars. I think you'll like them. With ice cream or whipped cream, they'll taste a lot like pies."

Frances' brow creased with doubt. "I don't know. We always have pies. It will have to do, I suppose. It's too late to make pies now. I just wish..."

"You're going to love these, Mom," Dan said. "I tasted the pumpkin cake. It's good."

"Dan. You didn't." Shelley frowned at him and he ducked and hurried out of the kitchen, depositing the pans in the dining room as he went. His sisters laughed as he left.

"Men!" Vera said. "They can't keep their fingers out of the dessert. But I'll take his word for it. They look wonderful, Shelley."

Frances turned her back on them and finished her salad. Then she started handing bowls and platters of food to each of the women. "Call the men, Annie," she said. "Livvy and Samantha, round up the children and make sure they all wash up. Dinner is ready."

The long table was set with white linen tablecloths and the lovely Thanksgiving china. Candles and flowers added to the beautiful setting. In the middle of the dining room table was a lovely centerpiece of sprigs of crab apple branches with bronze-colored leaves and tiny, shiny red apples. Perched on top was a bright-orange-and-black oriole. Shelley stared at it.

"Pretty, isn't it?" Frances asked, coming in behind her.

"Beautiful. Did you make it?"

"No. I bought it at the craft fair at the Cannery. I love orioles. Don't you?"

"Yes, I do. A lot."

Shelley was still thinking about the coincidence of another oriole sighting as she sat down between Dan and her father-in-law. Interesting that Frances liked them too.

Once everyone was seated, the din of the television turned off and the voices quieted, Ralph said grace, giving thanks for their many blessings. Then it took ten minutes to go around the table, each of them telling something they were thankful for.

Shelley loved hearing the children. Aiden was thankful for his dog Prize. Hailey was thankful for her friends and the turkey. Emma didn't understand, but she said she was "tankble," which got a chuckle from everyone.

Dan took Shelley's hand. "I'm thankful for my wonderful wife and my family." He squeezed her hand and smiled at her. It was her turn.

"I'm thankful for my sweet husband and my family and for the love and wisdom passed down to me by a special woman."

Frances beamed and dabbed at the corner of her eye. She'd thought Shelley meant her. Shelley had been thinking of Darlene Kearns, but she didn't say so. She and Frances didn't always communicate well, but she realized that Dan's mom also had, in her own way, passed on wisdom and encouragement to Shelley.

Shelley looked at the oriole centerpiece and thought about her relationship with Frances. Sometimes she had to laugh at her mother-in-law's backhanded compliments. She really meant well. And Shelley didn't have Darlene to turn to anymore. She certainly couldn't turn to her own mother. In an odd way, she had grown close to Frances. For all her critical comments, Frances was fiercely protective of her family, and Shelley realized that included her. Shelley wouldn't have chosen Frances as a mentor, but Frances had charged in and taken that role because she was the mother and she wanted the best for her family. Was the oriole centerpiece a sign for Shelley to see Frances in a new light? It dawned on her that even in her criticisms, Frances wanted Shelley to succeed and rise to her full potential.

After dinner, Shelley helped clear the table. Then Frances got out the good dessert plates.

"I'll let you serve the desserts, Shelley. I don't know how you intend to do that."

"I'll be happy to. Dan, could you get out the ice cream and whipped cream, please?"

Shelley lined up the large glass baking dishes that held the desserts. She set the ice cream and whipped cream at the end.

"Everyone serve yourselves. I suggest taking small amounts to start with. You can come back for seconds later. There's plenty."

"Sounds like a perfect plan to me," Hal said. "Only I'll have to have some of everything."

"That's the idea," Dan said. "And believe me, it'll be worth it."

Frances still looked doubtful, but she went along with the plan. Shelley noticed later that Frances took a second helping of every kind when she thought no one was looking.

Emma and Aiden fell asleep on the way home. Hailey laid her head against a pillow and looked out the window.

"Did you have a good time, Hailey?" Shelley asked.

"The best. I wish my mom could have been here. She'd have liked it."

"I know. I wish she could have been here too. I'm sure she misses you something fierce."

"Yeah." She closed her eyes.

Dan reached for Shelley's hand. "Your desserts were a big hit. Dad loved them. I just wish there'd been some leftovers."

Shelley had noticed how quickly they disappeared, but it was nice that Dan noticed too. "I can always make more."

"You were talking about your friend who died when you said you were thankful for a special lady, weren't you?"

"Yes."

"I thought so. It was nice that you let my mom think you meant her."

Shelley shrugged. "I didn't want to make her feel bad. And I realized in that moment that she's actually become a mentor and a support for me as well."

"Really? As much as she gets on your case? You're being generous. So did your friend help you make up your mind?"

"About Rusty, you mean? In a way. I got a lot of encouragement from her notes and the Bible verses she highlighted. And then there was the Baltimore oriole."

"The baseball team? How did they help?" Dan sounded completely confused.

"No, silly. The bird. It is a bird, you know."

"I know. Are you going to say yes to Rusty?"

"Would that be all right with you?"

"It'd be tough, but I told you I'd support whatever you decide, and I meant it. You're good, Shell. I don't know if you realize just how talented you are. Rusty knows."

"Thank you for believing in me. What I've discovered is that I really do want to keep my business going and someday I want to expand and grow it. I believe I'm capable, but I don't want to do something that will hurt you and the kids. So for now it'll be one step at a time, with the dream out in front of me. I put it on my bucket list. When the time is right, we'll have to work it out together. We're partners in everything."

"And that's a two-way street. You never complained when I was out of work. I'd reached the point where I'd have taken anything. You gave me the freedom and encouragement to find what I really wanted to do. That meant a lot to me."

"I'm glad. I'll talk to Rusty. It'll be up to him whether he'll find someone else or wait awhile. He said a year or two."

"Right. Who knows what things will be like by then?"

"I love you, Dan Bauer."

"I love you too, Shelley Bauer."

Shelley couldn't wait to share her thoughts with her friends.

CHAPTER TWENTY-TWO

A re you sure you feel up to this party?" Jessica asked Friday afternoon, after they got back from Diane's chemo treatment.

"I feel fine. A little tired. The chemo reaction doesn't usually hit me until the next day. If I have to, I'll slip off to bed. My friends will understand. Thanks for going with me today."

"I wish I was here to go with you every week. I'm glad Beverly insists on taking you. At least I know you're not alone. Now go rest while I get our leftovers ready. All we are supplying is turkey and gravy and mashed potatoes, right?"

"Yes. Beverly, Margaret, and Shelley are bringing the rest. I can help you set the table."

"No, you can't. Go rest. I can do it. I want to do it. After all, you're letting me join your special sorority."

Diane laughed. "We're not a sorority. We don't have lots of parties or fuss about hair and outfits and boys."

"Grown-up sororities don't do that. They're more like benevolent organizations, and you are always helping someone else or the town or your church."

"Well, since you put it that way, I guess we are like that."

"Go take a power nap so you'll be ready to party."

"All right. If you insist." Diane went to her bedroom and stretched out on the bed with her favorite lap blanket. She closed her eyes, intending to rest for a few minutes. She hated that the chemo treatments zapped her energy. She and Jessica had always enjoyed long walks together, but this week all she'd managed was short trips to the store and the walk from the parking lot to the infusion center and back.

The ringing telephone brought Diane out of her slumber. She heard Jessica answer it.

"She's taking a nap right now so she'll be rested up. The treatments make her tired, but she wants to have the dinner tonight. I think it'll be good for her. We'll see you in a little while."

"Who was that?" Diane asked, coming out of the bedroom.

"Shelley wanted to make sure you feel up to having them all come over."

"I'm fine."

"That's what I told her. They'll be here in about twenty minutes."

"Oh dear. I'd better get ready then. Shall I help you in the kitchen?"

"All done. The table is set. The leftovers are warming in the oven. And you look fine."

"I'm a mess. My clothes are wrinkled from lying down and my hair is a mess. I shouldn't try to sleep in the wig. I'll wear my other one."

"All right. Go do what you need to do."

Diane changed into knit pants and a pullover top. The soft fabric didn't irritate her sensitive skin. She washed her face and got out her fun wig. Just looking at her image in the mirror perked her up. She applied some foundation to cover her pale skin and a light dab of lipstick. The makeup worked magic. She felt better already. She heard the front doorbell and went into the living room. Jessica opened the door, and all three of her friends were there, chatting and laughing as they came in. Suddenly her home was filled with energy and warmth. The love flowed into her, warming her.

"Look at you!" Shelley said. "I love your spikes."

They all turned to look at Diane.

"Wow, Mom. You look more like my sister than my mother. I think you should cut your hair like that—I mean, after it grows back in."

Diane couldn't help grinning at their comments. "I wouldn't dare. I'd be accused of trying to be a teenager again. People would tell me to act my age."

"Nonsense," Margaret said. "It's very upbeat and makes your eyes look brighter. I like it."

"How are you feeling?" Beverly asked.

Beverly knew from taking her to her treatments that she felt totally drained by the time she got home. "I may fade on you, but I'm doing well."

"Come put your food in the kitchen. Does anything need warming?" Jessica asked.

"Not if we eat right away," Margaret said. She had a hot sweet potato dish.

"Then let's eat."

They took their places around the table.

"May I ask the blessing?" Jessica asked. At their nods, she bowed her head and began. "Dear God, I thank You for surrounding my mom with loving friends..." She went on to give thanks for the blessings and bounty they enjoyed. Then she unfolded a small piece of paper and finished by reading a verse from an old hymn:

> With grateful hearts we all are met
> To eat the bread of gladness.
> The ancient leaven now forget,
> And every thought of sadness.
> Christ Himself the feast hath spread,
> By Him the hungry soul is fed,
> And He alone can feed us.
> Hallelujah!

"Amen!" they all chorused when she finished.

"And dig in," Jessica added. "I haven't eaten this well in a long time." She passed the platter of turkey and the bowl of stuffing.

"This looks wonderful. I love leftovers. I wanted to bring over some of Jeff's stuffing, but we ate every bit of it," Beverly said. "It was an oyster stuffing. Really yummy. And I was surprised how gracious Mrs. Peabody was about having him in the kitchen while she was there. I stay out of her way when she's cooking. He totally charmed her."

"You had quite a houseful," Margaret said. "Did Celia come with Edward? They make such a cute couple."

"They seem to spend a lot of time together. Jeff is pleased that his grandfather has someone keeping an eye on him. Edward is pretty independent and capable, but Jeff's concerned about his living alone. I've got the same concern about my father. I'm wondering if Jeff and I shouldn't get our own place when we get married, though. Someplace close to my father. But at least we've settled that we will live in Marble Cove for the next few years, while Father's alive and I'm mayor."

"Good. I'd hate to have you leave. Our group wouldn't be the same without you," Shelley said.

They all agreed that they wanted to keep their foursome together. They had the perfect mix of ages and talents and personalities.

"I have a surprise," Beverly said, grinning. She got up from the table and went into the living room, then came back with three small packages wrapped in silver paper with blue bows. She handed one to Diane, then Margaret and Shelley. "I kept one for myself too. Go on. Open them."

Shelley got hers open first. Her eyes widened, then she smiled and held it against her chest so the others couldn't see it.

Margaret slowed down. "Hurry up," she told Diane.

Diane fumbled with the ribbon, then pulled it free. She opened the package and stared. "Oh my. What a...what a wonderful group of hams." She blinked back the sudden moisture that pushed into her eyes. Then she laughed. "Thank you for the sweet reminder, Beverly. That was a special day. But people must have thought we were crazy."

Margaret finished unwrapping hers. She looked and grinned.

"I want to see," Jessica said.

Diane turned her gift around. It was a framed picture of the four friends modeling their wigs and grinning for the camera. "This was the day we went to pick out wigs. I'll never forget how you all made that day fun for me. I was so upset and dreading having to wear these things again." She pointed to her spiky wig.

"It turned out to be fun for all of us," Beverly said.

"I love it," Jessica said. "How lucky you are to have each other."

"Lucky?" Diane said. "Blessed. You, my friends, have held me up and lifted my spirits more times than I can count."

"Same here," Margaret said.

They set their pictures aside.

Shelley brought out dessert. They all claimed to be full, but everyone took a piece of pumpkin dump cake.

"Now I want to know what you've discovered about the railroad station," Margaret said.

"Oh yes." They all leaned forward to hear.

"You know we didn't discover a lot from the newspapers, though we got a few tidbits we can use. But Augie Jackson remembers when the railroad pulled out of Marble Cove. It wasn't long after that letter we found in the station. The quarry shut down in November of 1951, and the last train ran in early 1952. And there's a mystery, besides the train whistles we've all heard."

"Really? What?" Shelley asked.

"Well, we told you we'd discovered the last stationmaster was named Elias Thorpe. We don't know for certain if he was a descendent of Jeremiah Thorpe, so that's something to find out, but he disappeared without a trace. He lived a lavish lifestyle, and left behind his house and all the furnishings. Even his personal belongings."

"Do you think he had an accident?" Shelley asked.

"Or met with foul play," Jessica suggested. "Maybe he had an enemy. Did he have money? Did it disappear too?"

"We don't know," Diane said. "We'll have to do some digging to see if we can find out. The house was auctioned off. We don't know if his property was sold all together or in pieces. Augie tried to find out about Elias, but he didn't discover what happened to him."

"Even his clothes and jewelry and that kind of thing?" Shelley asked. "Didn't he have family?"

"He was a bachelor. That's about all we know. Oh, and we found out the name of the people who owned the quarry. Their last name was Gentry. So we have that to research too," Beverly said. "I think we can put together enough history to get people interested in saving the station. But it would be better if we can piece together what happened to Elias Thorpe."

"What if you publicized the hunt for him? Maybe someone would come forward with information. And a mystery around the station might get people more interested in saving it," Jessica suggested.

"Kind of like an archeological dig," Diane said, her thoughts churning. This sounded like a great plot for a book. Maybe she would get some inspiration from the hunt. She couldn't wait to get through the cancer treatments and get back to normal. She glanced over at Jessica, who was grinning at her. Her daughter knew how to inspire her. Just present her with a good puzzle. A new problem to solve. It might be just what the doctor ordered.

★ ★ ★

Shelley noticed the sparkle return to Diane's eyes. Sometimes the best thing that could happen was a new challenge. Her own life was filled with challenges right now. "I don't know how I can help, but you've caught my curiosity. I want to know what happened to the stationmaster too. This has been an interesting month for me. Margaret, your bucket list got me to thinking about what I want to accomplish in my life. I started my own bucket list."

"Good for you. I think we all need goals. But let me warn you not to take your list too seriously. It has to be flexible. That's where I got hung up. I had lots of ideas that never happened, and when I found the list, I felt like a failure. Looking at those dreams now, I can see that they weren't that significant. I was fascinated to discover that I have accomplished the really important ones. And I'm so excited." Margaret's face became animated as she talked. "We're going to do the one item I've always wanted to do. Allan and I are going to Paris. And I believe I've found the perfect intensive art course to take while we're there."

"Good for you! That's fabulous," Diane said. "Yay for Allan."

"That's wonderful, Margaret. I'm so glad that you're going to do something from your list. That makes me think I'll be able to do the things on my list someday too," Shelley said.

"So what is on your bucket list, Shelley, if you don't mind sharing?" Beverly asked.

"It's kind of boring, in a way. Nothing as exciting as going to Paris. The usual things, I suppose, like raising my children and having grandchildren someday. That kind of thing. But there was one thing I was afraid to put on my list. I've agonized over my business. Now that Dan is on a secure career path, and the children will be needing more and more of my time with school activities and homework, I wondered if I should quit. Frances advised me to close my business, at least until the children are grown. But if I stop, I'd have to start from scratch to rebuild a clientele. And I'd be letting my current customers down."

"I should say so," Diane said. "But I know you're stretched thin, and you're always doing things for others, like cooking for me. I don't suppose it's in your nature to stop helping others. What do you want to do?"

"I want"—Shelley took a deep breath—"I want to keep my business going, and Dan agrees. But that's not all. Rusty asked me to take over the Cove for him when he retires. It wouldn't be right away, but down the road. I've gone back and forth wondering if it's selfish to want to accept his offer."

"Selfish? You? Not a chance," Beverly said. "No wonder you've been struggling with the decision. Knowing you, you've thought of every angle to see if you could make it work. I'll be happy to help you crunch the numbers and do a feasibility plan if you'd like."

"I don't know how I can help, but I'd be happy to do any artwork for menus or brochures or whatever," Margaret offered. "And I know Adelaide will want to babysit or help you with baking if you need her."

"I'll take Emma any day so you can work. And I can help you ferry Aiden and Hailey to school or activities," Diane said.

"I knew I'd have your support. You have no idea how much it means to know my friends are beside me, no matter what I do."

"I know, believe me," Diane said. "I couldn't go through this cancer without all of you."

"I wish I had a group of friends as special as what you have found with each other," Jessica said. "I have friends from church that pray together, and that keeps me going, but you have much more than that. So tell us, Shelley. Have you decided?"

"I have. I had reached a point where I just couldn't decide. I felt guilty for wanting to do this, 'cause I knew it was going to be a strain on my family. Dan said he'd support me, whatever I decided, but he wouldn't tell me I should or shouldn't do it. His mother was pushing me to quit. She didn't know about Rusty."

"It isn't her decision," Diane said in a gentle voice.

"I know, but sometimes she's right. I prayed about it and wasn't getting an answer. Then I got a package in the mail. It was from the daughter of my youth group leader when I was in high school. This leader was the person I leaned on and confided in when my folks were getting a divorce. She encouraged me and prayed with me and taught me to cook. I just found out she passed away."

"Oh, Shelley, I'm so sorry," Beverly said. "You must be heartbroken."

"I am. But I know I'll see her again. The package was her devotional book. In it, I learned that she had prayed for me every day. She left Bible verses for me. The last one was my answer. She had tucked my wedding invitation into the day of our wedding. When I read it, I knew this was what God prepared for me. Then I received a sign. How it came about, I won't even speculate, but I don't believe it was a coincidence. I heard a bird and looked up. It was a Baltimore oriole in a maple tree outside the pre-K."

"It's too late for the orioles to still be here," Margaret said.

"That's what I thought. That was Darlene's favorite bird. She said it made her realize God was with her."

"Wow. I'd say you received a miracle. I love it when God is so specific," Jessica said.

"Yes. It helped me put things in perspective and decide. I finally wrote on my bucket list that I want to have a storefront bakery someday. Maybe the Cove, or maybe something else, but it's my dream and it's okay to want to do it."

"Of course it is," Margaret said.

"But not now," Shelley added. "Right now, I'll keep running the Lighthouse Sweet Shoppe. It helped to see that you have all followed your dreams, but you waited until the time was right. That's what I'm going to do too."

"That's a great revelation, Shelley. And it's true that we can realize our dreams when the time is right. And it won't be too late. God is doing great things in each of our lives. I can't wait to see what He has in store for us next," Margaret said. She looked at each of her friends and grinned. "Look out, world. The ladies of Newport Avenue are on the move."

ABOUT THE AUTHOR

Award-winning author Sunni Jeffers is setting course for a new life adventure. After college, Sunni started her first adventure as a Navy wife and mother. Ten years later, she, her husband and kids moved to Denver to take over management of the family security business. When her children left home, she began writing books. In 1992, Sunni and her husband moved to a ranch in the Great Northwest to raise cattle, timber and hay and to give her the time to hone her craft and write stories of other women and their struggles and victories. Now Sunni's next adventure has begun. After downsizing to a cottage in town, Sunni and her husband are exploring the United States and Canada in their RV home. Taking her computer along, she will continue writing heartwarming stories of delightful women living out their faith in small-town America as they face challenges and adventures in everyday life.

A Conversation with Sunni Jeffers

Q. This is your first book for Miracles of Marble Cove. What has been the most challenging part of joining a series after it is well established?

A. This is the fourth series I've joined with Guideposts Books, and each has been well established when I got on board. I love the small town ambiance of Marble Cove, where roots go deep and friendships can be both complicated and precious. I grew up in a small town and after seventeen years in Denver, I live in a small town once again. This series has been most challenging because each book closely follows and adds to the previous book, so details and growth are vital and depend on all of the books in the series.

Q. Which of the four main characters' stories do you identify with most?

A. I relate to Margaret's story. I am near her age and my husband and I are going through a life change now, embarking on exploring our great country by RV. I went through a time in midlife when I wondered if God had something more for me to do. I was the accounting manager of our small business. I wondered if life had passed me by. I think we all face those moments in doubt. Years before, my husband and I each made a dream list, then packed it away. Finding that list after seventeen years spurred a life change for us, but it was gratifying to see that we had accomplished many items on our lists.

Q. What aspects or experiences from your own life became part of the story?

A. Diane's battle with cancer hit home for me. I was deeply involved with my mother-in-law's battle with breast cancer that spread into her bones. She had many trials and triumphs over sixteen years, and it was my privilege to walk with her and see her deep faith and strength and how God sustained her and all of us.

Q. The four friends in Marble Cove have experienced a number of intriguing miraculous events in the series. Have you ever experienced or witnessed an inexplicable or miraculous event?

A. I've seen lots of miracles. I have no doubt God is intimately involved in our daily lives. One big one. I was in a hospital in Mexico where my mother-in-law was getting alternative treatment for her cancer. All of her family were in Denver. After we'd been there a few days, one night she got extremely ill. I stayed in her room all night praying—crying out to God. She thought she was dying and so did I. It was one of the longest nights of my life. In the morning she was still alive and finally resting. The doctors came in. She was surrounded by Spanish-speaking men and they were talking and laughing. I was incensed until one told me in English that she'd had a miracle. A blockage had broken loose during the night. Now she would not need surgery. She entered that hospital in a wheelchair, but after that turning point, she got better and walked out of the hospital to go home.

Baking with Shelley

Pumpkin Pie Biscotti

3½ cups flour

1 cup packed brown sugar

½ cup white sugar

2 teaspoons baking powder

½ teaspoon coarse sea salt

2 teaspoons cinnamon

½ teaspoon nutmeg

½ teaspoon ginger

dash cloves

1 tablespoon finely chopped candied ginger

2 large eggs

¾ cup of pumpkin puree

2 teaspoons sorghum or molasses

2 teaspoons vanilla extract

Optional:

½ cup chopped walnuts or pecans

¼ cup chopped dried cranberries

Preheat oven to 350 degrees. Grease baking sheet or line with parchment paper. Mix together the flour, salt, sugar, baking powder, and spices into a large bowl. In another bowl, whisk together the eggs, pumpkin puree, sorghum or molasses, and vanilla extract. Pour the pumpkin mixture into the flour mixture. Mix together. Dough will be crumbly. Lightly knead the dough on floured surface. It will get sticky as you knead.

Form the dough on pan into a large log, roughly about fifteen inches long by six to seven inches wide. Or make two loaves crosswise on pan. Loaves will only be about a half inch high. Bake for twenty-five to thirty minutes at 350 degrees, until the center is firm to the touch, but not overdone.

Let biscotti cool for fifteen minutes and use a serrated knife to cut into one half- to three-quarter-inch-wide slices. Lay slices on sides on parchment-covered pan. Turn the oven to 300 degrees and bake for an additional twenty minutes, turning the cookies over after ten minutes. Cool completely. When cool, stand slices together like in loaf form and drizzle tops with half of maple glaze recipe or melted white chocolate. Let set until firm. For crisp biscotti, leave uncovered for several hours in a dry space. Serve and enjoy. Makes thirty to thirty-six cookies.

Maple Glaze

1 cup powdered sugar
1 tablespoon melted butter (not soft type margarine)
2 tablespoons maple syrup or 2 teaspoons maple flavoring
   and 2 tablespoons milk or cream

Cream together until smooth and liquid enough to drizzle on cooled biscotti. Can be warmed to make it spread easily.

FROM THE
GUIDEPOSTS ARCHIVES

This story, by Dale Pape of
Adrian, Michigan, originally appeared in
the February 1998 issue of *Guideposts*.

Bringing a train to a halt is no small thing, especially for reasons you can't explain. On a frigid January afternoon in 1997 I was an engineer on our short line, the Adrian & Blissfield Railroad, hauling tank cars. I was alone that day, and glad to be in the warm cab of the diesel locomotive.

As I rolled slowly along, something caught my eye. The driveway of a trailer home near the tracks hadn't been plowed. A small thing. But somehow it didn't seem right.

Stop and investigate! I tried to ignore the thought. Stopping a train takes valuable time and no small cost in fuel. Besides, I needed to get back home in time to pick up my wife and attend an important dinner party.

Yet the thought came again: *Go back!* I closed the throttle and pulled the brake. Tank cars clanked and thundered behind me. Fifteen minutes later, I'd backed up to the trailer home. Feeling foolish and certain I'd find nothing wrong, I swung down from the cab and trudged through four feet of snow to the house.

There I saw what looked like a kid making a snow angel. An elderly woman lay half frozen in the snow, her face red from frostbite. I helped her into the house, then called 911. The ambulance rushed her to the hospital. She'd been in the snow for three hours. Paramedics said she wouldn't have lasted fifteen more minutes.

The woman recovered after several days. I later learned that she lived alone. She had gone out to shovel her walk, fell, and couldn't get up. All she could do was pray for somebody to come along.

I'm just thankful that I paid attention to the nagging thought to stop my train and go back when I did.

Read on for a sneak peek of the next exciting book in
Miracles of Marble Cove!

Home for Christmas
by Anne Marie Rodgers

Margaret Hoskins stepped back from the plate glass window of the Shearwater Gallery, head cocked and eyes narrowed as she studied the fruits of her labor.

Last year she had painted a lovely scene of Bethlehem on her glass for the window-decorating contest held for the downtown merchants. Although it hadn't won a prize, she'd been very pleased with it. Every time she had seen it, she'd felt that the painting radiated peacefulness and joy. It had been difficult to make herself scrub it off when the New Year arrived.

This year, she was going with a secular theme, although as the idea had evolved, it had taken on a significantly spiritual twist. Thinking of last Christmas had reminded her of angels, as she remembered the mysterious figures that had appeared in Jeff Mackenzie's lighthouse photographs. She had decided to decorate a tree for her window with an angel theme. And then she'd added a few of the heavenly host in the upper corners of the window, sort of an angelic frame for the Christmas tree scene she was creating.

She'd painted a small backdrop with a fireplace and hung a handmade cross-stitched stocking in an angel pattern from the faux mantel. She'd set up an artificial tree, and she'd even found time to make an appliquéd tree skirt in an angel theme to cover its base. On the tree itself she'd hung the angel ornaments— two were antique metallic glass from her grandmother, while the rest came from a set of porcelain bisque and a few she'd found at recent Christmas craft shows. She was going to have to make or purchase quite a few more ornaments to fill up the tree, no matter how lovely the rest of her window was.

She hummed along with Frank Sinatra's "I'll Be Home for Christmas" as she affixed hooks to the little collection and spaced the ornaments out over the tree. As she started to climb out of the window display, Cindy Little hurried by, loaded down with shopping bags. Seeing Margaret in the window, she grinned and waved, juggling her bags. Giving a cheery thumbs-up, Cindy indicated the display and mouthed, "Love it!"

Margaret smiled and wriggled her fingers in appreciation at Cindy. It looked like her neighbor was accomplishing quite a bit of her gift-buying.

She needed to get busy with that too. A month ago, she had painted miniatures of the Orlean Point Light for her three dearest friends, which she had enclosed in small ornament frames that they could hang on their trees. But she'd done very little yet for Adelaide and Allan, and it was already the last Saturday in November. She knew Allan wanted a new scroll saw and a set of chisels for his woodworking projects, and she'd also decided he needed a new parka after she'd noticed how ratty his current cold-weather coat was becoming.

Adelaide was generally easy to please. She enjoyed pretty new clothes, especially if they were pink. Margaret had seen a pair of pink boots in a catalog that she knew would thrill her daughter. She'd have to run to the Hallmark store too and pick up the "Mischievous Kittens" ornament for this year. She'd begun the collection in 1999, the first year it came out, and now Adelaide had over a dozen of the kitten ornaments to decorate the tabletop tree they always set up in her bedroom.

After setting her brushes to soak, Margaret grabbed her coat and dashed out the front door. It was too bitter cold to be outside without protection, but she really wanted to see how her window decor was progressing from the view of passersby.

"Nice window." Ham Levesque, the postman, grinned as he trooped toward her pushing a large mailbag. Stopping, he flipped through the items he had pulled from the bag and handed her a stack. "My mother collected angels, and it's still my favorite Christmas theme. If I could choose the winner, I'd choose you."

"Thanks." She waved as Ham trudged off to his next delivery.

Still clutching the mail, she stood back and surveyed her window. The tree definitely needed a few more ornaments, but it was coming along nicely. She had left a space front and center for her mother's treasured handblown glass angel. Tomorrow she'd bring it in and hang it in the place of honor she'd reserved.

"Hi, Margaret." Shelley Bauer, her young neighbor, stepped onto the snow-packed sidewalk. She was far better insulated against the cold than Margaret, with warm-looking boots, a calf-length down coat, fleece mittens, and a snug watch cap pulled over her bright hair. Around her neck she'd wound a gorgeous scarf crocheted in a shell-stitch pattern.

"Hey. What are you doing without the kiddos?" Margaret rarely saw Shelley out and about without her two young children and her niece Hailey, who was living with them.

"They're out at Dan's parents' place having a cookie-baking party," Shelley told her. "I wanted to get my Christmas shopping started before all the shelves are bare."

"I was just thinking the same thing." Margaret eyed the tree critically, thinking that she needed to move one of the two antique angels farther away from its counterpart.

"That's going to be lovely," Shelley said, turning her attention to the window display as well. "I especially love the angels you've painted around the edges of the window. It makes me think of the borders I've seen on Victorian postcards or something."

Margaret was delighted. She hadn't been attempting to achieve that effect, but now that Shelley mentioned it, she could see exactly what she needed to do to enhance it. A bit of gilt filigree and some other embellishments would do the trick. "Thank you!" She clapped her hands in delight. "I need to add some things, of course, and I'm saving that space right in front for my mother's angel."

"Your mother's angel?"

"*Brrrr!*" Margaret shivered, then hugged herself. "Let's go in before I turn into an ice sculpture!" She led the way into the cozy warmth of the gallery. Over her shoulder, she said, "My mother gave me a handblown Venetian glass angel when Allan and I got married. My father brought it back from Venice after World War II. He was there at the end of April 1945 when the Allies liberated the city. A woman in Venice gave him the angel as a gesture of her gratitude."

"What a lovely story! Did you say it's not on the tree yet?" Shelley turned and craned her neck, trying to see the front of the tree again.

"No. I'll have to bring her from home." Margaret's face took on a faraway look as she thought of the lovely little piece of glass. "Oh, Shelley, she's just beautiful. Her robe is pale blue and her body is clear. The hair is golden glass with striations that really make it look blonde, and the wings are clear crystal with flecks of silver foil in them."

Shelley's eyes widened. "Wow. I can't wait to see it. It sounds gorgeous."

"It is. My mother treasured it. She said she always knew angels were watching over my father during his combat tour, and this was a confirmation of it."

Shelley put a hand to her throat, clearly touched. "Oh, that's lovely."

Margaret nodded, her mind traveling back to her childhood. "Every year when my mother would get out the angel, my father would tell the story of how he'd received it."

When she paused for breath, Shelley said, "Don't stop!"

Margaret laughed. "I exaggerated just now. It wasn't every year, because Mother sort of lost the angel for a few years."

"Lost it?"

"I was about a year old when he came home from the war. The angel always hung on our tree until I was a teenager, and then one year, my father took it to his office to show a secretary to whom he'd told the story. He kept forgetting to bring it home, and Christmas came and went, and we all sort of forgot about it.

"The next Christmas, Mother went to get out the angel—and it was gone. We all assumed it was at my dad's office, but he couldn't find it. The secretary remembered it, but she hadn't seen it either. Mother was really upset, but there wasn't much we could do." Margaret fell silent, recalling her mother's distress.

"But obviously you found it again," Shelley prompted, her blue eyes puzzled.

"Eventually." Margaret felt a familiar pang of grief shadow her mood. "The first December after my father passed away, my mother and I were going through some of his things that had been stored in their attic for years. One of them was a box of odds and ends he'd brought home from his office when he retired. My mother probably set it in the attic without ever even checking it. I started going through it, and in a little box near the bottom, there was the angel!" She smiled. "Mother and I were stunned. And thrilled, of course. We looked at each other and said, 'Fear not!'"

"Fear not?" Shelley looked puzzled.

"From the Nativity story. First chapter of Luke, verse thirty. My father used to tell me to remember the words of the angels." Margaret chuckled. "It sounds silly, but ever since I found that angel again after my father died, any time I had reason to be frightened or upset, I could hear him saying, 'Fear not!' As long as I've had that angel, I've felt his presence with me, giving me courage." Her smile faded a bit. "I strayed from my faith after my teenage years, and I didn't think about that again for a long time—not until after my 'miracle experience,' I guess."

"I think our personal miracles gave all of us a whole new lease on our faith," Shelley said, referring to the life-altering experiences that she, Margaret, Beverly, and Diane each had experienced and drew them together when they first became friends.

"It certainly brought me back to mine." Margaret said. She turned and regarded the place of honor where the angel would go.

"What a lovely story." Shelley's smile was wistful. "So when do we get to meet her?"

A NOTE FROM THE EDITORS

We hope you enjoyed Miracles of Marble Cove, published by the Books and Inspirational Media Division of Guideposts, a nonprofit organization that touches millions of lives every day through products and services that inspire, encourage, help you grow in your faith, and celebrate God's love.

Thank you for making a difference with your purchase of this book, which helps fund our many outreach programs to military personnel, prisons, hospitals, nursing homes, and educational institutions.

We also create many useful and uplifting online resources. Visit Guideposts.org to read true stories of hope and inspiration, access OurPrayer network, sign up for free newsletters, download free e-books, join our Facebook community, and follow our stimulating blogs.

To learn about other Guideposts publications, including the best-selling devotional *Daily Guideposts*, go to Guideposts.org/Shop, call (800) 932-2145, or write to Guideposts, PO Box 5815, Harlan, Iowa 51593.

Sign up for the
Guideposts Fiction Newsletter
and stay up-to-date on the books you love!

You'll get sneak peeks of new releases, recommendations from other Guideposts readers, and special offers just for you . . .
and it's FREE!

Just go to Guideposts.org/Newsletters today to sign up.